THE SECRET DRESSMAKER

JENNY O'BRIEN

Ebook ISBN: 978-1-83700-487-4
Paperback ISBN: 978-1-83700-490-4

Cover design: Sara Simpson
Cover images: iStock, Shutterstock

Published by Storm Publishing.
For further information, visit:
www.stormpublishing.co

To Kari

I think you have to pay for love with bitter tears.
Edith Piaf

PAST

Saturday 30 August – Sainte-Marthe-des-Anges Convent,
Paris 10 am

She folded up the last dress and placed it neatly in the box, her fingers brushing over the tiny, white and yellow daisies embroidered around the neck and hem. Two complete layettes. Dresses and coats. Vests and nightgowns along with hand-knitted bonnets, mittens, bootees and shawls. There were even two identical christening robes in the finest Lyon silk, which she'd spent a week on. She'd poured all the love she had for her daughters into the garments, reconciled by the fact that she'd never get to see them worn.

Blinking back a tear, she secured the lid, fastening it with a broad violet ribbon knowing she'd never be able to afford such glorious silks and linens, but that wasn't why she fumbled in her pocket for her handkerchief. It was the thought that her short time as a mother was coming to an end.

She'd been given a week and been told to feel thankful at the generosity of her benefactor. That most unmarried mothers weren't afforded such consideration. She was too numb to reply, powerless to change any of it. A week wasn't enough to squash all the memories into. The weight of their tiny bodies pressed against her chest. Their milky breaths and soft sighs. The feel of their fuzzy hair under her palm when she smoothed it back. The depth of their bottomless stares. She filed everything away from the smallest memory to the biggest, knowing they had to last a lifetime.

A little moan and she was reaching into the basket, a pain stabbing at her chest from the milk she hadn't been allowed to share.

'Bonjour, ma petite. Hush now. Your sister is still asleep and it's too soon for your milk.'

Staring down at her daughter, Flora's eyes and her arms added a new memory to the newly formed chamber of her heart. One of the last before the final, precious minutes trickled away.

'Let's see if we can find any sparrows in the garden.' She moved between the beds, admiring the profusion of marguerite daisies lining the path, and listening to the bees buzzing between the pot of lavender, the church bells ringing in the distance.

The blue sky was trailing heavy clouds, the bright day fading as the shadows across the garden lengthened and shifted. She didn't notice the change in temperature or the threatening rain. She didn't notice anything. Her eyes were trained on the man and woman walking through the garden gate, her hands busy winding a leftover twist of silken embroidery thread through her fingers, the basket beside her still bearing the impression of her daughters' bodies.

ONE

Friday 30 October, 1942 – Taylor's Mill, Carrickfergus

Once inside the mill, Flora unpinned her hat, setting it on the small shelf before slipping off her coat. With a quick hello to the other parachute packers, she took up her position at her workstation, a bundle of silk laid out in front of her. Working quickly, she started separating the strings that trailed from the chute, her lips pursed. It was a job that required intense concentration, but the monotony in both her life and her job was starting to wear her down. The thought that there was a war on did little to relieve her boredom.

The morning continued at a steady pace, the mill strangely silent instead of the chatter Flora had been used to at the wool factory down the road. It only took a quick glance at the notice pinned on the wall behind her to realise why.

Remember, a man's life may depend on every parachute you pack.

It hadn't been the job Flora had wanted when she'd signed up to join the Women's Auxiliary Air Force, or WAAF. With her husband out of work, she had to take anything she could get.

The door burst open, bringing a gust of cold air with it.

'Good morning, ladies,' Mr Lindley said, escorting an officer into the room. 'Squadron Leader Rives has requested to see one of our parachutes folded.'

'Hello there. And what's your name?' asked Rives, stopping in front of her table.

Flora tilted her chin to meet the gaze of the squadron leader.

'Flora Granville, sir.'

He paused briefly, studying her.

'You're French, Mrs Granville?'

'Yes, sir.'

'And how long have you been packing parachutes?' he asked in an accent she couldn't quite place.

'Three months. Before that I was in a factory, but it closed.'

'And what brings you to these sunny shores?'

'Well, it's certainly not the weather,' she quipped, nodding towards the next packer, expecting him to move on but he didn't. Instead, he waited for her to expand her reply, his hands shoved in his pockets.

'I met my husband in Brittany. I was working in a bar. I'm sure you can guess the rest.' She stopped abruptly, not wanting to explore the devastation that was her marriage.

'And what about your husband, Mrs Granville? What is his profession?'

'He's currently between jobs, sir,' Flora replied, concentrating on his tie. Regulation black, made from some kind of woollen material, probably like the fabrics they'd used to produce at the factory before it had closed.

Mr Lindley interrupted with a slight cough. 'If you've seen enough, it's time for the ladies' lunch.'

Flora watched them retreat into the office before grabbing her bag and making for the small kitchen. With money tight, she couldn't afford to eat in the canteen. She'd just unwrapped her sandwich and settled in the chair when a noise from behind had her turning in fright.

'It's alright, Madame Granville. Stay where you are.' Squadron Leader Rives raised his hand to emphasise the request. 'Do you mind if I join you? I have something important I'd like to discuss.'

The squadron leader's fluent English morphing into impeccable French had her speechless.

'You're speaking French?' she said, her eyes trained on him as he grabbed the other chair and turned it around, his arms folded along the back.

'And why not? I'm a French native just like you are.' He raised his eyebrows. 'I've recently returned from Paris,' he continued. 'An opportunity to brush up.'

'How is that even possible with the Germans?' she finally managed.

'Ah. That's a question I can't answer yet.'

'No, that's a question you're not prepared to answer, monsieur,' she replied, wondering what he was doing in Carrickfergus. By the look of things, she'd know soon enough.

He suddenly swung to standing, offering her his arm. 'I have my car outside. I'd like to take you to lunch, that is if your husband won't object. It's perfectly above board. As I said, there are some things I'd like to discuss away from the mill.'

Flora was startled at the invite but managed to hide it. The idea of lunch somewhere nice with someone from France was tempting, but it would never do. There was work and after work there was her dressmaking business. She still had a wedding dress to finish for one of her clients, which she'd promised to deliver tonight.

'It's important, and it comes with Mr Lindley's permission. He's given you the afternoon off, if you're in agreement.'

Flora took in his badly fitting uniform in contrast to his highly polished shoes, trying to work out what he wanted and whether she had it in her to refuse. A *French* squadron leader. She had cut ties with her home country after what had happened between her and Lucien.

Her stomach knotted at the thought of him. A man she never allowed out of the box in her mind.

She looked up, the squadron leader's little cough reminding her that he was still waiting for her answer. There could be no harm in lunch in a public place especially if it came with her boss's approval.

'As long as it's not Spam sandwiches and I'm not home too late. I cannot abide Spam.'

Dobbins Inn had been fashioned out of a medieval tower house. Its crenelated parapet, casement windows and lime rendered façade added a touch of elegance to the High Street. Flora had heard the rumour about a pair of ghosts walking the place at night. She didn't have a superstitious bone in her body, which couldn't stop her from quickening her steps every time she walked past on her way to the cobblers.

'I'm not really one for inns and the like...' she said over her shoulder, suddenly unsure of what she was doing. Doubt set in, as she walked into the dark panelled interior, the smell of beer and cigarettes mingling with wood smoke from the fireplace ahead.

'Chin up. You're perfectly safe.' He wandered towards the back. 'I've been told they have a garden. It should be quiet this time of year.'

'You don't say,' she replied, glancing at him in alarm.

He laughed, his face relaxing for the first time since she'd met him.

'I think we're going to do very nicely, Madame Granville. Very nicely indeed.'

Flora refrained from replying.

She was soon settled on a high-backed wicker chair with a thick blanket over her knees and one across her shoulders, not surprised to find that no one else was stupid enough to sit outside at this time of year. The only other person present was the barman, pad in hand ready to take their order.

'Bread and soup do? It appears that's all they run to.'

'Perfect.' They'd switched to English as soon as they'd entered the inn. With the barman hurrying inside to the comfort of a lit fire, they switched back to French.

'I know you'll think me odd at best, stark raving bonkers at worse for making you eat outside this time of year, but the fewer people who know about what we're up to the better. The same goes for speaking English in company. Don't want to panic the locals.'

She leant forward. 'I had thought you were trying to seduce me, monsieur. The cold is a welcome relief. I hear men don't do so well in the cold.'

The colour in his cheeks went from pale to pink and back again, causing her to relax for the first time since he'd invited her to lunch.

'Well, that's honest.'

The sound of the door opening behind them had them sitting back in their chairs while the barman placed a platter of thick Irish soda bread and bowls of steaming soup in front of them.

'Before I start, Madame Granville, there's something about you that—'

'You may call me Flora,' she interrupted, picking up a slice of bread. 'No formalities here.'

'I'm Tomas,' he said. 'As I was saying, there's something about you that doesn't quite fit the parachute packer profile. What am I missing?'

'That depends on what you're looking for,' she said with a shrug, the bread back on her plate. 'You know that I'm French, born in Paris, spent most of my life there before moving to Belfast on meeting my husband. We moved to Boneybefore a few years back.'

He leant forward. 'Most of your life? What about the other part?'

'Oh, nothing really.'

He pushed his bowl aside, giving up any pretence that they

were there to eat. Instead, he placed a small brown envelope in front of him. 'There's something I'd like to share with you?'

Flora flicked him a look as she selected a cigarette from her pocket, before working on lighting it. She'd felt relaxed, now she was struggling to strike a match.

He removed four photographs from the envelope, laying them face down.

He turned over the first. *A woman.*

Sabine Lumineau. Lucien's wife.

Flora stared at the woman's perfect features. Wide, guileless eyes. Creamy complexion and a provocative bow of a mouth. Her hair was a shining cap, topped off by a beret tilted off to one side. Flora's stomach twisted, her hands flexing in her lap. The woman that Lucien had chosen as mother for their twin daughters.

The image wavered in front of her, her head starting to swim. 'What is this?'

'Wait and see.' He quickly placed the next photograph beside it, giving her no time to question him further.

Lucien. Still elegant, his blond hair brushed back from his forehead. Immaculate but aged. His face lined, his mouth down at the corners. He wasn't happy, but he didn't deserve to be. Not after taking her daughters.

She waited for the next photograph, her mind running through the possibilities, the ash from the tip of her cigarette tumbling onto the grass without her realising.

It was a studio portrait of a blonde-haired young woman, aged sixteen or seventeen, dressed in a simple tea dress with a Peter Pan collar, white gloves resting across her knees. High cheekbones. Straight nose, a confident look in her eye.

'Violette.'

The word came out in a whisper, the cigarette falling from her fingers onto the blanket over her knees.

'Careful!' Tomas picked it up and stubbed it out in the ashtray before resting back in his chair.

Flora barely noticed.

She knew it was Violette in the same way her lungs knew how to breathe and her heart knew how to beat. Her daughters might have been twins, but they'd had very different features and personalities right from the beginning. Blonde Violette had seemed robust and self-contained. Even in those first days, any of the nuns had been able to pick her up. Flora had told herself that it was a blessing. She'd never quite believed it. Marguerette, with her dark hair and eyes, was different. In her first week of life, she'd screamed if anyone came near her. She'd only wanted her mother.

Tomas flipped over the last image slowly, his finger touching the corner.

Marguerette. Gone were the pale features and downy hair. Instead, there was a glamorous creature with long lashes and painted lips, her dark curls styled into loose waves, her dress long and figure-hugging.

Flora picked up both photographs, her eyes heavy with tears.

'Who exactly are you and what are you doing with my daughters' pictures?'

He took Marguerette's photograph and held it up. 'Marguerette has been working at Le Moulin Rouge.'

Le Moulin Rouge.

She clamped her lips together, determined not to betray her dismay, her gaze fixed on his face. It wasn't the kind of news any mother wanted to hear about their daughter, but what was it to him?

'I'm not sure why you've come all this way to show me some pictures and to tell me that Marguerette is working in that place. And what of Violette? Is she there too? I'm sure the Lumineaus must have something to say about that?'

Flora watched as he gathered the photographs up into a neat pile, her daughters' faces disappearing back into the envelope. It felt as if her heart was breaking all over again as he tucked the packet back in his pocket.

'You're right. There is another reason. Violette is fine. The

Lumineaus squirrelled her out of Paris days before the Germans came.'

She shrugged to disguise the relief flooding her veins.

'And Marguerette?'

'Marguerette is a singer at Le Moulin Rouge, but she's also working for the resistance and is the reason I'm here.'

'Marguerette is working for the resistance?' she repeated, trying to make sense of words that made no sense. 'Why are you telling me all this?'

'Her relationship with her father is invaluable to us,' he said, picking up a slice of bread. 'His fashion house has close ties to the Germans.'

'A collaborator.' Flora's eyes widened, but she wasn't surprised. The Lucien she remembered was all for putting his own wants and needs first. 'I still don't understand why you've...?'

'It's easy for us to assume that everyone in Britain is on the side of the allies, but that's not always the case, Flora. The war office is looking to corral patriotic Europeans willing to fight for their country, in the form of a secret army.' He glanced around the empty garden briefly. 'For instance, if I was to ask you to go to France on a special mission for the War Office, what would your answer be?'

Flora stared at him, her cheeks growing hot despite the freezing temperature. 'You're asking me to...?'

'No, I need to know where your loyalties lie first.'

'My loyalties will first and foremost always be to my daughters, Tomas, followed closely to my country. If I can combine them, so much the better.' She bit her lower lip briefly, drawing courage from the simple act. 'If you're here then you must know I let them down when they were babies and that's something I won't allow to happen again.' She paused, thinking of something. 'How do you know about me? No one knows.'

'Marguerette does. Lucien told her.'

'I don't believe you. He wouldn't.' She waved her hand through the air, nearly knocking over her glass in the process. 'Why would he do that?'

Tomas placed the end of his bread down, dropping his napkin on top. 'Marguerette has been working for us for about four months or so. We recruited her as soon as we realised the connection between them, which then led us to you.' He placed his bowl on top of his plate, the spoon rattling against the china.

'And what about Violette? I take it she knows too?'

'No, only Marguerette.'

'I don't understand.' Flora sat back, folding her arms across her chest, everything she thought she knew collapsing in a heap around her.

An uncomfortable silence stretched between them.

'We suspected that they might not have got word to you.' Tomas eyed her briefly before rummaging in his pocket and dropping a couple of coins on the table. 'Let's get out of here. Damn stupid idea having lunch in the cold.'

She gripped his arm to stop him from standing, her voice taking on an edge. 'I'm not leaving until you tell me what's going on, Tomas? You can't start something without finishing it.'

He stopped, his expression conflicted. 'I didn't intend to upset you, Flora. Please remember that's the last thing I wanted.'

'Just tell me, please.'

'We don't know the full story about the adoption. Only what Marguerette told us and her information... Well, let's just say it was pretty sketchy. The Lumineaus' private lives are carefully controlled.'

Flora pressed her fist into her mouth to hold back a scream, her eyes stricken, willing him to stop even though she knew she had to hear the rest.

'What else?'

'Flora, I...'

'What else!'

He ran his hand over the back of his neck, before shoving his hands back in his pockets. 'Through a process of elimination and eventually catching up with Violette's old nanny, we were able to piece together that Sabine didn't like the idea of twins and, as soon as you left the convent, they returned Marguerette to the nuns where she was subsequently fostered out to another family. I'm sorry. Truly.'

Flora felt her world shatter. Everything she'd been told by the nuns. Everything she'd thought and hoped for her daughters. Everything Lucien had promised. All lies. She'd only agreed to give the girls up because she knew he'd be able to give them a better life in a household where money wouldn't be a problem. Instead, they'd returned Marguerette and kept Violette.

'My God. How could he?'

She'd thought she'd felt hate when he'd chosen to marry Sabine instead of her, but that was mild in comparison to the sudden rush of anger melding with despair. There would be no forgiveness for what he'd done.

She stood suddenly. 'I'd like to go home now. It's not far. Only a mile up the road.'

'You wouldn't like to go somewhere to discuss this further?' Tomas asked gently.

'It's far too cold for that. You can tell me about Marguerette and how I can help on the way.'

'Right.' He took her arm, his expression impossible to read. Older than she'd initially thought. Forty-two or three, and with a smattering of grey peeking through the dark brown. She wondered if he'd volunteered for the mission or if he'd been sent.

Once in the car, he started to speak, almost as if there'd been no interruption to their conversation.

'As you can imagine, there's no love lost between Marguerette and her father. Not after she was returned to the convent.'

Flora lifted her hand to stop him. 'You need to back up a bit, Tomas. How did they meet?'

'He's started visiting Le Moulin Rouge, Flora,' he said, following the road sign for Boneybefore up ahead. 'A very unhappy man if Marguerette is to be believed, and there's no reason not to. He's taken solace in spending time with her and... She also told me that you were the love of his life.'

She closed her eyes briefly, knowing that to be untrue. 'I still don't understand why you need me involved? Surely you must have people in position already?'

He shook his head before she'd even finished speaking. 'Our only contact has been arrested. There's no one else that we can think of to get close to him, to find out what he's up to and why. It's vital to the networks or they wouldn't have sent me here. My boss is working on an ambitious plan to unite the resistance groups across France, but we need to weed out people like Lumineau first and all of his German contacts. We must have someone get close to him, find out his secrets, and with Marguerette gone...'

'She's left Le Moulin Rouge?' Flora interrupted, her hand to her throat.

Tomas nodded. 'She was doing a good job of gaining his trust. We were hopeful he'd tell her what had made him turn traitor, but she left. We set the hares running to track you down instead, simple enough now everyone has an ID card. You're our last hope, Flora. We have to know what's going on at Maison Lumineau. Who's involved. Who their contacts are. The source of the information they're leaking. Lumineau was only on the fringes, helping us sneak arrangements for evacuations as opposed to being involved with the actual escapes, but things have changed and we need to know why. We can handle Lumineau, but it's if anyone else is involved at the fashion house or if he was acting alone. We simply can't afford to lose any more people to the enemy.'

The sight of Boneybefore up ahead came far too soon for Flora to get her head around what Tomas was trying to tell her. Her mind was whirling. Violette safe but Marguerette working at that place. And Lucien a traitor, conspiring with the enemy instead of helping the resistance. She remembered thinking only a short time ago how bored she was with her life, never imagining that it could change so radically.

Tomas pulled the car to a stop and, removing his pocketbook, withdrew a piece of paper. 'It will be easy enough to find you a job in the sewing room at the dance hall. The perfect cover. This is the number of Miss Maxse, our liaison in London. She's expecting your call, one way or the other. Please, think about it. If you need anything in the meantime, I'm staying at the inn until tomorrow. I've added their number on the bottom.'

Flora glanced at the paper in a daze. 'I'd be able to meet Marguerette, and Violette too.'

There was a brief pause while he restarted the car and manipulated the gears. When he next spoke, his words dropped into the conversation like pebbles in a deep pool, the ripples spreading in increasingly large circles.

'That's the other thing I've been meaning to tell you. Marguerette hasn't just left. She's disappeared.'

TWO

Tomas insisted on driving her home, or as near to her home as she'd allow. Flora had a reputation to uphold and Boneybefore was as narrow-minded as the rest of the country. For her to be seen in the presence of a man who wasn't her husband or a relative would only cause raised eyebrows and gossip over the fence. Life wasn't fair and, in close communities like Boneybefore this disparity was emphasised.

She climbed out of the car and strode away without a backward glance. There was no point. She'd made her decision. She'd help the resistance find out what Lucien was up to. And she'd be able to search for Marguerette too. All she needed was to come up with an excuse for Brian, something to do with work, before heading to Belfast. Then it was the steamboat to Scotland, a train to London and, after, Paris.

Simple.

She stopped off at the corner shop to pick up a newspaper, a packet of cigarettes and a soda bread, reading the news headlines as she walked the short distance to their old fisherman's cottage, the sight of the thatched roof raising a smile. A lounge and a bedroom with a kitchen bolted on the back and an outside toilet for the grand total of eight shillings a week. They'd never been able to afford to buy and they never would with Brian perennially out of work.

The street was quiet at three o'clock in the afternoon, the children still in school, the men still at work. The women would be having a well-earned break, a few minutes respite until they had to think about what came next. She didn't wonder at what Brian was doing. She didn't care.

She let herself into the cottage and closed her eyes, allowing the small hall to settle around her. Gauging the mood of the place she'd never accepted as home.

Unpinning her hat and removing her coat were as automatic as sliding out of her shoes and stuffing her feet into her slippers. The hall stand was an old hand-me-down made from some indeterminate wood with pegs for coats and a shelf above the brown flecked mirror. She ignored it except on a Saturday when she ran a duster over the surface. Now she smoothed a hand over her cheek and stared at her reflection. The same face as Marguerette's if Tomas was to be believed, and why would he lie?

She was trapped in a loveless marriage with no way of escape. France would only offer a temporary reprieve. It might have been different if they'd been able to have children, but the barren early months of their marriage had quickly turned into barren years. Their perfect home altered without her even realising it, to somewhere to eat and sleep. Brian spent his evenings in the pub and she couldn't blame him.

With a sigh, she wandered into the kitchen and, dropping the bread on the counter, plucked a glass from the shelf. She ran the tap, the sound of the gushing water filling the air as it slopped over the dirty dishes left in the sink for her to wash. Two mugs, a pan and a plate. Nothing new apart from the second mug, and the smear of pink lipstick on the rim.

She turned off the tap.

Her hands flexed into fists, her nails digging deep.

Where was he? It was too early for the pub. It had been a long time since she'd worried about how he spent his days. Mostly, she thought he lounged around in bed until she came home.

She walked across the room, ignoring the broken tile where he'd dropped a full basket of turf. He'd been promising to fix it for months now. There were a lot of things he'd been promising.

Something shrivelled and died deep inside as she pushed open the bedroom door, the smell of cheap booze and cheap perfume filling the air, the bed a crumpled mess. She could say the same about the couple staring back at her in horror.

'Hello, Brian, and Mavis. I've seen you in the corner shop, but we haven't been formally introduced. I'm Flora. Brian's wife. I'll put the kettle on, shall I? Oh, and do put some clothes on, Brian. You'll catch your death in this weather.'

THREE

Monday 2 November – London, 8.30 am

The train pulling into Euston Station had Flora reaching on the rack for her suitcase and her gas mask before following the throngs out of the station. She fell into step behind a young woman with a toddler hanging off each arm, feeling numb at the speed she'd left home. Tomas had helped by agreeing to speak to Mr Lindley and arranging for her WAAF card to be stamped before he left. All she'd had to do was pack her bag and drop off the finished wedding dress on her way to catch the train to Belfast and the boat beyond. Her life irrevocably changed by a man she'd only met that morning.

When she arrived at Whitehall, she left her suitcase with the porter before being escorted to Miss Maxse's office.

Miss Maxse settled behind her desk, the large, button-backed chair almost swallowing her small frame. She looked more like someone's maiden aunt than chief of staff, but her welcome was effusive, and the tea strong and hot, just the way Flora liked it.

'Right then, down to business. Squadron Leader Rives has commissioned me to set you up with some accommodation while we source a full wardrobe of French clothes and shoes. The first part is easier than the second,' she said, pulling a large desk diary towards her, a pair of black-rimmed glasses perched on the end of her nose. 'Luckily for you, one of my team has recently moved on to pastures new, therefore freeing up quite a nice apartment in Portman Square, which I can let you have temporarily.'

She paused briefly, her gaze resting on Flora's plain navy dress and coordinating hat. 'The problem I have is in kitting you out.' Her fingers thrummed the top of the desk, her frown deepening along with the silence. 'Things are very busy currently and our team over at Thatched Barn are up to their necks in work. Ask me to disguise a cow as a sheep, and I'll find a way, but I can't help admitting you pose a problem, madame.'

Flora stared down at her practical outfit, as understanding finally hit. If she went to France tomorrow, she'd stand out by the cut of her clothes and the shade of her stockings.

'I'm sure I'll be able to manage a wardrobe, if the appropriate fabrics are available. Assorted French cotton. Some plain for blouses, some with small flowers for under garments,' she said, counting off on her fingers. 'I'll also need a heavy wool blend for some kind of jacket or coat as it's winter. Either serge or flannel will do, along with a lighter weight for a skirt, and a couple of dresses. There's also buttons, hooks and a selection of threads.' She smiled at the softening in Miss Maxse's expression now she'd taken one problem from her shoulders. 'I can also knit. I have needles but I'll need French wool in navy or grey. Oh, and if you can procure tools for darning, I'll need to age some of the items. A humble seamstress wouldn't be able to afford new. The garments would be well worn and, in some cases, hand-me-downs.' Flora pulled a face as she glanced at her shoes. 'The real problem here is footwear. My last pair of French boots fell apart years ago.'

The knock on the door had her sitting back in her chair as Miss Maxse's secretary strolled in with a bright smile and a fresh pot of tea.

'What size feet?' said Miss Maxse.

'Four.'

'Leave it with me.' Miss Maxse gestured towards the teapot. 'If we don't have any in stock, I'll have one of my team scour the pawnbrokers, charity shops and market stalls from here to Portobello Road. In fact, we might as well look for some other items too,' she added, picking up her cup and taking a small sip. 'Fabrics we can manage but shoes, belts, hats and other sundries...' It was her turn to shrug, her cup back in its saucer.

Flora leant forward. 'That's a great idea. Can you get them to pick up French clothes too.'

Miss Maxse nodded approvingly. 'Bravo, Madame Granville. I have the name of a couple of contacts in Bond Street and Soho for French fabrics and I believe the best place for appropriately sourced trimmings is Hatton Gardens. I'll ask my secretary to supply you with the details before you leave.' She pulled open the top drawer of her desk and withdrew a small bunch of keys, which she slid across the desk. 'The apartment is number 3, Portman Square. One of the porters downstairs will arrange for a taxi. You can charge your purchases to the War Office.'

Flora hadn't expected that. She smiled as if she had. She'd have liked to ask what the wages were, but she didn't quite have the nerve. Tomas had her sign the Official Secrets Act in the car before dropping her off. It felt like a lifetime had passed since then.

She placed her cup and saucer back on the tray and reached down to collect her handbag from the floor.

'Now is there anything we can do for you? This is a risky undertaking and all in a rush. We are very happy to offer our services in return.'

Flora stared at her, her mind racing through all the possibilities, but the truth was, there was only one thing she needed right now.

'You wouldn't happen to know a good lawyer by any chance?' Rummaging through her bag, she pulled out a crumpled letter. 'My husband has agreed to a divorce in writing so it should be quite straightforward.' She hoped so.

Miss Maxse eyed her briefly before taking the letter, her hand resting on top. 'The one thing Whitehall has is a surplus of lawyers, madame. I'll get one of them onto this straight away.' She smiled. 'I do believe you're going to be a huge asset to the War Office.'

Flora struggled to get comfortable on the narrow seat, the webbing of her harness biting into her shoulders through the thick, green-and-brown camouflage of her parachute suit. Tomas looked to be asleep opposite, his head lolling to one side. That he could sleep at all with the roar of the Halifax bomber's engines filling the main fuselage was a mystery, but then this wasn't his first jump.

Two weeks at RAF Ringway in Manchester had been an experience she never wanted to repeat. After today, any experience that involved jumping out of a plane with a parachute packed by someone else, was going to be added to her never again list. That Tomas had decided to keep her company during her training by undertaking a refresher course, was a bonus. His presence had helped, as had being billeted with the fatherly vicar of St Mary's, who'd taken it upon himself to drop her off and pick her up from her training sessions, no matter the time of day or night.

Everything had been prepared with military-like precision for her parachute drop into France. Her new French wardrobe was packed in a thick canvas bag, which would follow her straight after the jump and, as for footwear... She glanced down at her second-hand boots which had been bandaged to her feet. Losing one would be disastrous. They were the only footwear she had.

A trickle of sweat dripped down her neck from the overheated interior of the main fuselage in the Halifax. Despite the calendar month, the air inside was muggy, heavy with the stench of oil, sweat and engine fumes. The floor thrummed beneath her boots as the aircraft climbed. Somewhere up ahead, the navigator shouted instructions to the pilot, but it was impossible to hear the words over the roar of the engines.

With Tomas still asleep, she fumbled to check her straps and that the status cord was hooked and ready. Her hand brushed against a lump in her pocket. The shape of her Czech 32 pistol. Tomas had taken her to a shooting range at the back of the airfield after her parachute training, insisting she knew how to both look after and work a gun. She had no intention of firing it, but she wasn't prepared to tell him that.

The gun sat alongside her ration card, clothing coupons and identity card, all made out in her birth name of Flora Toussaint. An important detail in all of this as she wasn't going to France to play a part. She was going as herself. She also carried 30,000 francs in neatly bound notes, and a handful of small change, along with a flashlight, a knife, a compass and even a small trowel. Everything she might need in France straight after plunging through the floor of the bomber.

'Wakey wakey. Over the coast. Ten minutes to go,' the flight engineer's voice boomed.

Flora watched, wide-eyed, as the hatch opened, the moonlight sky scudding beneath. She'd felt calm, excited even, at the thought of returning home and seeing her daughters. Now, with France somewhere below, panic started to build. She knew more than most that there was no margin for error when packing parachutes.

Tomas leant forward, patting her knee briefly. 'It will be alright, Flora. As easy as riding a bike.'

She managed a weak smile.

'Right. Get yourself ready. Tomas, you first.'

'Righty ho.'

'Go.'

Flora shifted closer to the opening in the floor to watch, the cold rush of night air hitting her face like a slap. The black void stretched out below with no lights to break the monotony. Tomas disappeared briefly, until the faint glow from his parachute silk picked up the light cast by the silvery moon.

She closed her eyes, breath seeping out in relief.

Paris was up ahead, but that's not where the drop was. There was a narrow field somewhere beyond the hedgerows, lanes and scattered farms. The map was burnt into her brain: two barns, a line of trees, a small road to the east. A church steeple in the distance.

'Go!'

And before she knew it, it was her turn.

She threw herself forward through the gap, the sudden silence of the sky replacing the deafening thunder of the Halifax. The wind hit her full in the chest, tumbling her into a spin. For a second, she couldn't tell up from down as sky and ground merged into one. Then she yanked hard on the rip cord just the way she'd been shown.

The parachute burst open with a crack and a violent tug that wrenched her upright. The straps bit into her thighs and shoulders, the harness tightening as the canopy billowed above her. Risking a glance down, she saw the blur of a grey field surrounded by black hedges and trees, a small cluster of roofs in the distance. The Halifax was already banking away, the sound of its engines dissolving into the night air.

They were on their own.

The ground rose faster than she expected, grey turning into dark green as she bent her knees, bracing against the drop. The landing was nothing like the textbook she'd been promised. A jolt through her legs sent her sprawling onto all fours. For a long moment she stayed still, chest heaving. The smell of wet earth and crushed grass filled her nose, her vision a blend of brown and green, the noise from the departing plane only a memory.

Then instinct took over. She pulled herself to her feet, unclipped the chute and gathered it in, faster than she'd ever managed at the mill, fingers flying in the dark. Within a minute, it was a neat, wrapped bundled tight beneath her arm. She glanced left then right before racing to the bank of trees up ahead.

Staying out in the open was tantamount to a declaration to the enemy. She'd use the trowel to bury the parachute and then she'd wait.

She didn't have to wait long. Tomas slid out from the cover of knotty bark, closely followed by a farmer type in a thick jacket, a beret squashed flat on his head.

'What the devil kept you? I've been waiting ages.'

FOUR

Monday 23 November – Rue de Villejust, Paris, 7 am

Flora drank in the scene out of the window as the truck rumbled along the street before pulling to a stop. Surprisingly it didn't seem so very different to the last time she'd been in Paris. The bare streets at that time of the morning, when she'd expected to see soldiers. Scanning the road, she fixed upon a couple of swastikas hanging from a building halfway along.

A salutary reminder that this wasn't her Paris anymore.

'Thank you, Octave. I'll be in touch.' Tomas clasped his friend on the shoulder before helping Flora out of the truck, his hand staying on her elbow slightly longer than necessary. With a rucksack slung over his back, he picked up her canvas bag and walked beside her up the steep street, stopping halfway outside an elegant, grey Haussmann building.

'I don't think you mean for me to stay here, do you?' Flora said, her gaze shifting from the opulent, glossy green door to the tall windows framed by wrought-iron balconies. 'It's far too elegant for a humble seamstress like me.'

He laughed. 'No one would ever call you humble, Flora. Come on. It's too early to be wandering the streets. This way.' He took her arm and escorted her past the building and through an arched gate off to one side, clicking the latch in place behind him.

Flora held back, overwhelmed at the garden unfolding in the pale morning light. Curved paths weaved through clusters of bamboo and large, black urns. The oriental theme continued in the long black benches carefully positioned in a circle around an ornamental pond. Her gaze finally landed on a small pergola set against the back boundary wall, red paper lanterns swinging gently in the light morning breeze. It was an oasis of peace and calm in one of the busiest parts of the city.

As a seamstress, she knew she couldn't stay here. Setting her up in accommodation she clearly couldn't afford on her salary was the kind of misstep the Germans would be looking for.

She turned back to Tomas, her mind a whirl with one thought front and central.

'I think you'd better tell me what's going on?'

'Come and sit a minute.' He waited until she'd sunk onto the nearest bench before joining her, their bags propped up against one of the urns.

Like her, he'd changed out of his parachute suit. Gone was the RAF squadron leader and in his place a smartly dressed businessman with the weight of the world on his shoulders. She'd been told that he was acting as a wine merchant. He looked the part.

'Right then. I haven't been entirely honest with you. I haven't lied but...' He waved a hand at the luxurious garden before turning to glance at the shuttered windows behind them. 'L'Etoile de Kleber isn't a pension, or even a hotel, but the woman who owns it is sympathetic to the cause.' He cleared his throat, his face losing what little colour it had after a night of travelling. 'She's also good friends with Lumineau. He's known to visit every couple of weeks or so, which makes it an ideal spot for you to bump into him. It has the added advantage of having rooms to rent on the third floor. The attic room, which Marguerette was renting until recently, is free. Madame Billy, that's the owner, has agreed that you can take it over until she knows what's happening with Marguerette.'

Flora felt her heart drop to her boots. It wasn't what he'd said. After all, as a married woman, she was a madame too. It was the inference he couldn't hide. His staccato speech and clear discomfort filled the gaps that his words had missed.

'Stop. Right. There.' She looked at him without blinking, her heart picking up tempo as all the strands of the conversation pulled together into a seam of understanding.

'I'm afraid so. L'Etoile de Kleber is *une maison close*, but I have to tell you that Marguerette is a singer at Le Moulin Rouge. That she isn't... has never been a...'

'A call girl. A...' Flora wouldn't allow her thoughts to be tainted by the word heading for her lips. For all its beautiful gardens and beautifully presented façade, L'Etoile de Kleber was nothing more than a brothel.

Her fingers clenched inside her worn gloves, the outline of her knuckles visible under the thin fabric as she struggled to speak.

'Look, I'm sorry. I should have been upfront with you about the accommodation. It seemed perfect with Marguerette having rented it and with Lumineau being a frequent visitor. You need to understand how important he is to us. Vital, in fact. Most of the couturiers closed in 1940, some fleeing to Biarritz then England, some even making it as far as America. Our interest has always been in the ones who remained. Designers who found themselves having to negotiate with the Germans in terms of their collections. While the rest of France is wearing rags, there are a small, select few who go about decked out in furs and brightly coloured silks.' He flicked the back of his hand through the air dismissively. 'If that was all, then we'd turn a blind eye. The fashion industry employs many workers, men and women who rely on their wages to feed their families. They'd have to find alternative employment when there isn't any. But the problem is far greater than running up a few frocks for the wealthy, Flora.' He removed his hat and placed it on his lap. 'We managed to persuade Lumineau early in the war to help us with one or two things. Fashion houses are perfect foils for resistance work. Many of the German officers bring their wives to

Paris for the shopping and some women are born chatterboxes, but it's not just eavesdropping or idle chitchat we're interested in. It was essential that we forged links between Free France and the north, only to find the link was already in place. You probably know about Lyon's silk industry?'

'Everyone in the fashion industry knows about Lyon, Tomas.'

'Well, this blasted war has put most of them out of business, except for the high-end market. The couturiers can't seem to get enough of the stuff, in spite of the German ban on exports. Every week without fail there are bundles of silk transported across the border. What better way to sneak plans between the two zones.' He stood abruptly and started pacing as if he couldn't bear to be still a moment longer. 'It was all going perfectly until Lumineau's handler was arrested and taken to 84 Avenue Foch, the headquarters of the intelligence branch of the SS. He overheard one of the officers mention Lumineau by name and managed to get word back to us.'

Flora gaped at him, not quite believing what she was hearing.

'What did they do with him?'

Tomas looked bleak. 'We haven't heard news of him since he was transferred to Sachsenhausen.'

Flora's breath caught. 'Sachsenhausen?'

'It's a concentration camp somewhere north of Berlin.'

Flora braced her shoulders, ashamed of where her thoughts had been heading moments before. Tomas wouldn't have chosen the accommodation without good reason.

She rose to her feet.

'I think it's time I met with this Madame Billy, don't you?'

FIVE

The housekeeper appeared to be dressed in mourning. Her high-necked robe stretched down to her ankles, the only adornment a bunch of keys pinned to a belt at her waist. Her iron-grey hair was drawn back from her forehead, revealing a severe face creased with wrinkles.

'Tomas. Now this is a surprise.' She broke into a smile, stretching out both hands before reaching up on tiptoe to press a kiss on each of his cheeks.

'Mimi. You're looking great. Not a day over twenty-one.'

'Hah. Get away with you. And who is this, mon chéri?' she asked, surveying Flora, her eyes twin beads of navy blue.

'My sister, Madame Toussaint. A new seamstress at Le Moulin Rouge. Madame Billy seems to think there's a room for her on the top floor?' He turned back, saying, 'Flora, this is Mademoiselle Merret, but we all call her Mimi. Need to know anything at L'Etoile, Mimi is the person to ask.'

Mimi cracked a laugh. 'I'll take you up. No point in waiting for Madame Billy. She doesn't normally show until after lunch.' She walked over to the stairs. 'I do hope you like singing, madame. Tragic if you don't.'

Singing?

Flora raised her eyebrows as she followed the woman, uncertain of what she was letting herself in for.

The third floor was very different to the floors below. Instead of plush fabrics, cherub statues and gilt furnishings, there was a mixture of cracked plaster and bare floorboards. The light was a single bulb hanging from a dusty filament. There was silence here too. No sound of singing, she thought, wondering if she was starting to go mad. It had certainly been the strangest day and, with the sun barely in the sky, it had only started.

Of the three doors ahead, two were firmly shut.

'Your room, madame. I'll leave you to unpack. You'll find us in the small room on the left, at the bottom of the stairs.'

Mimi closed the door gently behind her, leaving Flora to get acquainted with her new home.

It wasn't much. Faded floral wallpaper and a single iron bedstead with a thin mattress. Beside the bed there was a small table, holding a chipped jug and basin. There was no wardrobe – instead, a rickety chest of drawers with one of the knobs missing. But the room was clean, the air holding the faint smell of lavender; she noticed the sachet hanging from the sash window. She caressed the gauze pouch briefly, her gaze drawn to the rooftop view outside.

Marguerette's room.

The sharp sound of tapping drew her gaze to a little sparrow staring back, causing her to laugh. She'd forgotten about the rooftop sparrows of Paris and how she'd always kept crumbs to pop on her windowsill. Had Marguerette done the same? By the intense, black-eyed stare of the bird, it seemed likely.

'I don't have anything for you, ma petite, but come back again,' she said tenderly, her palm pressed against the windowpane.

With her coat and hat removed, she sat on the edge of the bed, rubbing her arms although she wasn't cold, far from it. The house was warm, even the top floor. She spotted the stove in the corner and the full coal skuttle, along with a basket of firewood soaked in resin, which filled the room with its acrid perfume.

She finally left the room, pulling the door closed behind her. The house was quiet as she descended the stairs to the hall. When she entered the dining room, the sight of the plate of croissants on the table dragged her straight back to the Paris she'd almost forgotten.

Tomas jumped to his feet. 'Everything alright?'

'Fine, thank you,' she lied. 'The room is perfect.'

The croissants were warm, straight from the oven, while the coffee was the best she'd had since leaving France. Proper coffee instead of that chicory nonsense. She would have liked to stay longer. Have another cup in the quiet room, delaying whatever it was Tomas was planning. It was there in the way his restless hands fiddled with his spoon, clicking it back and forward between his fingers.

'We should check in with Le Moulin Rouge,' he said, dropping his spoon into the saucer with a clatter. 'There's no time like the present.'

Le Moulin Rouge was at the foot of Montmartre Hill, only a short walk from the Basilique du Sacre-Coeur and a half hour journey on the Metro.

Flora sat beside Tomas, staring at the map of the stations displayed above the window opposite instead of the German soldier sitting underneath, one leg folded across the other, his hand resting on the hilt of his gun.

'This is us. Ready?'

She squinted at the glare of light spilling into the carriage after the darkness of the tunnel, her eyes still determinedly turned from the soldier opposite.

'Ready,' she replied softly, taking his arm.

Le Moulin Rouge was a clash of red in the otherwise grey street. Grey buildings and pavements. Grey suits. Grey uniforms and, slap bang in the middle, the red windmill. The air oozed with the sound of German voices instead of familiar French ones. Parisians forced into a silence that wasn't in their nature. It made her more determined than ever to do her bit for the war effort.

The dance hall was the only light relief among the grey. A little faded and the front surrounded by sandbags, but ostensibly the same.

She barely had time to glance at the glitzy entrance papered with bright, colourful posters before he'd walked her past to an almost invisible door set off to one side. The stage door.

Once inside, she followed him down a long, dank corridor, smelling of a mix of paint and stale cigarettes.

The cabaret was a world inhabited by glamorous women and handsome men, not dissimilar to working with the clientele at Maison Lumineau. While Lucien's salon was white and blue, the workrooms above were shabby. Freezing in winter and far too hot in summer, the windows sealed shut from the threat of smog and dust.

Le Moulin Rouge was no different.

The walls were bare, stripped of the brightly coloured posters that lined the entrance. A three-legged chair leant haphazardly against one wall, a pile of rope next to it along with an empty tin of red paint. There was no one around, but she could hardly expect the dancers and cabaret stars to be up. They'd be sleeping off the excesses, their bellies full of cheap wine and even cheaper words.

She grimaced, her thoughts turning to Marguerette. Was this the sort of life she lived? How could she stand it?

Tomas headed for the stairs, and she followed. A man who had obviously been here before. What was his story? A French spy walking through the innards of Le Moulin Rouge as if he owned it. What had made him turn to the RAF instead of fighting alongside his own men? Up to now, she'd only thought of him in terms of his role. Now, for the first time, she saw him as others must. He was handsome enough and he'd certainly been able to charm Mimi when it was easy to see that the woman was no pushover. Yet with her he was different. Professional. Even reticent. She frowned. Because she was a stranger or because of something else?

The stairs were steep, a thin metal handrail screwed into the wall. Where was he taking her?

Flora gripped her handbag tightly, her gloves showing signs of where she'd repaired them with careful stitches, the thread the exact colour of the clotted cream linen. Tomas felt reliable enough in his tailored suit, his hair neatly brushed back from his forehead, but that meant nothing. The hardest of lessons, but the most valuable, had been to put faith in her instincts. If something felt wrong, then chances were that it was.

She paused, her foot hovering between steps, her attention shifting from Tomas to what lay just out of sight. It wasn't too late to turn back. There were plenty of places she could hide. It would mean she wouldn't have to meet Madame Billy. She could concentrate on finding Marguerette and Violette instead of some half-baked scheme that involved Lucien. She'd be happy never to set eyes on Lucien Lumineau again. As an inexperienced seventeen-year-old, she'd been taken in by his soft words and even softer hands. As a mature thirty-six-year-old woman, all she could do was grieve for the stupidity of her younger self.

The familiar noise of sewing machines was as comforting as it was familiar. It was also a reminder that she'd entrusted her Singer sewing machine with her neighbour before leaving Boneybefore. It wasn't as if she could take it with her.

The stairs opened into a large workroom where three women were busy sewing flutes of fabric.

Flora sighed, her shoulders relaxing under her jacket.

The workroom was different to Maison Lumineau and yet eerily familiar. Racks of colourful costumes, each one unexplainably marked with a number. Shelves of sequins in a kaleidoscope of colours. Bolts of silk and tulle lining the back wall. No sign of rationing here. If it hadn't been for Lucien, it was the life she'd still be living instead of all those years wasted in Boneybefore, she thought bitterly. This had been her world from the age of fourteen.

Her formative years had been spent learning the feel of the cloth as it pulsed through her fingers. But it wasn't just the business of sewing, she remembered, glancing at the other seamstresses. It was the feeling of comradery.

'Monsieur Rives!'

The woman nearest was coating a length of thread with beeswax. Flora watched as she jabbed the threaded needle in a pincushion before pushing to her feet and rushing over, pressing a fierce kiss on each of his cheeks.

'Bonjour Madame Guilloux.' Tomas laughed, picking up the woman and swinging her around in a circle before placing her back on her feet.

'It's been ages, mon chéri. Our wine cellars are nearly empty. Poor André has been wringing his hands in despair.'

'I'll believe that when I see it, Odile. Where is he? In his office?'

'Where else!' She spread her hands before turning to Flora. 'And who's this? Hopefully the seamstress you promised.'

Flora fixed a smile as the woman examined her.

Odile was small and thin. All sharp corners, her chin pointy, her eyes two black blazing buttons in an otherwise unremarkable face. But it was the woman's outfit that captured Flora's attention, not her face. The simple, white poplin shirt with important-looking sleeves teamed with a plain black skirt in an enviable cut. She couldn't have done better herself.

'Flora, this is Odile, the chief seamstress.' Tomas propelled her forward. 'Odile, my younger sister, Madame Flora Toussaint, an expert with a needle.'

'So I hear.' She didn't sound convinced, more like resigned. 'I hope you're intending to stay more than a few days, madame? The work is hard and the dancers... temperamental.'

'Bonjour, madame.' Flora removed her glove and offered her hand. 'I have nothing against hard work, and as for the dancers.' She shrugged. 'Their work must be... difficult. Your role in supporting them equally a tricky one. All I can promise is to do my best.'

Odile eyed her sharply before giving a brief nod. 'Go and find André, Tomas. Madame Toussaint will be perfectly safe. We'll get word to you when you can collect her. Now, madame, tell me about your experience?'

Tomas had told her to stick to the truth so that's what she did. It wasn't as if anyone knew about her relationship with Lucien apart from Sabine and the nuns.

'I left school at fourteen and apprenticed at Atelier de la Chapelle. After, I was lucky enough to get a job with Maison Lumineau. I was there about six months before I decided to get married. For the last eighteen years I've continued sewing at home. Mainly wedding dresses.'

'So, it's unlikely anyone at Maison Lumineau will remember you,' Odile said, her thin eyebrows disappearing under her fringe. 'And what about your husband? He's keen for you to go out to work?'

'He's dead, madame. And I need to support myself.' It wasn't a lie, not really. Brian was dead to her even if he wasn't six feet under a ton of soil. The only part that remained was her wedding band, which was necessary for the role. She planned to sell it as soon as this farce in France was over.

Odile observed her keenly. Sizing her up, trying to read her mind. Flora would have felt uncomfortable under such intense scrutiny if she'd cared about the outcome of the ad hoc interview.

'We're not Maison Lumineau, madame. We only have a ball-room and a few showgirls these days.' She nodded in the direction of the two seamstresses who'd both paused in their work, their expressions kindly. 'Of the original eight, there are only Amantine, Juliette and me to manage the workload, which leaves us at least two seamstresses short. Long gone are the celebrated artists and revues we had before the war. In their place, we have a cinema.' She curled her lip. 'We do what we can, but if you're expecting haute couture then you'd be wise to leave. The door is behind you.'

'If you don't want me to take the job...' Flora started to turn, only to stop at Odile's next words.

'Don't be so quick, madame.' Flora watched as she made for the rack of dresses, selecting one at random.

'Each dress's many petticoats require forty-five metres of fabric, which are then sewn onto a boned bustier. As you can see, the shoulders are left exposed. There are no sleeves. These garments aren't our only responsibility. There's all the lingerie too.' She beckoned her forward and, with a heave, passed over the costume. 'I hope you have muscles under that jacket, Flora. Each dress weighs six kilograms.'

Flora secured the gown back on the rail, her attention on the intricate stitching and the careful positioning of sequins to catch the light. The craftsmanship on the red, white and black gowns was exquisite and, despite the woman's words, the detailing was as fine as found on one of Lucien's creations.

'How many costume changes per show?' she finally asked, in awe of the scope of the work.

'Before the war it was twelve but, we've had to reduce it to three. There just isn't the availability.' She nodded in the direction of the fabric bales along the wall. 'It might seem like a lot, but there are rips to repair every night. Remember the dancing is intense, particularly Le Can Can. All that jumping, kicking and the final split mean the dancers leave the stage dripping. The dresses have to be carefully washed after each performance. The delicate fabric simply can't take it.' She moved to the rail on the other side of the room, where the dresses were even more spectacular. The shelf above displayed large feather festooned hairpieces. 'It's not only the dancers, of course. We have other performers too. Not so many now. We can't force them to perform to a German audience, but enough to keep the Bosch happy.'

Flora eyed a particularly fine red silk dress, with a high neck and long, narrow sleeves. Had Marguerette worn such a gown while serenading the enemy instead of her countryfolk?

If she'd been in Marguerette's position, what would she have done? The simple truth was, she didn't know.

It was time to reshape herself into the woman Tomas needed her to be. A seamstress at Le Moulin Rouge and, more importantly, a former... friend of Lucien Lumineau.

She slipped off her jacket and started pulling out her hat pin. 'What if you put me to work for what remains of the morning.' She smiled briefly. 'After, we can decide what comes next.'

SIX

Flora loved every minute of her day. Madame Guilloux became 'Odile' as soon as she saw the quality of her stitches and her quick accuracy on the sewing machine. Lunch was bread and cheese provided by the kitchen. A wheel of mouth-watering, ripe camembert from Normandy, which almost dripped off the knife when she'd tried to spread it. Surprisingly there was wine too. A light, crisp Sancerre, which had her rolling back the years to happier times.

If this was going to be her life from now on, she might never leave. If only she could find her daughters, it would be perfect.

'You've done incredibly well for someone new to La Moulin Rouge, hasn't she, Juliette?' Amantine said as soon as Odile left the room, her hands reaching up to adjust a pin in her dark hair.

'Without question,' Juliette replied, stretching up on tiptoes to hang up her finished dress.

'Here, let me do that for you. You know I don't mind.' Amantine grinned, patting the much shorter Juliette on top of her blonde bobbed hair with a laugh as she easily fixed the gown in place.

Flora smiled at the banter. 'Thank you. It's not so very different to working on my wedding dresses,' she replied as she lifted the finished gown onto the same rail, taking her time to check the skirt for any stray threads. 'We all know how fussy brides and mothers of the brides can be.'

Amantine rolled her eyes. 'A dressmaker's worst nightmare. I far prefer working here.'

'Have you been here long?'

'Two years. Our husbands joined up as soon as war broke out. It keeps our minds off what they're up to and where.'

'I'm sorry.' She felt the underside of her wedding ring with her thumb. Making herself a widow had seemed the easy option. No difficult questions to field.

'There's no need. We're only telling you because of Tomas.' Amantine covered her machine with a dust cover before packing up her scissors and measuring tape into a little pouch.

'Tomas?' Her voice was casual, her fingers busy as she worked on pinning her hat to her hair.

Amantine stopped what she was doing, her voice low. 'Tomas and our husbands are firm friends and... compatriots. Any... er... friend of his is a friend of ours, with no questions asked, although...' She leant in. 'You're not a spy supplied by the management to check on the quality of our work, are you, because if that's the case...?'

Flora laughed, liking her new friends more and more. That they knew about Tomas and suspected her of helping him in some way made things easier. Fewer secrets to trip over. 'Well, now that you ask. Absolutely not.'

'Good.'

She watched as the women started gathering the offcuts of fabric left over from their day, placing them in a large bin at one end of the table. Nothing was wasted but, looking at the bales of fabric, she suddenly wondered at the need to save the slivers of material. The French had the same make do and mend philosophy as the British, but surely Odile would have no use for the scraps. They were too small to be of value. She was about to question her when Amantine beat her to it.

'I see you've noticed our little project.' Amantine reached for her bag and pulled out a patchwork quilt with a flourish. 'With fabric impossible to come by, we couldn't justify throwing away even the tiniest offcut so, instead, we make these, backing them with whatever we have to hand. Not that we know what to do with them apart from give them out to the needy.'

Flora touched the multicoloured patchwork, the pieces by necessity postage stamp size, but arranged in a starburst design and reflecting the red, white and black of the dancers' dresses.

'I can't get over that you made this from that,' she said, nodding at the overflowing bin.

Amantine folded the quilt and placed it back in her bag out of sight. 'Well, we had to do something. It's just a shame we can't work in a code. Help our resistance friends share information between different cells across France and beyond. Think about the allies who suddenly find themselves on French soil with a German or two on their tail, Flora. There must be a way of getting word to our people, at both the ports and the Pyrenees, that we have a "package" that needs safe passage.'

'Which is admirable,' Odile said, from the doorway. 'But with all our many *guests* arriving from the east we have to be careful,' she added, a note of rebuke in her tone. 'I agree that it would be splendid to include a secret message somehow or even documents, but the one thing the Germans aren't is stupid. Every parcel I receive from my sister in the south has been opened and inspected. Clothing has been turned inside out, including the pockets, the food packages opened and mostly confiscated, our letters black-lined.' She darted a look at Amantine's bag. 'Please don't be too clever, Amantine. There's a lot at stake here. One false move and we might end up without a job or, even worse, arrested.'

Flora glanced between the three women before focusing on Amantine's bag; an idea for a simple patchwork quilt starting to build in her mind. One that included a code. She filed the idea away for later. She'd need peace and quiet and a pencil and paper to work out the maths. Instead, she asked, 'How can I get involved?

Do we meet here or take the scraps home? Tell me how it works. I'd like to help.'

A beat of silence. Then Juliette reached across and covered Flora's hand with her own, her eyes bright.

'Tuesdays, Thursdays and Fridays – we stay an extra hour after everyone else leaves, including Odile despite her cautious words. You're welcome to take some scraps with you to get started. Every little helps.'

The four seamstresses looked at each other.

Flora felt something she hadn't felt in a very long time – the particular warmth of women who had decided to trust each other.

She grabbed a handful of scraps and added them to her bag.

Tomas was waiting for her at the entrance, his arms folded as he languished against the wall, an unlit cigarette dangling from his lips, which he removed pronto. 'There you are. I thought you'd never be done. How was it?'

'Oh, you know. Work.' She shrugged dismissively, not wanting to reveal her joy at being back in an environment she hadn't realised she'd missed.

He eyed her keenly as he pushed away from the wall, clearly not believing a word, but Flora didn't care about that. She'd agreed to help him find Lucien. She hadn't agreed to share her innermost thoughts on the matter.

'Fair enough. Where to now? Back to Madame Billy's or a coffee somewhere, if you're not too tired?'

Flora was past tiredness. With no sleep on the plane and little on the drive into Paris, there was no energy left, but the quilt had ignited a spark. She wanted to probe him to see if her idea might work as an alternative to hiding messages in fabric bales.

He coughed, reminding her that he was still waiting for her answer.

'What time is blackout?' she asked.

'Nine, so we have four hours unless we have a pass, or an exemption.'

She looked at him, her mind working through his words. 'Exemptions are for doctors, night workers. Of course, Germans?'

He nodded, his expression darkening. Flora was suddenly thankful that they were on the same side. Tomas was a man she shouldn't underestimate. 'Midwives, cabaret stars, collaborators too.'

'Which means Lucien can come and go freely while I can't. Typical. How often does he visit Le Moulin Rouge?' she continued, looking at the red windmill, its sails motionless. Odile had told her that the war had curtailed their use of electricity. The sails might be frozen while power was heavily rationed, but they were able to use their sewing machines so it could be much worse. It was all very well objecting to their clientele, but not when the alternative was starving.

'When Marguerette was singing it was most evenings. The place opens at seven and runs into the small hours. Why, what are you thinking?'

Flora wasn't sure. It wasn't as if she'd be welcome in the place unless she was on the arm of someone and, with no suitable dress, that would be impossible. Even the thought of entering as a guest was an anathema. The cabaret wasn't for working women like her. She'd be completely out of her depth to the point of drowning.

She tucked the ends of her scarf inside her jacket, trying to work out what to do for the best. It was all very well knowing Lucien's routine, but managing to bump into him accidentally was going to be difficult. Unless it was at Madame Billy's, she thought, dismissing the idea almost immediately.

The sound of a chair scraping across the pavement drew her attention to the other side of Place Blanche and the elegant café opposite. The Café de Palmier was ideally situated for the entrance to the metro, but also for the cabaret. A waiter in a three-piece suit and ankle-length white apron was wiping down a table under a bright red striped awning. A young couple were sitting outside huddled in their coats. Their heads were close, as if sharing a secret. A rumble of wheels against road before a military truck appeared at the end of the street. The woman raised her head, her face a white mask against the glow of dusk. The waiter paused, the cloth pressed into the table before continuing to wipe the surface.

'A coffee,' Flora said, still looking at the waiter. 'Let's sit and plan.'

They were soon settled on an ornate, carved wooden banquette just inside the door, dainty white cups in front of them. The place was busy, most of the seats taken, the air full of the aroma of ersatz coffee and the sound of muted conversation.

'Do you mind if I smoke?'

Flora turned from where she'd been looking at the young couple throw a few coins on the table before hurrying into the darkness. 'Not at all.'

Tomas tapped his cigarette packet. 'Like one?'

Flora shook her head, watching as he went through the little ritual of choosing one before striking a match. Brian had smoked a pipe. A messy, complicated affair that seemed far too time consuming. All that emptying and refilling. The house was littered with tobacco strands and pipe cleaners. She'd once caught him using the end of her knitting needle, which had caused one of their worst rows.

The door pushed open on a crowd of fashionable young women who quickly crammed around the table across from them.

These must be some of the dancers, she thought, trying not to stare. Women who'd known Marguerette. Women she'd laughed with and confided in. Women who might know where she was and why she'd disappeared.

She gripped the porcelain cup. If she was braver, or if she could come up with a good enough excuse, she'd lean across and ask them.

'Anything wrong?' Tomas said, his voice soft, his breath carrying the lingering aroma of cigarettes and coffee.

'You've been telling people I'm your sister,' she improvised, not wanting to talk about her daughters. 'I have no family, Tomas. When Lucien finds out – and he will – what then?'

'Good point. Well, it's too late to change it now,' he mused, a deep frown forming. 'You're sure he knows?'

'Not exactly.'

It was difficult to remember what she'd said all those years ago, but Lucien had been interested in her from the very beginning. He'd wanted to know her life story, everything about her from the smallest to the biggest of things.

Since then, Flora never talked about her past. She'd told Brian that her parents had died in a train crash when she was fourteen, which had closed down the conversation. The scars on her back were more difficult to explain as were the changes wrought by her pregnancy. Being whipped by her foster mother until she'd collapsed was something she couldn't bear to describe. Brian had seemed satisfied with her explanation when she'd told him she'd been seriously injured during the train crash. That her whole life was a train crash seemed more fitting.

'My mother abandoned me when I was born.' She placed her cup back in its saucer, her hand steady, her words matter-of-fact.

'You never knew who your parents were?' Tomas sounded stunned.

She shook her head slowly. Her upbringing was one no child should ever have. She'd never had anyone to belong to. No home. She took a breath, air filling her lungs before she exhaled the lot. No wonder she'd latched onto the first man to offer her any kindness.

'I was found in a gutter. My cord still attached. The Assistance Publique placed me with a foster family on the outskirts of Paris and, when I turned fourteen, I apprenticed with a seamstress.' Her gaze rested on the perfect features of the pretty, blonde-haired woman at the next table. She admired her poise and elegance. The angle of her head and the way tendrils of her hair artfully framed her face. It was all about confidence, something she'd taken years to develop after what had happened with Lucien. She also admired her simple, elegant two-piece in claret silk, and wondered at the designer. 'I'd hate for you to feel sorry for me.' She smiled across at him. 'I insist that you don't.'

He set his cup down, the porcelain rattling against the saucer, the back of his hand brushing against hers in the process, his face tense. 'The family you were placed with. They were kind?'

Flora thought back to the cold indifference on the farm. The expectations that she could never meet. The film of ice on her water jug in the mornings. The biting cold where heating was a luxury. She'd done her best, but it was never enough. She'd still have been there if...

'Flora?'

She blinked, drawn to the light pressure of his hand covering hers.

'They placed me with a family near Étampes. A small sheep farm. Fields and sheep. The only outing was to church.' She managed a lopsided smile, withdrawing her hand and placing it on her lap. 'If you have any sheep that need shearing or wool to be spun, I'm your woman.'

'Alright. That only changes things a little. I can be your foster brother.' He looked pleased with himself at having solved the problem and why wouldn't he, she thought, unable to share in his triumph. There was so much that he didn't know, would never know. She certainly wasn't going to tell him.

Marcel.

The image of her foster brother popped into her head like a jack-in-the-box, bringing the memory of that last day with it.

'Excuse me. I just need to...'

Flora didn't finish the sentence. She couldn't. Instead, she pushed away from the table and headed to the back of the restaurant in search of the toilets.

She'd forced herself to wipe that time from her mind, only for it to come hurtling back almost as soon as she'd landed in France.

With her bag on the ledge beside the sink, she stared at her reflection in the mirror. Skin so fine that faint lines were starting to fan from her eyes and crease the corners of her mouth. A face bearing little resemblance to the young girl she remembered.

Running the tap, she dampened her wrists before pressing them to her brow and the sides of her neck, tears of annoyance and shame blurring her vision. Twenty-two years on and the memory of Marcel launching himself at her fourteen-year-old-self in the sheep shed still had the power to break her. His hands on her shoulders, propelling her back, the smell of his rancid breath, perspiration so thick that she'd gagged.

His mother, on hearing her screams, had dragged him off before turning on her with the handle of her broom.

It had been her fault for leading him on, the stroke of the handle emphasising every word. She'd whipped her until Flora had lost consciousness. Darkness had fallen by the time she'd finally come to. She'd hobbled the four miles into town, her torn dress clutched to her chest, her back beaten to a bloody pulp. It was only thanks to the kindly priest that she was still here today.

The sound of the door suddenly opening behind her was closely followed by, 'I'd recognise that hair anywhere, ma cocotte. Where have you been, Marguerette?'

Flora lifted her head from the ornate art deco sink, locking eyes with the smiling woman reflected in the mirror behind. The woman in the claret two-piece who'd been sitting opposite.

A beat, then two before the woman's smile collapsed, her delicate features staining puce red. 'I'm sorry. I could have sworn that you were...' She broke eye contact, clearly embarrassed as she moved to the other sink and started pinning her hair, her actions hurried.

Flora closed her eyes briefly, releasing her hands from where they'd been clutching the edge of the sink.

'It's an easy mistake to make, mademoiselle,' she replied. 'I've come to Paris to find her.'

The woman paused, her expression uncertain until Flora turned to face her. Tomas had said they could have been sisters, a statement which she'd put down to kindness. Apparently not.

'You're her...?'

'We're related,' she said firmly, holding out her hand. 'I'm Flora. Anything you can tell me about Marguerette would be welcome.'

'I'm Coralina, a friend from Le Moulin Rouge.'

'I really need to find her, Coralina. Marguerette and I... lost touch... a while ago.' Her voice was laden with a sorrow she didn't try to disguise. 'You don't happen to know where she is?'

'I was about to ask you the same question. No one does. One day she was here and the next, vanished into thin air. Disappeared from her lodgings along with her belongings.' Coralina paused briefly, giving up any pretence of repairing her perfect face and hair in the mirror. 'You know where she was living?'

'I have lodgings there too. Maybe we could meet?' Flora said. 'I've just started in the sewing department with Madame Guilloux.'

The noise from the door opening had them both freezing in surprise. A skeletally thin woman skewered them with a suspicious look before heading into one of the cubicles.

Coralina leant forward, her voice whisper soft. 'We need to find her. I'll be in touch.'

SEVEN

Flora and Tomas stayed for another hour, but they were both flagging by the time they got up to leave. Flora felt she'd achieved far more than she'd dared hope. There was no sign of Lucien, but she wasn't worried about that. In less than a day, she'd got to meet her daughter's friend and settled back into working life as a seamstress. That had to be enough.

Seven was still early when viewed through the lens of Parisian nightlife. L'Etoile de Kleber was quiet, with none of the hustle and bustle she'd imagined. Her mind had been going full throttle since Tomas had walked her through the oriental garden earlier. The reality of the quiet, upmarket townhouse was far less exciting.

'Let's see if we can find Madame Billy. She's bound to be in the drawing room.'

'What about my coat and hat?'

He smiled gently. 'I wouldn't worry about that. It's all very casual here, as you'll quickly discover.'

The drawing room was painted in rich creams and dotted with mirrors, exotic greenery and dainty side tables and chairs in the style of Louis XVI. The focal point was an impressive piano, which looked perfectly at ease in such glamorous surroundings.

The woman sitting on a low couch by the lit fire wasn't what

Flora had been expecting. In truth, she hadn't known what to expect. It wasn't as if she'd ever met a brothel owner before. Someone flamboyant maybe, with careless clothes.

She was probably mid-forties, with a bold aquiline nose dominating an otherwise exquisite face. Laughter lines fanned out from a pair of fine blue eyes that sparkled in mischief. Her pale hair was pinned neatly into tiny curls.

There were no adornments. No jewellery at all and very little make-up, if any. She could have run a bookshop or been a teacher, but she wasn't.

'Bonsoir Aline. I'd like to introduce you to Madame Toussaint. Flora, this is Madame Billy, Aline to her friends.'

'Ah, dear Tomas. How good of you to grace us with your presence.' She allowed him to press a small kiss on each cheek before waving him away. 'Our wine cellars are in need of some attention.'

'I'm not sure I'm going to be much help.' He wandered over to the fireplace, his back to the flames. 'You'd do better to have a word with one of your esteemed visitors. With the Weinfurter's requisitioning all our good wines for transport to Germany, we've been left with the undrinkable and the unremarkable.'

Flora watched as Madame Billy made her way across to him, her hand smoothing over his shoulders. 'This isn't for the Boche, mon ami. I'd like a few bottles for my own paltry cellar. Something full-bodied instead of the vinegary slop we serve to our clients.'

He smiled down at her, his eyes alight with laughter. 'I'll see what I can do, after all you're doing for us, but it won't be easy.' He considered a moment. 'Keep back any bottles of 1910 Château L'Ancien Pont Bordeaux from the next order. It was a particularly wet year so unlikely that anyone light-fingered will be tempted. The harvest is well known for being poor, the wine thin, acidic and with undertones of mould.'

'Sounds vile.'

He smirked at the laughter accompanying her words. 'It is, but your bottles won't be holding it.' He flicked his wrist. 'I have one or two special vintages left, which I can easily decant. They'll have to be drunk quickly though.'

'Don't you concern yourself about that, chéri. Drinking them won't be the problem.' She turned to Flora, patting the seat beside her. 'Come sit, Madame Toussaint. You look like your daughter. Marguerette is such a wonderful young woman. Voice of an angel. I was saddened when she left.'

Flora settled beside her, but at a slight angle. There was so much she wanted to ask about Marguerette, but formalities had to be followed. Madame Billy looked nice enough, but it was difficult to guess what was really going on behind her smooth expression and intelligent eyes. She'd have to tread warily. 'It's very kind of you to let me stay.'

'Kindness doesn't come into it, chérie. Tomas and I have a little arrangement. I help where I can.' She sighed briefly, her knitting back in her lap, her hands settled on top. 'Although I don't think I'm going to be of as much use as I'd hoped. Dear Lucien hasn't been to see me in weeks. It might be to do with the quality of the wine, but I don't think so. Something is worrying him. We're all worried, chérie. When I bought L'Etoile, I never could have imagined that the Gestapo would settle their headquarters in the next street.'

Flora's eyes widened, her gaze seeking out Tomas, who'd relaxed onto one of the chairs opposite, a large white cat busily kneading his lap.

'Yes, I'm afraid it's true, but it shouldn't make any difference. Some of your best customers, eh, Aline?'

Madame Billy threw back her head and laughed, a long guttural rasp that exposed her expanse of white throat and yellowing teeth. 'The kind of customers I can do without, but as long as they pay their bills and know who's in charge of this little establishment.' She shrugged her thin shoulders. 'Now, there are some things you need to know, madame.'

'Do call me Flora,' Flora insisted. Toussaint, or *all saints*, was the name given to her by the Assistance Publique, in line with their policy of naming foundlings after feast days. It was a name she'd come to despise, and one of the reasons for her inopportune marriage to Brian. It was difficult to remember whether she'd been attracted to him first or his perfectly serviceable name of Granville.

'And you must call me Aline.' She pushed to her feet, suddenly all business, her heeled shoes digging into the expensive-looking rug. 'This room is out of bounds for you from 9 pm each evening, as is the bar and the restaurant.' She grinned, her eyes glinting with amusement. 'The same goes for both the first and the second floor. There is a private staircase you can use, which leads directly from the kitchen to the attics above.' She turned to Tomas. 'You'll stay for supper, Tomas?'

'If I'm invited.'

Flora opened her mouth only to close it again. She hadn't considered that he'd be staying elsewhere, but it made sense. As a wine merchant, he'd probably have a shop somewhere.

'My home is in the village of Ancinnes, but I also have a small apartment above my store in the Rue de Passy, although I'm rarely there,' he said, as if reading her mind.

'Of course you're invited, you silly man,' Madame Billy said, her eyes sliding between them, her expression unreadable. 'If you're lucky, you'll get to meet my other tenant on the top floor. She might even play for us if she's not performing later.' Aline lifted her hands to her hair, securing one of the pins just so. 'A word of warning though. She keeps late hours but, when you hear her sing, you'll understand why.'

EIGHT

Flora sat at the table in her bedroom, a fresh sheet of Madame Billy's best notepaper in front of her along with a pencil and a ruler she'd borrowed from Mimi. This would be her sixth attempt. The other five had been scrunched into tight balls and aimed in the general direction of the wood basket.

The problem wasn't the maths. Dressmakers had to be good at numbers or garments wouldn't fit. It was designing a patchwork quilt that would enable the receiver to pinpoint a certain date and time. By necessity it also had to be a simple arrangement of squares, the simpler the better, but with the added stipulation that it also had to hoodwink the Germans. Odile had rattled her with her talk of pockets being turned out and seams examined. There could be nothing hidden, nothing to alert the enemy that the quilt wasn't what it seemed. A vibrant addition to a baby's cot using the three colours they had available. Red, white and black. That they were the same colours as the flags dotted around was something she wasn't going to think about.

She chewed on the end of the pencil until the acrid taste of lead had her spitting it out and scrubbing the back of her hand against her mouth. The seemingly insurmountable problem was in making 361 uniform squares into 365, the number of days in a year needed for her idea for a calendar quilt. It hadn't taken her long to realise that $19 \times 19 = 361$. A eureka moment until she remembered she needed another four squares for her idea to work. Maths wasn't something she could mess with.

Flinging the pencil across the room in disgust, she wandered over to the stove. With the door open, she stuffed it full of her rejected designs before jabbing it with the poker and slamming the door shut.

After, she plonked herself on the floor with her handbag in front of her, fabric scraps of all different shapes and sizes scattered around her. She picked up her triangle of tailor's chalk in one hand and her measuring tape in the other. Within twenty minutes she had a pile of one-inch squares with a little extra added for the seams – 50 instead of the 361 she needed, but enough to play with.

Stretching her neck, she stared at the ceiling and yawned. It had been a long day. Too long to be sitting on the floor playing with scraps, which didn't want to turn themselves into a quilt. Then she remembered Amantine and Juliette and their husbands. Their eagerness to do their bit, but not knowing how.

She'd give it another half an hour before she gave up for the night.

She determinedly worked on setting the squares down in front of her in alternating colours, staggering consecutive rows to make a stair effect. With six rows of six, she had the perfect square, in the same way she would with nineteen rows of nineteen.

It took ten minutes of concentration and the start of a headache to realise what she was missing. A border on the quilt to turn 361 to 365 with the added advantage that the Germans wouldn't know what they were looking at.

She stood and stretched before moving to the table and, with a few quick lines, created the pattern she'd been struggling with for the last two hours, feeling a spark of delight at what she'd achieved during her first full day in Paris.

. . .

It wasn't surprising that she couldn't sleep. A strange bed and strange noises from the floors below. There'd been night noise in Boneybefore too, she remembered. Men wandering home after chuck-out from the pub. The milkman's horse-drawn cart, bottles rattling in the back. Coal trucks going to and from the mills in Carrickfergus. The roar of the occasional train that ran between the back of the cottage and the sea. Even the sound of the baker's van rumbling along the cobbles to the shop on the corner, but the sounds in L'Etoile de Kleber were different. Unsettling. Doors banging. The occasional shout and scream. People racing up and down the stairs. Cars screeching away from the premises.

By 2 am the house had finally settled into a quiet harmony, the tension of the day replaced by the familiar pre-sleep lethargy.

She wasn't sure what woke her. Pulling her shawl around her shoulders, she pushed her feet into her slippers and made for the door, her ear pressed to the wood.

Music and singing. Loud enough to go through three floors. Loud enough to wake the dead, along with the neighbours if the hammering on the door directly below her window was anything to go by.

Flora hurried down the stairs, ignoring the piano music coming from the drawing room. If she didn't open the front door, they'd break it down.

'Open up!'

She'd barely pulled the bolts back when the door burst open and a couple of burly policemen burst through, almost knocking her over in their quest for the drawing room. Flora turned to shut the door behind them, only to find Madame Billy descending the central staircase, immaculately dressed in a plain black gown.

'Ah, I see that Edith has finally turned up. Do come and meet her, Flora.'

The music from the salon was swelling to the finale, a diminutive woman with rust-red hair thumping away at the piano keys, her smoky voice raised in song.

'Here they are!'

The police stood, mouths slightly open and seemingly starstruck as Edith swung to her feet, slamming the lid closed.

Flora wasn't sure who was more surprised. The police, or her at the sight of the tiny Frenchwoman producing such a transfixing sound.

Edith appeared full of contradictions. Small, not even five feet tall, and dressed in a nondescript dark frock. There was nothing that stood out in her pale, heart-shaped face, except for her luminous eyes. Flora stood in the doorway, unsure of her place, but no one was looking her way. They were all enthralled by Edith, and why not. She couldn't tear her eyes away even if she'd wanted to. The woman's presence filled the room, one hand on her hip, the other picking up a glass of amber-coloured liquid from the nearest side table. On stage she'd be magnificent. In Madame Billy's salon, she had the power to make Flora forget about everything apart from the music.

'Bonsoir, messieurs. Perhaps I was a trifle loud, non.' She gave a little bow of apology. 'It is late and my wits are starting to fail me. Just one more song? A soft lullaby to see you on your way.' She waved them to sit. Flora wouldn't have believed it if she hadn't seen the two men doing exactly that. Madame Billy winked before easing onto the edge of the sofa, indicating that Flora should join her.

The song, 'L'Étranger', was indeed a ballad. A soft serenade that brought a sigh to Flora's weary heart even if she was unable to summon up a smile. The music was new to her, the words a balm in a Paris that felt as unfamiliar as the stranger in the song. When Edith finally trailed to a finish, the gendarmes nodded their appreciation before hurrying to the door. No doubt there'd be neighbours to placate but, for tonight at least, the impromptu music session at L'Etoile de Kreber was over.

'Bravo, ma petite, but you should be in bed. Even if you can't think about yourself, what about my beauty sleep?' Madame Billy smoothed her fingers over her cheeks, her eyes alight with laughter. 'Those policemen will be talking about you for weeks to come.

And, in the meantime, I'd like to introduce you to Madame Flora Toussaint, Marguerette's mother. Flora, this is Edith Piaf. You may have heard of her already. She's quite famous. Now, off to bed with you both.' She strode to the front door, bolting it shut before watching like a headmistress on duty until they'd mounted the stairs.

Edith waited until they were on their own floor before beckoning her into her room.

'A little drink to help us sleep.'

Flora expected a duplicate of her bedroom and she was both right and wrong. The size, the shape and the window were the same, as was the stove, but that's where any similarity ended. The room felt half the size of hers and in need of a good tidy. What space there was had been filled with an old piano.

'Sit.'

The chair Edith gestured to was covered in a mountain of sheet music, which she quickly dumped on the floor, pushing it into a messy pile under the window.

She then removed what looked like half her wardrobe scattered across the bed and tossed it carelessly into a corner with a shrug.

'Calvados do? It's all I have.' She produced a small flask, tipping a generous measure into a glass before handing it across. 'You look like Marguerette.'

Edith slipped back on the bed and leant her head against the wall, her feet barely touching the edge of the narrow mattress. With her flask between her legs, she pulled out a squashed packet of Gauloises. Within seconds the room was filled with the distinctive earthy smell of rotting leaves.

'Want one?'

Yes, but she wouldn't. It was too late and the packet didn't appear that appealing. 'No, thank you.'

Edith shrugged again, her smile gamine and decidedly cheeky.

Flora didn't know what she was doing in the room. In four hours she'd have to think about getting up, but there was an opportunity here.

'I've come to Paris to find my daughters, Edith.'

With the sentence out in the open, she took a tentative sip from the glass, letting the small trickle of fiery liquid burn a path from her mouth to her throat.

Edith stared at her through a haze of smoke, her dark eyes appraising. 'Marguerette told me a little of her background, ma chérie. Her childhood was a happy one, but not in the traditional sense. I'm not judging you,' she added, when Flora went to speak. 'I'd be the last person to do that, but you have to realise that Marguerette might not want to be found.'

Flora bit her lip, her throat tightening from the combination of cheap liquor and threatening tears. Looking around the mess on the floor, she imagined Marguerette sitting in this same chair sharing her secrets. What else had she shared? How had she been? What had she felt? And finally, where had she run away to and why? There was nothing she could do to change the past but, if the likes of Edith wouldn't help, Flora wouldn't be able to alter the present or the future – her dearest wish. It might be too late to rectify her failings as a mother, but now she was back, she'd never stop trying.

Dropping her gaze to her glass, she lifted it to her lips and tipped it back in one. What Edith really meant was that Marguerette might not want to be found by her.

She swallowed, feeling shame at the younger woman laying the facts before her, facts she knew already. 'I have many regrets, Edith, but nothing greater than leaving my girls.'

'I know from personal experience, ma chérie, that there are always two sides to every story. If you'd like to tell me yours, Flora. I'm a good listener.'

The olive branch, presented in such a gentle, quiet way was enough to propel tears to the back of her eyes. Flora knew she'd found a friend at Madame Billy's. It was unbelievable that she was even staying in the same building as the famous singer.

NINE

Flora stared in the bathroom mirror, her eyes heavy from lack of sleep. She'd lain awake thinking all sorts, but primarily about how she was going to broker a meeting with Lucien. Only after, would she be able to concentrate on finding her girls.

It couldn't be at either his home or his work, or indeed the brothel if Madame Billy was to be believed. That Tomas had put his faith in the latter was a blow to the mission. He'd looked to her for ideas but, the truth was, she didn't have any. She'd never got to know the real Lucien. That side of him had remained well hidden.

The sound of sudden rain and wind bashing against the window brought a memory with it. The day she'd first met him.

The streets had been awash with water that day too, she remembered, closing her eyes against the bland ceiling. She'd been slipping on the wet pavement outside Maison Lumineau, the soles of her shoes letting in water when a car had pulled up alongside.

'Get in. You're like a drowned rat.'

Flora held back, tongue-tied at the sight of the famous Lucien Lumineau stopping the car and speaking to her. 'I can't, Monsieur Lumineau. I'm all wet.'

'You'll dry, as will my car seat, mademoiselle.' He'd eyed her legs as she folded them inside, her skirt riding up her knees until she yanked it back in place. 'You know who I am?' he said after a moment, his voice full of surprise.

'Of course. I'm one of your seamstresses,' she replied primly, wanting to brush her hair back from her face where it was dripping down her neck in icy cold drops.

'Then we certainly can't have you catching your death. Where are you off to?'

'Place St Pierre. There's a little ribbon shop...'

'I know it well.' He held out his hand, his fingers long and slim. 'I'm Lucien, enchantée, mademoiselle.'

She placed her hand in his, embarrassed at her raggedy, bitten fingernails and roughened skin. 'Flora Toussaint.'

'Flora.' He rolled her name over his tongue, as if savouring each letter and syllable. 'The Roman goddess of flowers,' he mused, still in possession of her hand as if he'd forgotten it was there, his gaze settling on her hair. 'I should have guessed. Titian would be delighted with his namesake.' He released her hand only to replace it with a strand of her hair, smoothing it out between his fingers as if transfixed. 'The colour of honeyed amber, and as soft as silk.'

'Titian, monsieur?' She'd heard the name but couldn't quite place it. Her mind was reeling, not quite believing what was happening. That the famed couturier was even speaking to her. Things like that didn't happen in her world. She went to work and, after, she went back to her room. That was it. Her life in two steps. There had never been a third, until now.

'His painting of you hangs in the Uffizi in Florence. A prize among treasures.' He sat up suddenly as if coming to a decision, his attention back on the road. 'A quick trip to Montmartre for this very important ribbon and then supper, I think.'

Flora gaped at him, her voice holding a wobble. 'No, I mustn't.'

'Why not, mademoiselle. A husband, boyfriend?' He quirked an eyebrow, ignoring the sharp toot from the car behind. 'A lover perhaps?'

'No, you don't understand. Mademoiselle Crambert will be expecting me, and the ribbon too,' she added, suddenly reminded of the urgency of the errand.

He patted her leg, leaving his hand longer than necessary. 'As the ribbon is for me, there's no problem. We can even drop it off first if you're that worried.'

Flora unscrewed the lid of her tooth powder and spread a little on her toothbrush, the morning rush to get to work on time forgotten as her first day with Lucien continued to unfold. Their supper at Café de la Rotonde in Montparnasse. He'd chosen well. She had to give him that. Rare roast beef sandwiches with a trio of mustards. A meal she'd recognised. The warm, crusty bread a staple even if the tender meat wasn't. The accompanying bottle of champagne had been her undoing along with his soft words, his gaze fastened on her honeyed hair.

The gas lamps had already flared to life by the time they'd left. It had made sense to her champagne-clogged brain to accept his invitation to have a coffee to finish the evening off.

'Bonjour, Flora. Just the person.' Odile hurried across the room, a bale of aquamarine silk tucked under her arm, which she proceeded to grab in thick handfuls, the fabric streaming around her. 'Coralina has just been appointed the new resident singer. We need a dress for her by tonight. Something spectacular, and we've nominated you.'

Flora looked between the fabric, Odile's expression and the way Juliette and Amantine had their heads buried over their machines. She'd planned on having a quiet word with them about her design for the quilt. Now it looked as if it would have to wait.

'What kind of thing are you looking for? And I'll need Coralina's measurements,' she said, with a smile, an idea already forming in her mind. Blue was a good choice for the blonde woman. She'd make Marguerette's friend look fabulous.

Odile nodded approvingly. 'Glamorous and eye-catching to

show off her figure but not too much of it. We don't want to send the men into a frenzy. Apart from that...' She nodded at the mannequin in the corner. 'I'm happy to leave it to you. Use whatever you like as an embellishment. We'll take care of the repairs. You'll find a bolt of muslin to work with and a list of her measurements on the cutting table.'

'Right.' Flora unpinned her hat before removing her coat and gloves and donning her overall.

Running the silk through her fingers, she gathered it into pleats before setting it aside in favour of pencil and paper. Odile wanted glamorous so that's what she was going to get. An asymmetrical neckline, supported by one shoulder strap, in the Grecian style but with a fitted bodice to echo the dancers' dresses. A little horizontal ruching at the waist and the hips before draping to the floor.

There were no measurements at this stage. Only a preliminary design, which was where the muslin came in. The cream fabric was inferior quality, the type only suitable to wrap cheese, but that wasn't important. She was only using it to test the pattern.

With her pincushion at her side, she draped and tucked the muslin to the mannequin until she was sure the shape and form were what she was looking for, starting to enjoy herself with the adventurous design. The gown would only come alive when the final pattern was executed in silk.

Over an hour had passed by the time she removed the muslin panels and laid them down on the thick brown paper they used to build their designs. With Coralina's measurements to hand, she used a ruler to mark out the pieces, remembering to add a generous seam allowance, sections for the front and back bodice along with the skirt panels and extra for draping and facings.

By lunchtime, she'd cut out all the pieces and tacked them together. After lunch, she prepared the seams before assembling first the bodice then the skirt. Next it was back to the mannequin to work on the ruching. It was three o'clock by the time she'd completed the sewing, but Flora wasn't finished. The gown was stunning. Graceful, romantic, sexy even, but it wasn't spectacular.

It took the addition of appliquéd, cut out satin and artfully placed sequins to have the three women rush over just as the clock ticked to five.

'I'll admit, I didn't believe you when you said you'd worked at Maison Lumineau, but this is exquisite.' Odile hurried to the door. 'Wait there a minute. I'll see if Coralina has arrived. She said she'd be here early for a fitting.'

Flora rolled her shoulders, her hands pressed into her lower back, her eyes gritty with fatigue. She was tired beyond belief, but there was no time to bask in Odile's praise. With a quick glance at the empty corridor outside, she opened her bag and pulled out the collection of squares she'd worked on last night along with the sheet of Madame Billy's notepaper. It wasn't that she didn't trust Odile. She couldn't forget her words. Helping the resistance was too big a risk and, as lead seamstress, Odile had more to lose than the rest of them.

'Were you serious about what you said, Amantine, or am I about to make a complete fool of myself?' she said, placing her scissors and bag of needles and thread beside the pile of squares.

She watched the two women exchange glances, their eyes glinting in anticipation. 'Absolutely. I knew there was something about you when I met you yesterday. This dress proves it. I said as much to Juliette on the walk home, and why should our husbands have all the fun?' she said, moving her chair closer.

Flora thought it unlikely that fun was the right word for what their husbands were involved in. Blowing up bridges and disabling train tracks as part of their sabotage activities couldn't rank alongside a bit of low-risk sewing. She paused, taking her time in arranging the squares she'd cut out last night. There were going to be risks. If they were caught...

'I've come up with a design for a baby's patchwork quilt. A calendar quilt,' she amended, pushing her concerns aside. There would be time enough after she'd shared her idea. 'A simple design. It needs to be simple, or they'll suspect something.' She pulled a face. 'As Odile reminded us yesterday, it's impossible to send items across France without them being turned inside out. And a baby's quilt because it's smaller.' She laughed briefly. 'Less work.'

'Sounds amazing, if you think it will be effective.' Amantine squinted down at the pattern, sounding far from convinced at the sight of the alternating red, white and black squares.

'Oh, it will be effective and relatively easy to make. The question is, are you prepared to take the risk? If we're caught then...'

'If we're caught then we'll deny all knowledge,' Juliette said firmly. 'Although I'm not sure how a blank quilt is going to help.'

Flora smiled, unable to disguise her joy at having worked out the design. 'Why don't you count the squares,' she continued, tapping on the notepaper.

She watched as Juliette started adding, muttering the numbers under her breath, her finger marking her place on the small squares.

'Three hundred and sixty-one?'

'Not quite, nearly.' Flora pointed to the white border with the four coloured squares, one in each corner. 'Three hundred and sixty-five, or nineteen rows by nineteen rows, which luckily for the resistance makes a perfect size for a baby's quilt. A single stitch out of kilter in the design, invisible unless you're looking for it, to denote the date and the time a drop is expected.'

'I still don't quite get...?'

Flora grabbed the template and a pencil from the table, marking a small line in one of the squares.

'Imagine there's a parachute drop coming in, or that you're trying to send a downed British airman over the border to Spain and there's no way of getting a message to alert those that need to know. The phones are monitored and using radio is almost as bad. Then a quilt arrives. The black squares at the top are to tell the reader which way to hold the quilt up.' She started counting, tapping the tip of her finger on each square, stopping at fifty-nine, where she'd placed the dot. Then she strolled across the room and plucked the calendar off the wall, and repeated the exercise before stepping back from the table with a smile. 'The next drop is on 28th

February and if you see where I placed the line, or stitch if you like, at the top of the square, or the twelve o'clock position.' She frowned down at the quilt. 'The only things I need to work out is how to alert them whether it's during the day or during the night, and what to do in 1944 when it's 366 squares instead of 365, a leap year.'

There was a stunned silence before Juliette reached across and pressed a deep kiss on her cheeks, much to her embarrassment, the woman's eyes brimming with sudden tears. 'You amazing, fabulous woman for making a calendar and a clock in one go. Do you know how useful this is going to be? And the brilliant thing about it is when the stitch is removed, we can reuse it. There's going to be a lot of quilt-making going on, and we can always think again in a couple of years, but the war might be over by the next leap year. Here's hoping.'

The sound of feet on the stairs had Flora tucking the pattern in her bag, her expression set to neutral at the sight of Odile and Coralina hurrying over.

'Flora is a genius, Cora. Look at what she's made for you.'

It was times like these that reminded Flora of why she'd decided to become a seamstress. To see Coralina's pure delight as she examined the dress before quickly trying it on was only heightened by the fact that the gown required no adjustment in either the fit or the length. A rare enough event to make Flora glow with pride.

'I feel like a princess.' Coralina danced around the room, her arms twirling over her head in delight.

'You look like one. The blue was a great choice, Odile.'

'The last bale, Flora. I can't see us getting any more.'

'There are a few pieces left.' Flora folded them into a neat pile. 'I'm sure you can use them for something.'

'I think *we* can use them for the quilts, Flora.' She deliberately tilted her head in the direction of where Flora had left the pieces she'd painstakingly sewn together last night, before turning back to

Coralina. 'In our spare time, we make quilts for the needy. Every stitch counts.'

Coralina smiled, before shrugging helplessly. 'If only I could sew like dear Marguerette. Not even a button.'

Slipping off the gown, she handed it back to Flora, her voice pitched to a whisper. 'I've been asking around. No news yet but I'll keep trying.'

TEN

Sunday 29 November – Rue de Villejust Paris, 8 am

Lucien,

It has taken me eighteen years to find the courage to write to you, but it is time. I do not know what you will think after a gap of so many years. There's too much to explain in a letter. Can we meet at a time and place of your choosing?

Flora scrunched up the paper in annoyance. She'd got up early to see if she could write the letter she'd been promising herself since Monday, but thinking about it and turning her thoughts into words were two different things.

Grabbing her coat, hat and bag, she made for the door. A walk in the crisp air might be just the thing she needed to come up with a way of accidentally bumping into Lucien instead of the letter she couldn't seem to write and the growing stack of quilts that had taken on a life of their own. She'd put aside her knitting and had managed to piece together three, although they wouldn't be finished until the final stitch was added.

She didn't bother with breakfast, instead she slipped out of the gate and turned into the street, choosing to avoid Rue de Passy and Tomas's wine shop in case she ran into him. The last thing she needed was to be questioned about whether she'd managed to contact Lucien yet. She'd seen nothing of him since Monday, which had surprised her until Madame Billy let it slip that he was on a wine procurement trip to the vineyards.

She'd also seen nothing of Edith, who was performing every night to a packed ABC Club. Occasionally, she'd been woken by a sound from her room in the small hours, but it felt mostly as if she was the only one living on the top floor.

Sundays were busy at Le Moulin Rouge, with a matinee performance squeezed in as well as the evening one. It was also Flora's day off and one she'd been looking forward to. She'd overheard some of the girls at Madame Billy's discussing Marguerette's disappearance in the salon, but it was all conjecture. She'd stood in the doorway anyway, unable to move until the conversation had drifted onto something else.

She'd taken to working on her quilt in the Café de Palmier after work as an excuse to watch the comings and goings at the dance hall, but it was too early for Lucien and, with curfew on the horizon, she couldn't risk staying late. Maison Lumineau was out of bounds. Without Tomas to advise her, she was at a loss as to know what to do next.

She heard the bells of the Église de la Sainte-Trinité and looked towards the steeple at the end of the road.

Flora wasn't a church-goer, not since she'd fallen pregnant. It was always going to take something momentous to drag her inside. The twins were that reason. Sister Maria Clara had been her friend and one of the few people aware of her history with Lucien.

If anyone knew of Marguerette's whereabouts, it would be the kindly nun. Her search couldn't only be about Marguerette, though. There was also Violette to think of. Being squirrelled away by Lucien somewhere in the country could mean anywhere. France was a big place.

She slipped through the thick wooden door of the church and found a space at the back, her coat pulled around her, the smell of incense and candle wax as familiar as breathing. It was here that she'd been dropped off as a baby and where the priest from Étampes had delivered her after her foster mother's attack. If it hadn't been for his kindness and Sister Maria Clara's skill, she didn't know where she'd be now.

The ornate church was packed, the congregation a mixture of old and young, the sound of a baby crying somewhere towards the front drowning out much of the priest's words.

There was no comfort in the hymns, the familiar verses rising above her head in a swell. There was only the thought of what came next, a worry to add to the growing pile.

After the service, she waited in the shadows, watching as the parishioners rose from their pews and made their way up the aisle. Elderly couples propping each other up. Young children racing on ahead, harried parents behind. Her gaze skimmed over them, not really seeing. A conglomeration of Parisians in their Sunday best, their coats three years out of date, their shoe leather worn at toe and at heel.

A shaft of expensive perfume heralded a change. A slight deviation as the congregation moved aside to let a woman through. Someone distinguished.

Not just a woman. A couple.

Sabine and Lucien Lumineau.

Flora blinked then blinked again, unwilling to believe what her eyes were telling her. Lucien attending church when she'd been racking her brains to think of ways to meet him. She suddenly remembered conversations from the early days of their relationship and how he'd had no time for religion. She'd tried to argue, but he'd been too clever for her with his fancy words and intransigent views. To find him attending mass when she'd spent all week trying and failing to think of ways to bump into him was almost laughable. She hadn't given church a thought.

Her hands tightened around the back of the pew, her fingers biting into the mellow wood.

Instead of Lucien and memories, she forced herself to study his wife first.

Sabine suited her name. Tall, slim and elegant, her hair a burnished halo of pale gold under her peacock-blue felt hat, the large brim hiding her eyes. Her coat was fur-lined and with the wasp waist detailing that the designer, Mainbocher, had introduced in the late 1930s. The dress peeking through was scarlet silk. There was nothing practical about the outfit. The bias cut, which used more fabric and created more waste, felt like a snub to the women making their way to the entrance in their serviceable browns, blacks and greys. The only colour in their practical outfits was a slash of scarf at their neck, and maybe some lipstick if they had any left in the bottom of the tube.

Flora might not be able to afford haute couture, but she was experienced in pattern design, cutting, fabrics and sewing. Sabine's trifle of a hat would have cost a year's wages, her dress and coat triple that.

Lucien coughed, his handkerchief pressed to his mouth, drawing her gaze. He matched Sabine in height and good looks, his blond hair swept back from his brow. His black suede coat was bespoke, the cut shaped to his shoulders, the drape over his back some of the best tailoring Flora had ever seen, but even the best tailoring couldn't disguise a heaviness that hadn't been there before. A thickening around his waist, a slight stoop to his shoulders. His face was lined, his jaw blurred at the edge where before it had been sharply defined. His eyes were tired. Disillusioned. She'd heard that the war had affected his business, which wasn't a surprise. There were far more important things to worry about than hem lengths and, with Sabine's fortune behind him, money would never be a problem.

'Do hurry, Lucien. I don't want to be late for lunch.'

'Just coming.'

They moved away, propelled forward by the wave of people flowing towards the priest waiting at the entrance. Flora sank against the pillar, relief clouding her vision. She'd felt nothing, not even the slightest flicker of the love she'd once held so dear. It was like seeing a stranger in the street. In truth, that's all he'd been. He'd gone to great lengths to divert her when she'd tried to bring the conversation around to him. As for Sabine... hatred flooded Flora's veins and honed her vision to pinprick clarity. Sabine's refusal to have children of her own had forced Lucien to look elsewhere for the family he craved.

Flora stayed where she was. It was only when the last nun, the one she'd been waiting for, hurried up the aisle that she took a step forward.

'Sister Maria Clara.'

'Yes.'

Flora noted her look of confusion. After all, nearly twenty years had passed. She was confused too. Up close the nun didn't resemble the woman she remembered.

If Lucien had aged, she barely recognised her friend, Sister Maria Clara, only ten years her senior and with the roundest apple cheeks and twinkling eyes. This woman looked old and drawn, her skin dropping off her bones. Her eyes were sunken, and her lips so pale that it almost seemed as if the blood had left her body.

'It's me, sister,' she said softly. 'Flora Toussaint.'

The nun's eyes widened, her hand flying to her mouth, the black arc of her sleeve revealing her stick-thin arm and fragile, almost translucent skin.

'Oh, my dear. I've often prayed for you and your beautiful daughters.' Her smile was tremulous, her eyes rimmed with glistening tears, the faint trace of her Germanic roots still present in her words. 'God is good to have brought you back to us. You must tell me everything. Where you've been all these years.'

'My daughters are why I've come. Could we go somewhere and talk?' Flora looked anxiously towards the entrance, not wanting to bump into Lucien. Meeting him again was a foregone conclusion, but not with Sabine by his side.

'Of course.' The nun drew her further into the body of the church and away from the main door. 'It's only a short walk to the convent.'

The convent of Sainte-Marthe-des-Anges was situated halfway along Rue Jean Baptiste. It was nothing to look at from the outside. A tall, faceless building, which concealed a rabbit warren of rooms and a kindness that Flora hadn't experienced in the first fourteen years of her life living on the sheep farm. The nuns had let her stay with them, feeding her up and rubbing a soothing mixture of pungent-smelling herbs from the garden onto the weals criss-crossing her back. She'd stayed only long enough to realise that the food they'd given her had been taken from their meagre post-war rations. Arranging an apprenticeship at a small fashion house had been easy once the owner had seen the quality of her work.

'Come into the garden. It's a beautiful day.' Sister Maria Clara spread her hands in joy at the sight of the cloudless sky. 'I'll make us some chamomile tea.' She drew her into the convent before pushing open the door to the private walled garden at the back.

Flora was happy to follow despite the cold. With Sister Maria Clara off fussing over the hot drink she didn't want, she sank onto one of the wooden benches and stared at the flower beds, the soil frost hard until the onset of spring. There weren't many things she'd miss about Boneybefore. Only two she could think of. The tentative friendships she'd formed with the girls at the mill, and her beautiful garden. Brian wouldn't bother and Mavis wouldn't recognise a turnip from a swede even if it was labelled, she thought cattily. Gardening wasn't all about pretty flowers. She'd had a healthy vegetable patch, and a boundary wall crammed with espaliered apple trees. During the autumn months she'd bottled and jammed enough fruit to last them through the harsh Irish winters. As much as Brian might moan, she'd always provided a varied diet full of her home-grown produce.

The sound of cups rattling in their saucers had her springing to her feet, ready to take the tray from a far from steady Sister Maria Clara.

'Sorry I took so long.'

'Here, let me.' Flora set the tray down on the rickety, wrought-iron table and started arranging crockery and teaspoons, the sweet smoky smell of chamomile causing her to glance at the other side of the garden where the beds lay. Sister Maria Clara was a knowledgeable herbalist, having learnt from her father as a small child. As well as growing their own vegetables and fruit, the nuns produced herbal concoctions for a range of conditions from insomnia to eczema. Flora knew she had her to thank for the way her back had healed, the traces of the silvery scars barely visible.

'About the twins...' With her cup held between her hands, there was no reason to delay the inevitable.

'Fine young women, my dear, despite what happened to Marguerette.' Sister Maria Clara spoke gently, her gaze trained on the old beech tree up ahead. 'No one could have foreseen, or wished her return in the way it happened, but we managed to place her with a good foster family.'

'So good that she ended up a singer at Le Moulin Rouge?' Flora said, her voice breaking. She knew all about foster families, and didn't try to disguise the tears building up behind her eyes. 'I would have come back for her if I'd known. I could only have just left and I did write to you when I was settled in Brittany.'

'We did think of that, child, but Révérende Mère forbade it.' The nun smoothed her habit over her knees, the black fabric faded to a dark grey. 'She told us God must have decreed it and that it wasn't up to us to interfere in his work.'

Flora was broken by her words, simply because it was too late to do anything about them. A silly decision by a silly old woman had robbed her of the chance to raise her daughter.

'Tell me about them, dear. What are they like?'

Sister Maria Clara smiled, her skin creasing into a myriad of folds. 'They're a credit to you, Flora. Truly. Violette takes after her father. Her blue eyes and blonde hair are all his, but the rest is you.

Always so independent. The Lumineau's staff had their work cut out trying to look after her.'

'The Lumineaus sent her away, I believe?'

'And thank the lord for that. Whisked into the country as soon as the threat of invasion became a reality.' She picked up her cup and took a lengthy sip. 'The dear child even sent us a letter from Chateau Beau Marin to put our minds at rest.'

Flora felt a glimmer of hope explode in her chest, even as her eyes started to fill. Chateau Beau Marin. Everyone who kept up to date with French news knew that the chateau was Sabine's award-winning champagne estate in Épernay. To write to her would be too risky. What if Sabine got hold of the letter. But to know where she was... To see Violette's words. To know she was safe from all this madness.

She swallowed hard before saying, 'I'd love to see the letter, if I may?'

Sister Maria Clara nodded. 'I'll ask Révérende Mère. Sister Cecile manages that side of things.'

So, the old bat is still alive. She managed to hide her feelings. *She won't let me see it in a million years.*

Flora didn't regret her un-Christian thought. What had seemed like ninety when she'd been a teenager was probably nearer sixty. There'd never been any love lost between the two of them. Sister Cecile, despite her good works and devotion to the Lord, had always looked down on Flora. And the saddest part was that Flora couldn't blame her. Deserted at birth and not knowing who her parents were, only for history to repeat itself when she'd fallen pregnant with the twins.

Flora had lost her faith somewhere on the gentle hills of Étampes, her many bruises never given a chance to heal. She'd been too tall, too plump, too slow. Her sins were too many for her to ever find favour with the Lord. Her foster mother had been keen to recite the scriptures to her at every turn. A religious woman who attended mass three times a week but never seemed to practise the humility and forgiveness required for such devotion. Flora suddenly remembered the kindly priest's words the day she'd turned up at the church, her back slashed red raw from her foster mother's broom-handle. As a shepherdess minding her flock, it had struck a chord that had never left her.

Though your sins are like scarlet, they shall be as white as snow: though they are red like crimson, they shall become like wool.

The priest had saved her life that evening, tending to her wounds before arranging for her to travel to the convent she was now sitting in. While the Révérende Mère had never raised her hand to her, Flora knew that the nun had thought of her in the same way the farmer's wife had. Two sides of the same coin. Two women who should never have been put in a position of power over the less fortunate.

'And what of Marguerette?'

'The dearest girl.' Sister Maria Clara plucked a handkerchief from her sleeve and blew her nose gently. 'We found her a good home with a music professor at the Sorbonne. Professor Lang and his wife weren't blessed with children, so it seemed ideal.'

'It *seemed* ideal?' Flora pounced on the nun's words, unable to understand how the daughter of a professor could end up working as a singer in a dance hall.

'The war happened, Flora. It was the perfect arrangement until Hitler invaded Poland and then France.' Sister Maria Clara placed her cup down on the tray, her hands folded in front of her. 'Professor Lang and his wife, as Jews, knew they couldn't stay. They made arrangements for Marguerette, which sadly didn't work out.'

'I still don't understand. How would you know all this if she was brought up Jewish?'

'After hearing a little of her history, they decided to honour the religious side of her upbringing.' She smiled gently. 'You could say we raised her together. The priest and the nuns looked after the religious side of things, while the Langs looked after the day-to-day aspects like feeding, clothing and educating.'

'Where are they now?'

'We think America, but we haven't heard confirmation.' She angled her head, looking at where Flora had secured her auburn hair into a roll at the back of her neck. 'Marguerette looks very much like you did when I first met you. The same eyes and retrouseé nose along with the same rich colouring. She's generous too. Generous and kind.' She lowered her voice even though the garden was empty, apart from a lonely sparrow perched on the beech tree ahead. 'She only stopped attending mass when she was sixteen. Madame Lumineau was most upset about having to see her every week, not that any of the congregation knew. A secret between the Lumineaus and the church.'

Flora stared at her in surprise, the same surprise she'd felt when she'd seen them earlier. 'Monsieur Lumineau never struck me as the religious type?'

Sister Maria Clara's eyes flared briefly. 'He's been attending mass every week for years now. A huge support to the church and the convent. I don't know quite where we'd be if he stopped.'

Flora wondered what had changed him, something drastic or something to do with Marguerette? It would have been his only opportunity to see her.

'Did she ever ask about her birth parents?' Flora asked, the question surprising her almost as much as it appeared to surprise Sister Maria Clara. She knew what Tomas had said, but this might help her understand what kind of person her daughter had become.

'That's difficult to answer. The Langs were always open with her about being fostered, leaving it to Marguerette if she wanted to follow it up. We would, of course, have told her if she'd asked...'

'But she never did?'

'No.' Sister Maria Clara fidgeted with her cross, her gaze focused somewhere in the distance. 'The Langs came to see us before they left, asking for advice. It was decided that she'd be safer staying in France instead of fleeing, which came with its own dangers. If they were stopped at the border, who knows what might have happened with no formal adoption papers and a birth certificate in the name of Marguerette Toussaint.' She lowered her voice even though the garden was empty and the shutters at the back of the convent closed to keep the cold out. 'All the Langs ever wanted was her safety and happiness. A friend of theirs at the university offered her a home. It was working perfectly until the Germans started taking an interest in the woman's resistance activities. We managed to secure temporary accommodation at L'Etoile de Kleber.' The nun pressed her lips together. 'Despite everything, Madame Billy works hard to help the resistance in any way she can.'

'And now Marguerette has disappeared. What can you tell me, Sister Maria Clara? It's my dearest wish to see both her and Violette again.'

'I don't know if...' The sound of church bells ringing drowned out her words. 'Oh my. I'm late. I have to go. Leave the tea things. I'll get them later.'

Flora watched as she hurried away.

What had the nun been about to say before the bells had interrupted her? She'd been within seconds of discovering the truth only for it to be whisked away.

Taking a deep breath, she picked up her bag and wandered across the garden, following in the nun's footsteps in the hope of seeing her, but the corridor was empty, the place silent.

Stepping into the street, she blinked a couple of times as her eyes adjusted to the light, a gust of cold wind encouraging her to hurry.

A hand on her arm. Sharp. Sudden. She wrenched back, pulling away.

'Flora.'

Flora swallowed, recognising the voice. The faint hint of his familiar aftershave.

Lucien.

ELEVEN

'My God, Flora. I never thought I'd see you again.' Lucien started the engine and pulled into the street, his gaze flicking to her before flicking back to the road, almost as if he couldn't bear to drag his gaze away. 'That you're here. You even look the same when...'

Flora managed a laugh, not a happy sound. 'We've all aged, Lucien. Eighteen years is a long time.'

'And all my fault.'

She raised her eyebrows at that, not recognising this version of him. She'd expected someone older, but ultimately the same. A man who knew what he wanted and ensured he got it, without a thought for anyone else. That's what she'd thought she was getting when she'd agreed to lunch. The clues were there in the modern dress of an assured man-about-town. The black fedora, and suede overcoat hiding a camel-coloured jacket and coordinating waist-coat. His trousers were charcoal grey, which shouldn't have worked, but the overall look was both casual and elegant. In the old days, he'd favoured blue velvet and flowers in his buttonhole, which she'd thought ostentatious.

Now she considered whether his change in dress was more than skin deep. He seemed softer. Less arrogant. Only time would tell if she was right.

'The Café de la Rotonde do? You used to like it there.'

Once inside the café, Lucien removed his hat and coat and handed them to the waiter, giving his order at the same time.

'A bottle of the 1928 Veuve Clicquot if you please.'

Flora's mouth firmed. Not so very different then. Lucien had always demanded the best of everything.

He reached across to pick up her hand, but she lifted it to her head instead, pretending to fix a hairpin before placing it on her lap out of reach. She wasn't ready for the feel of his hand. She wasn't ready for any of it despite the duty she owed to her country and the promise she'd made to Tomas.

'Salut.' Lucien lifted his glass in a toast, his eyes holding an expression she never thought she'd see again, and she didn't want to see now.

Flora closed her eyes briefly. A small respite while she assimilated what was written across his face. He couldn't think that he was in love with her. It wasn't possible, not after what he'd done, or what he'd let Sabine do.

'Salut. I can't believe I'm back in Paris and here…' She glanced around at the familiar red banquettes and marble-topped tables, trying to steer the conversation away from the troubled waters they were sliding into headfirst. The walls were crammed with paintings. Some artists she recognised. Picasso and Modigliani. The rest were a blur of colour and design.

'Such artwork,' he agreed. 'It's a place I love. Our place and, whatever you might think, I've never brought Sabine here.'

That's because she wouldn't have come.

'I'm surprised you remember,' she said, focusing on the one thing she could comment on.

'I've never forgotten a moment of our time together, chérie.' His eyes dwelt on her hair. 'Your crowning glory. So very soft. If I close my eyes, I can almost imagine the feel of the strands between my fingers. I was such a fool. I still am.'

She glanced around to see if anyone was listening. All they'd need was for the wrong person to overhear his words and pass them on to Sabine. He hadn't asked her where she'd been or what she was doing back in Paris, which was interesting. Why hadn't he? After all, it had been one of the first questions Sister Maria Clara had posed on their walk to the convent.

'I didn't think you'd still come here,' she finally said, determined to stick to safe topics.

He shifted his gaze from her hair to her face and reached again for her hand. This time she let him.

'When I first came to Paris, it was all I could afford. I'd sit in the corner with my sketch pad and a coffee, which would have to last me all evening, but,' he shrugged, 'it was warm and there were people to talk to. Far better than sitting alone in my garret counting my centimes.'

Flora found she couldn't look away, her thoughts in freefall.

The Lucien she remembered had acted as if he'd been born to a life of wealth. He was impeccably dressed and always knew what to say and what to do. Even down to which champagne to order. Only the best for Lucien. If that was a lie then what else had he lied about? Her breath hitched. It felt as if someone was ripping up everything she thought she knew about him, everything she remembered. The manipulative charmer replaced by something gentler.

'Why didn't you tell me?'

'It's not something I bandy about, ma chérie.' He gave a lopsided smile, his hand tightening its grip. 'Bad for business. My customers like to buy into the mystery that surrounds my fashion house and rise to fame. That I started out as a motherless street urchin on the boulevards of Cannes would ruin the image somewhat. In fact, I'm taking a risk telling you. Even Sabine doesn't know the whole truth, perhaps because she never asked.'

Flora felt her heart contract at the thought of Lucien as a child trying to manage among the rich and famous of Cannes, and of the woman who'd never cared enough to find out about his past. At least she'd had the nuns to help when things had got brutal at the sheep farm. Without it, she dreaded to think where she'd have ended up. Probably in the gutter like her mother. She clenched her teeth, biting down so hard that her jaw started to ache. She wouldn't feel sympathy for him, not after he'd betrayed his countrymen to the enemy.

'I'm sorry, Lucien,' she managed, the words choked for the boy he'd once been and not for the man he'd become.

'Oh, no need to be.' He managed a smile. 'I learnt quite a lot in my early days. My father was a lamplighter. Spent his life illuminating other people's lives, only to miss the point entirely in his own.' He threw back his head with a chuckle. Something had amused him. Flora waited to see if he was going to share it. 'He did inspire me to change my name though. Lumineau for the lamplighter's son – apt, don't you think?'

'Well, your secret is safe with me.' She slipped her hand from his grasp, and picked up her glass instead. 'Did you always want to be a designer, or was it something you fell into?'

He inclined his head at her question, his blond hair catching the light. 'In another life I might have tried my hand at painting but, when I arrived in Paris the place was crawling with starving artists with far more talent. I was always too fond of money for that.' He raised his hand, tapping the edge of one of the canvases on the wall beside him for emphasis. 'It took Picasso a long time to achieve anything like the money and prestige his talent deserves.'

With her gaze trained on the painting, she said, 'I think money takes on an importance of its own when you don't have enough to live on, Lucien. Poverty is a great leveller.'

'And the reason why, at fifty, I'm still working despite having sufficient money to meet my needs. However much I tell myself to the contrary, I still think that something or someone will come and relieve me of it.' He shrugged again. 'Madness, I know.'

'No, not mad.' She dragged her eyes from the vibrant painting. 'I never travel anywhere without my sewing kit. Threads, needles and scissors,' she elaborated. 'My tools of the trade so that I can always be assured of an income.'

'And now that I've found you, you'll never have to worry about that side of things again.'

'That's not how it works,' she said, dismayed that he thought her stupid enough to repeat the same mistake. She wrinkled her brow, remembering Brian. Even if Lucien wasn't a collaborator, they were both married and she would be no man's mistress. 'Tell me about Violette and Marguerette, Lucien? I'd love to hear about them even if seeing them might be impossible with the war.'

She watched his cheeks flood with colour before draining to a sickly grey, his attention shifting to his glass, which he emptied before beckoning to the waiter for a refill.

'I need to tell you something, Flora. Something I'm ashamed of.' He darted her a glance before returning his attention to his champagne flute, his fingers playing with the fragile stem. 'We found that having two babies at home instead of the one we'd been expecting was more difficult than we'd envisioned and, well...'

Flora let him squirm for a moment before speaking.

'I already know, Lucien. Sister Maria Clara told me, and...' She paused, her gaze intense as the lie tripped neatly off her tongue. 'I don't blame you. It must have been difficult. Tell me about Violette and everything you know about Marguerette.' She placed her hand over his, squeezing gently. 'Please, Lucien. It's important.'

He stared down at their hands, his voice low, his champagne glass forgotten. 'Violette is the most perfect daughter, Flora. Perfect in every way. She's creative too. Knitting, sewing, tapestry. She always has a project or six on the go.' He lifted his head, his eyes shining bright. 'The world is a far better place with her in it.'

Flora smiled, warmth sweeping across her chest. She remembered the photograph that Tomas had shown her. Their clever, beautiful daughter. 'Sister Maria Clara told me you sent her away?'

'Paris isn't the place for her. France isn't either,' he added, his brow drawn into a deep frown. 'She's safe at Sabine's vineyard for now. It's not ideal but better than here.'

Flora eased her hand away before sitting back in her chair,

feeling a little happier. That he cared deeply for their daughter was comforting.

'And Marguerette?' She lifted her hand briefly, when he went to speak. 'I know about her foster parents, if that's any help. By all accounts good people, and for that I'm grateful. But after, Lucien? How come she started singing at Le Moulin Rouge and, more to the point, where is she now?'

Instead of calling the waiter, he poured the last of the champagne into his glass, upending the empty bottle in the ice bucket.

'I knew nothing about Marguerette's life after the Langs left. One minute she was this child in plaits I saw at mass every Sunday and the next, she'd stopped attending. I tried asking around, but if anyone at the church knew they weren't telling and I couldn't press, not with Sabine around. When a friend mentioned that he thought he'd seen her singing at the windmill, I couldn't believe it. Gave me the biggest shock. Thought it was you for a moment.'

He glanced at his watch, an elegant gold timepiece with a plain leather strap, his expression changing to one of disappointment. 'I'm afraid I'm going to have to take a rain check. While I don't mind bailing out of one of Sabine's lunches I can't bail out of our party when I was the one to arrange it. A pity but there will be other meetings, other trysts.'

Flora knew he was running away, but there was nothing she could do about that. She'd met him and she'd meet him again. Small steps, she reminded herself. Re-establish a connection. Gain his trust and take it from there.

Within half an hour they'd pulled up at the bottom of the Rue de Villejust, Madame Billy's building only a few steps away.

'You're staying here?' He turned in his seat, his face ashen, a muscle flickering in his cheek.

'And what of it? I know for a fact that you're a frequent visitor. I wonder you never saw Marguerette here during one of your assignations. There's a separate staircase leading to the attics, but even so.'

He fisted his hand. For a moment she thought he was going to hit her. 'Aline is a friend. I have never paid for the company of a woman in my life.' He unfurled his hand, his voice lower but no less offensive. 'When you said you had to work, I didn't expect that you meant...'

'That I meant what, Lucien?' Flora asked, wanting to hear him say the words. 'What's good enough for *my* daughter, is good enough for me.'

She shook her head in disbelief, her heavy hair starting to come adrift from its pins. In all the times when her purse was empty and her belly rattled against her spine in search of food, the thought of selling her body hadn't once crossed her mind.

'That's different.' His jaw hardened. 'Marguerette is a talented singer while...'

'I'm a talented seamstress and proud of it.' She undid her seatbelt, pushing the car door open before climbing out.

'Goodbye, Lucien.'

There was a finality in her tone, which was impossible to miss.

Slamming the door, she stormed up the hill through the garden, seeing nothing and nobody until she heard her name being shouted across the flower beds.

TWELVE

L'Etoile de Kleber

'Where are you off to in such a hurry?'

Flora was halfway across the garden when she stopped and turned, blushing at the sight of Tomas leaning against the pergola, partially hidden in the shade.

'Probably to pack.'

His eyebrow arched while he waited for her to elaborate.

'I finally met up with Lucien, but I wasn't as clever as I could have been.' She wrapped her arms around her, the reality of what she'd done pushing the last remnant of anger away. Instead, all she felt was disappointment and, suddenly, incredibly tired. It had been a long week and, apart from the quilts, all she'd achieved was to alienate the man she'd been tasked to befriend.

Tomas offered his arm. 'Come on. Let's get out of here for a bit. I'm in need of a change of scene.'

Flora glanced from his tired face to her watch, not quite believing that it was already past five. Madame Billy would be coming downstairs soon, her knitting on the table beside her along with her notebook and a glass of decent wine, while the girls would be making themselves ready for their guests.

Cristelle, Isabel, Jade, Anouke, Marthe and Lilou. She'd met them en masse on her second day at the brothel. They could have been shop workers or waitresses. Even seamstresses. Flora hadn't known what to expect. She'd felt ashamed after brief introductions had been exchanged. Next time she'd do better. Be friendly, instead of reticent. Ensure that what they did for a living made no difference to how she behaved.

If there was a next time.

She placed her hand through the crook of his arm, determined to make an effort. 'Where were you thinking? I'm quite tired, and I think you must be too. All that gallivanting among the vineyards is bound to take it out of you.'

He laughed. 'Is that where you think I've been?'

'Well, it's what Madame Billy said, but...' She frowned up at him. 'Wasn't she right? I know it's your cover, but also your job.'

'It's best not to believe everything you hear, Flora.' He patted her gloved hand briefly. 'I've been west instead of south. It was a tiring trip, I'm in need of a few home comforts, if you're happy to come to my apartment. I only have chicory coffee I'm afraid, but I promise to act like a gentleman.' He managed a laugh. 'I'm too bloody tired to be anything else.'

Tomas's shop looked exactly as she would have imagined. Dark wooden shelves, mostly empty. A large counter, with a tray of upturned glasses. An old-fashioned cash register. A couple of comfortable chairs upholstered in emerald-green velvet. A door at the back, which led upstairs to his apartment.

A man's apartment if ever there was one. A sofa, and a chair. A radio. A large bookshelf piled high with books. A grate with no trace of a fire. No ornaments. No photographs. None of the trappings of comfort like a cushion or a blanket.

'It's not much, but then I'm rarely at home.'

She tensed, remembering she was here under false pretences. There was no room for small talk after what had just happened between her and Lucien. 'I need to tell you that I've sent Lucien packing.' She shrugged. 'He was rude so...'

'Hah. Did you indeed?' He turned and started filling the cafetière. 'And you think he's going to believe you?'

'What do you mean?'

'Exactly what I say, Flora. A man like Lucien. Someone used to getting his own way. Someone who...' He grimaced, his expression a little less certain, and suddenly he was backpedalling. 'You know him better than we do. We'll go along with whatever you think is best. Wouldn't want to get you into a situation you couldn't easily get out of.'

What kind of situation is he talking about?

Flora felt her heart trip, realising how stupid she'd been. They'd always intended for her to get close to Lucien *in that way*. Why else had they housed her at Madame Billy's, a place he frequented.

'Let me get this right, Tomas. You dangled the carrot of my daughters in front of me, expecting me to jump at the chance of seeing them again.' He opened his mouth to speak but she stopped him. 'No, wait until I've finished. Of course, all on the pretext of regaining Lucien's trust, if indeed I ever had it,' she added. 'You suspect him of collaborating but need proof. Something that links him to the enemy, and you thought I might be able to help you discover... what?' She lifted her brows, her eyes wide, the room suddenly filled with the scorched smell of roasted chicory. 'Don't you think it's time you told me what proof I should be looking for?'

He eyed her briefly before turning away to pour the coffee, only speaking again when he'd placed the cups on the table.

'Something that links him to the Germans, which could be anything. It's impossible not to leave some kind of trail behind. There would have been meetings, maybe even money exchanged. That sort of thing.'

'So letters, cash deposits – Lucien likes money – photographs, diaries and invoices. Anything untoward.' She shifted her cup to prop her elbows on the table, busying herself with lighting a cigarette before shoving the packet in his direction. 'If he does contact me again, what about if I try and get into his home and his showrooms? There's an office, not that I ever had reason to go there. Or, even better, if I manage to get his keys, then you can accompany me.'

Tomas looked at her briefly, before nodding as if he was making his mind up about something. 'Getting an impression of his keys sounds ideal. Just as long as he doesn't suspect. I wouldn't want to put you at any unnecessary risk.'

Flora stubbed out her unwanted cigarette. 'That's very kind of you, Tomas but I knew what I was getting into when you got me to sign the Official Secrets Act. Even Miss Maxse commented on the risks involved when we met.'

'I'm sure she did. I'll just get the putty.' He went to stand only to sit down again, slapping his hand against his forehead. 'Miss Maxse! How could I have forgotten. I have a letter.' He reached inside his jacket and pulled out an envelope. 'She asked me to give it to you next time I saw you.'

Flora glanced at him before withdrawing the folded sheet.

It wasn't much, only a couple of sentences, but they were so final that she felt the sudden need to cry.

She folded the letter and placed it back inside the envelope, not quite believing that news of her divorce could affect her in such a way. It had been such a long time since she'd loved Brian and yet they'd made a life together. A life that had spanned eighteen years. That life was now over and it hurt more than she could believe possible.

Lifting her head, she caught the tail end of Tomas's gaze as he placed a small tin on the table before retaking his seat.

Flora liked that he hadn't asked her about the letter, when he must be eager to know what all the secrecy was about. If it hadn't been a private matter, Miss Maxse would have entrusted him with a message instead of risking writing. And suddenly she wanted to share her news with him.

'Miss Maxse was kind enough to find me a lawyer,' she said softly, her voice a husky rasp. 'You see before you a bona fide divorcée.'

He stared at her, his grey eyes darkening, but his words were normal enough. 'And you're happy about that?'

'Of course.' She shifted her gaze. 'Why wouldn't I be?'

'You don't seem very happy, but maybe I'm wrong. I don't know you very well.'

You don't know me at all, but you're not doing too badly with the guesswork.

'Brian was seeing someone. I found them together the day you dropped me home.'

He winced. 'That must have been difficult and divorce inevitable. You've been together a long time.'

'Thank you.'

She didn't know what else to say. Discussing her divorce seemed like crossing a line when she was there on a mission. Picking up her bag, she dropped the letter inside and spotted the patchwork squares. Seeing them couldn't have come at a better time. With her coffee moved further into the middle of the table out of the way, she carefully set out the squares, much to Tomas's amazement.

'Is that patchwork?'

'It is. That you recognise it makes this much easier.' She started arranging the squares in a pattern before placing the four extra squares at the corners. 'You'll probably think I'm mad but I've come up with an idea about how you might still be able to share information to other cells across France, without having to depend on the likes of Lucien. Currently it's only in calendar form, so dates and times of meet-ups and drop-offs, but it's a start.'

'Are you serious! Flora, I'll take anything you've got.'

His expression collapsed from excitement into sudden sadness, the mood dropping a few notches in the process.

'Everything alright?'

He nodded briefly when Flora knew he was lying. 'A friend was working on something similar. Would you believe knitting in code?'

'I'll believe anything in this war, Tomas.' She rested her hand on top of his, in tune with the change in atmosphere. 'What happened?'

He stared down at their hands and, with an easy movement, placed his on top. Solid. Secure. Comforting. 'It's still used. Mainly in the camps to get information both in and out.'

He removed his hand and braced his shoulders, moving the conversation on.

'Tell me everything you've got.'

THIRTEEN

LUCIEN

Lucien snuck into his apartment like a thief in the middle of the night. The party wasn't for another two hours, but he needed to think. That Sabine was still out at one of her all-afternoon lunches was a blessed relief.

Seeing Flora again had slammed home what a mess he'd made of things. Her sudden appearance had opened the carefully sealed gate to his emotions. Her scent, which wasn't a scent at all. The way she wore her hair, hair the exact shade as Marguerette's. Darling Marguerette, the daughter Sabine had forced him to give up. He'd chosen Sabine's money over happiness and had been miserable every day since.

Outside his study, he unlocked the door, his fingers easing the mechanism into action before slipping inside, reversing the procedure and pocketing the keys. Locking himself into his private domain was the only way he got any peace these days. It hadn't taken Sabine long to realise she could do whatever she liked to their new home, with little or no interference from him, as long as she left him one room to call his own. She'd proceeded to rip the heart out of the place with no thought for the culture and history of the building. Since then, apart from his study, he only used the place to eat and sleep.

Shrugging off his jacket, he hung it up along with his scarf, gloves and hat, before striking a match to the fireplace. There was only one key to the room, which was either in his pocket or in the chest beside his bed. He allowed the maid in once a day to set the fire and sort out his drinks cabinet, but only in his presence. They thought him paranoid about his work and they were right, but it wasn't the staff he was worried about.

It was his wife.

He eyed the drinks cabinet but, after all that champagne, more alcohol was the last thing he needed. Instead, he poured himself a glass of water from the jug and made for the sofa, the flames starting to streak the back of the fireplace as the wood caught. There was work he needed to do. An evening gown to design for the Countess de Valcroix.

Evening gowns were his speciality. Long, flowing dresses in flattering silks that sculpted the wearer, turning a caterpillar into a butterfly. He'd been putting off this dress for weeks, primarily because the countess was more of a slug than a caterpillar.

He threw down his drink before refilling his glass and moving to the window. The sky was doing that tonal shift from pale blue to grey, then purple as twilight inched across the rooftops. The Germans might have occupied his homeland, but there were some things they could never change. The beauty of the blue hour was one of them. If he'd been an artist, he'd have picked up a paintbrush, but he was wise enough to know that he didn't have the skills required to blend the colours just so. His talents lay elsewhere.

With a flick of his hand, he twitched the blackout blinds in place before reaching for a piece of charcoal from the small pile in the pot on his desk.

The countess's dress came first. Only after, would he allow himself to think of Flora.

The gown must be in black, in spite of the woman's insistence on jewel colours. A deep V neckline to make use of her impressive bust, he thought, his eyes slipping to his bookshelves and where the source of his inspiration lay. He didn't need to revisit François Gérard's painting of Bonaparte's Joséphine, as he considered what to do with the skirt. He could see it in his mind's eye as he drew sweeping strokes to represent the empire line he was after.

Most evenings were spent sitting in silence flicking through one or other of his books. Paul Poiret was a huge inspiration for the tone and feel of his creations. When he'd first come to Paris, he'd spent hours staring at the couturier's flamboyant designs in the window of his salon along the Rue Auber. He'd even taken to following some of his customers as they'd weaved their way to the Place de l'Opéra to stroll among the wealthy, their nose in the air when they caught sight of his scruffy presence. But that was thirty years ago. The designer had disappeared off the scene. Rumour had it that he'd lost his design spark, which had scared Lucien more than he'd ever care to admit. Being brought up in poverty had given him an aversion to ever returning. He could easily do without the trappings of wealth, but not to be able to afford to eat...

His hand swept over the paper, his fingers inspired by the hours spent living and breathing fashion across time and continents. Cap sleeves to hide the top of the countesses' arms. An over skirt of the finest gauze, that started from under the bust to disguise her lack of a waist. With a final flick of his wrist, it was done.

Voilà!

He smiled slowly, admiring the drape of the gown, which would do far more for the autocratic countess than she deserved. She treated him like a slave, but as long as she paid her bills on time, he'd learnt to live with it. Reaching forward, he signed his name with a flourish, a little quirk of pride. If his friend Pablo could sign his work then so could he.

Flipping over the page, he stared at the paper only to see Flora's face reflected on the blank sheet. He'd managed to keep her tucked away in the back of his mind. The phone call from Sister Maria Clara earlier had brought her flooding back.

Poor Sister Maria Clara. She was determined to try and put right what should never have happened. He'd known Flora was special the first time he'd seen her. Before her there'd been few women and after, no one apart from Sabine, who'd been purely a business arrangement. Sabine had decided that the only way she could live the life she wanted was to add a layer of respectability to her name, which her lifestyle in Paris had muddied. Being rich and beautiful wasn't enough to gain her entry into the places she desired. When she'd learnt that her reputation was starting to be whispered in and around the drawing rooms of the women she coveted invitations from, she knew she had to do something. Modelling for Lucien was the push she needed. In return for respectability, he'd got the money to pay off his creditors with enough left to purchase the quality satins and silks craved by his wealthy clientele.

He pressed his head in his hands, his heart racing at the thought of the foolhardy pact they'd made, but he'd been young and scared, the past biting at his heels. The son of a deadbeat, destined for the same future if he didn't do something to drag himself out of the debt he'd got himself into. The wealthy, for all their posh houses and cars, never paid their bills on time and he couldn't live on air, just as he couldn't present his collections in inferior fabrics.

The only caveat to their arrangement was his desire for children, something that Sabine couldn't give him even if she'd wanted to. A backstreet abortionist had put paid to that. Flora falling pregnant had seemed fortuitous at the time. Sabine would achieve instant respectability as well as moral recognition for taking on a motherless waif. The problems started when she'd realised it wasn't just one baby and that Lucien had fallen in love with the mother, despite his best efforts to hide it.

They'd been in the drawing room trying to get used to having two babies to care for when he'd learnt that Flora had left Paris. He wasn't clever enough to disguise his distress. Instead, he'd grabbed his keys and had run out of the house, desperate to bring her back. When he'd finally returned, empty-handed, she'd broken the news that she'd arranged for Marguerette to be taken back to the convent in his absence. It wasn't all she'd crowed about that evening, he remembered, pressing his fists into his eyes, her words bellowing across the years.

You have a choice, Lucien. If you return from the convent with your bastard, I'll ensure you never see Violette again.

Instead of responding, he'd stormed out. No bar could have been big enough to sink his sorrows, but he made a good attempt. After, he'd driven to the convent where he'd passed over a sizeable donation to ensure that Marguerette would be found the best family available. Someone who would provide her with the love he couldn't. When he'd finally returned, it had been to devote himself to Violette, something he'd never regretted.

Now, Flora was back and Sabine... He took a deep breath, trying to steady his thoughts. And Sabine was cuckolding him with the enemy. Sabine, who wouldn't allow herself to go without, had discovered early in the war that the only way to achieve it had been to prostitute herself. But why had she chosen him of all people? Otto Reiner. A ghost from the past. A man Lucien had hoped never to see again, only for the war to thrust him back into their orbit.

Because she could. A way of turning the knife in a wound that was already bottomless.

He picked up a new piece of charcoal, weighing it in his palm, his mind veering to a place he rarely allowed it the luxury of visiting. A place where sadness grew out of the choices they'd made the evening Flora had gone into labour. The night he'd stolen her right to be a mother.

With the tip of the charcoal hovering over the paper, he suddenly swept it across in fluid strokes, a slight scrape filling the silence.

Within minutes it was done.

Standing back, he smiled at the simple lines of the dress, which relied on the figure of the wearer and the quality of the cut and the fabric instead of the design tricks he'd used on the countess's gown.

For him the dress was more than a few strokes. He knew it was his best work. It encapsulated his heart.

He scrubbed the back of his hand across his eyes before pulling open the top drawer of his desk where his diary lay. There was something he had to do. Something that couldn't wait. Turning over the leaves, he stopped at the last few, before ripping them out, the paper crackling between his fingers as he scrunched them into a tight ball.

He'd been foolish in pouring his heart out on the pages. Revealing secrets that weren't his to share, yet.

FOURTEEN

Monday 30 November – Le Moulin Rouge

'Ah, Flora. Bonjour.'

Odile hurried towards her, her arms full of cloth bales. 'Thank goodness you made it.'

Flora glanced around at the otherwise empty room, closing her eyes briefly in case Juliette and Amantine materialised in the brief interval. She was to be disappointed.

'Yes, alors. As you can see, we're on our own today. Juliette has a migraine and Amantine a cold. A disaster. There are three dresses with major repairs after last night. The dancers – clumsy oafs, the lot of them.' She tutted, dropping the fabric on the counter and starting to unwind the satin in large handfuls. 'You'd think they were galloping in a field instead of exotic dancing. A horse could do better, or perhaps a donkey.' She cackled briefly, her mood improving by the second now she knew she had help. 'I think I'll suggest it to the manager.'

Flora smiled briefly, slipping off her coat and unpinning her hat before stripping off her gloves. Her overall came next, starched white gleaming against the grey of her dress. 'Where would you like me to start?'

Odile walked over to the rail and the three limp dresses, their hems a raggedy mess. 'If I start work on these. I'm afraid Coralina's is the worst. All your work...'

Flora's heart sank at the sight of the large rip in the skirt. 'These things happen. Leave it to me.'

With the aquamarine dress billowing out on the worktable in front of her, she worked through the silk to inspect the damage. The tear wasn't a clean split, more an unravelling where the fine fabric had snagged, ruching right up to the waist. Part of her wondered what could have happened to cause such extensive damage while the larger part worked on how best to repair it. The ideal would be a new skirt, but she didn't have either the time or the silk for that. Instead, she stretched out the area and, using a sliver of tailor's chalk, marked a deep triangle before attacking the fabric with her sharp scissors. After, she made a template of the piece and was soon threading cotton onto a needle and doing what she loved best – hand sewing the fine fabric with stitches so small as to be almost invisible to the naked eye.

Any scraps of fabric were added to the pile, her mind spooling back to last night and how Tomas had gobbled up her calendar idea. When they'd parted outside Madame Billy's, he'd taken a rough diagram of the quilt sketched on the back of an invoice, along with a brief set of instructions, which he intended to take to London as soon as he could. That her little idea might be adopted across other European networks was as astounding as it was terrifying. What happened if she'd miscalculated and the enemy were able to see right through her quilt? Then she remembered something Lucien had taught her from the days when she'd had to turn his drawings into patterns. Simple designs were the most popular, but also the most difficult to execute. She hoped the same was true when it came to getting one up on the enemy. There was nothing fancy in the stitching and nothing untoward in the choice of the coloured squares. Nothing to alert the Germans that there might be something strange going on.

Coating her thread with beeswax, Flora remembered the way

Tomas's expression had crumpled when he'd spoken about his friend. His grief. Something he couldn't speak of. In that moment she'd instinctively wanted to pull him towards her, but she hadn't. There were layers to their relationship she had to navigate first.

By lunchtime she'd finished the dress and had started on the next while Odile went to speak to the chef about rustling them up something to eat.

'Hello. I was hoping I'd find you here.'

Flora paused, her needle poised between two stitches, her fingers clenching briefly before securing the needle and looking up. Lucien stood in the doorway.

Pushing away from the table, she smoothed her hands over her overall, feeling at a distinct disadvantage. She'd never expected him to visit her in the sewing room.

'This is a surprise,' she finally managed.

'I came to apologise.'

He ran his hands down his face, the shadows pressed like bruises under his eyes, the knot on his tie loose, the top button of his shirt undone.

'What must you have thought?' he finally said, lifting his hands only to drop them to his side. 'I know you're not like them. How could you be? You'd never sink so low as to sell yourself.'

Flora didn't know how to reply to the sideways remark. The last thing Madame Billy's girls needed was his contempt. If it hadn't been for the priest in Étampes and the nuns in Paris, she might have been forced into a similar situation. Heaving a sigh, she suddenly remembered Tomas and what she'd promised. There was only one way of handling Lucien, and that was to keep her thoughts in check. She had a job to do for the British government which was far more important than a few upset feelings.

'I made a decision earlier that you're part of,' he continued, removing his hat and placing his keys inside.

She waited, unsure of what he was going to say next. There was an eagerness in him which she hadn't seen since the first time they'd met in the rain outside Maison Lumineau. In that moment she could almost feel the sting of raindrops on her skin along with the warmth of his gaze, the sky overhead metal grey. She shuddered.

The day her world changed forever.

He coughed, drawing her into the present and the decision hovering between them. It could be anything from offering her employment – she'd have to think carefully about accepting – to asking her to become his mistress. Her stomach rolled. In her view, there was little difference between a demimondaine and a brothel worker, apart from an apartment and pin money. It was a proposition she wouldn't consider under any circumstance, no matter what Tomas said.

'The truth is, I should never have married Sabine. I think I went mad when the girls were born. The joy of being a father overtook everything else. By the time I finally worked out what was important it was too late. When the nuns told me you'd left... I searched...'

Flora stared at him, her mind in sudden disarray. 'You followed me?'

'I jumped in the car with a bunch of flowers and a willingness to agree to anything. My dearest wish was to keep you in my life in any way possible.'

'I never knew.'

Would it have changed things? It was impossible to tell, but his words were enough to set up an inkling of doubt. Lucien, the confident couturier rushing across France after an eighteen-year-old that he imagined himself in love with, didn't equate to Lucien the rogue. She frowned. Which one was he, or was this an act?

She watched as he ran his hand through his usually immaculate hair, his movements jerky and unsteady. It didn't look like an act.

'You only had a half hour start, but in which direction, Flora? I searched the streets, the train and the bus station but no one had seen you.'

All these years, she'd imagined Lucien and Sabine playing

happy families with the twins when nothing could have been further from the truth. That he'd tried to follow her changed everything she'd previously thought about him. That no one had told her felt like a punch in the gut. She'd contacted the convent as soon as she'd found work in Brittany. Nothing.

'I grabbed a lift to the station. There was a train pulling out. I was in no frame of mind to even know where it was heading.'

'I was going to ask you to be my mistress.' He shook his head as if trying to gather his thoughts. 'I know now that you would never have agreed. I was doing you a disservice by even thinking it.' His expression changed from worry to something softer. 'I love you so very much. I always have. When I found out that you were pregnant it was both the best and worst of news, given that I'd just proposed to Sabine. I need to make that right.' He flexed his shoulders back as if bracing himself for the next bit. 'I intend to divorce her if the church will let me. And if they won't, I'll seek an annulment. It's not as if we've ever been married in the true meaning of the word. When it's finalised, I'd like you to agree to be—'

'Stop, please!'

Flora took a step back in horror. What she thought she knew and what Lucien was telling her were two completely different versions of what seemed like someone else's story. Not hers.

It was too much to take in. If she hadn't run away, what then? If he'd asked her to stay, what would she have done? It was all very well thinking she'd never have agreed to be his mistress, but that was the grown-up in her talking. She'd been grown-up then too, she remembered, but only just and so innocent.

With her legs starting to buckle, she backed away until the edge of the worktable stopped her.

He looked at her thoughtfully, frowning a little. 'Are you alright, Flora?'

She lifted her head from where she'd been staring at the cube of beeswax.

Her life in Brittany, meeting Brian and moving to Carrickfergus had all happened on the rebound, her tender heart bruised and battered from what the cad Lucien had done, but that wasn't the truth. She could see it in his eyes and the way he couldn't quite hold her gaze. She didn't love him, not anymore. That had died a sudden death on the train somewhere between Paris and Brittany. But did she still feel the same burning hatred that used to cramp her stomach and flood her veins with vitriol? Closing her eyes, she examined her feelings, prising them apart one by one before deciding that all she felt was numb and confused.

'I don't know what to say,' she began, picking up the beeswax and kneading it between her fingers.

'You don't have to say anything, dearest. Let me do the talking, I have a lifetime to make it up to you.'

'Bonjour, monsieur, but you shouldn't be here. This area is private.'

Odile stormed into the room, a laden tray between her hands.

'I'm sorry, madame.' He gave a small bow of apology. 'I...'

'It's my fault,' Flora interrupted, her face warming.

Odile looked between them, her left eyebrow arched. Flora wondered how long she'd been waiting at the bottom of the stairs for the right moment to interrupt their tête-à-tête. Long enough.

Picking up Lucien's keys and his fedora from where he'd discarded them, she turned her back briefly, making a pretence of brushing the brim.

'You always had exquisite taste in hats.'

'Exquisite taste in everything, chérie.'

Flora laughed, as she slipped the beeswax cube into her overall pocket, careful not to touch the clear impression of the two keys pressed into the waxy surface.

'Your hat and keys, Lucien.'

He nodded his thanks. 'When can I see you again?'

Flora shot him a look, aware that Odile was back behind her sewing machine and tuned into the conversation. 'I'm not sure...'

'Saturday. My place,' he said softly, swooping in and pressing a kiss against her cheek. 'Sabine is away so we'll have the place to ourselves. I'll pick you up at seven.'

• • •

'I was hoping you weren't going to leave with him. We still have a lot of work to get through,' Odile mumbled through a mouthful of pins, her fingers running material through the machine. 'Monsieur Lumineau is quite a catch.'

Flora chuckled as she removed the lump of beeswax and placed it on the table.

'But he's not my catch, Odile. Far from it.'

'If you say so.' She removed the pins, pressing them into a raggedy pincushion in the shape of a frog before nodding at the tray. 'A quick break for lunch then back to work but in the meantime...' She grabbed her bag from under the table and pulled out a calendar quilt, the multicoloured patchwork squares some of the best sewing Flora had ever seen.

'Oh my goodness. That's wonderful. I wasn't sure if you were comfortable being part of all this.'

'It's difficult not to be with Juliette and Amantine always rattling on about the war.' Odile folded the quilt and tucked it back in her bag. 'It's easier and yet more difficult for them with husbands fighting. Quilts I can do.' She nodded at the beeswax. 'Be careful, eh. The Lumineaus aren't to be trifled with. Friends in high places.'

Flora nodded, feeling a sudden comradery with the older woman. There were many tools used to fight a war. Bombs, blades and guns but also fabrics, stitches and wools. Women could play their part too.

Five o'clock passed, then six. It was a quarter to seven by the time she snipped the last strand of thread before shaking out the final dress, the skirts a mass of white frills and ruffles.

'At last. Thank you, Flora. I don't know what I would have done without you.' Odile patted her on the shoulder in passing. 'Come in at ten thirty tomorrow, I insist.'

Flora was hooking the dress on the rail when the door burst open, a parade of chattering women launching themselves into the room in search of their outfits, each one labelled with their unique number. Coralina pounced on the newly mended dress, her hands rummaging through the silk for any sign of the tear.

'Madame Guilloux, you're amazing.' She stooped to hug the woman only to be flapped away.

'You have Flora to thank, not me, and next time you decide to rip your gown, spare a thought for the poor seamstress, eh.'

Coralina pulled a face. 'It wasn't my fault, I swear. I was lucky to escape with only a torn dress.'

'She's right,' a tall redhead, with luminous green eyes and a pout, interrupted. 'Monsieur André must be careful with his clientele or there'll be more than a torn dress to account for.'

'Tut tut.' Odile changed from dragon to mother hen in an instant. 'Don't worry, ma petites, I'll speak to him. It's a long time in coming. Without you girls, no business, eh?'

Flora watched the exchange from her position in the corner. What the dance hall needed was a Madame Billy, but she wasn't the right person to suggest it.

'Flora.' Coralina wandered over, holding on to her dress like a prize. 'If you're finished, I could show you our dressing room. It's a bit chaotic but we could talk.'

FIFTEEN

Flora followed Coralina into the pandemonium.

Through a haze of cigarette smoke and cheap perfume, she watched, wide-eyed, as the dancers, in various stages of undress, were helped by a small group of matronly types. One was busy pinning ostrich feathers onto a statuesque woman's blonde bob, while the dancer beside her was rolling black silk stockings carefully along her leg, her foot propped up against the wall.

'Hurry up, Cora. You're late,' one of the dressers shouted across the noise.

'I'm coming, ma chérie,' she replied, stripping off her gloves and beret before removing her coat. 'Two minutes for me to put some muck on my face.'

Perching on one of the high stools, she patted for Flora to sit next to her as she started layering creams and powders onto her smooth skin with an eye-watering speed that had Flora blinking.

'You want to know about Marguerette, chérie, but I want to know about her too.'

'There's nothing I can tell you.' Flora felt her throat close and her eyes sting. She knew nothing about her daughter except what others had told her. The thought was enough to break her into tiny irretrievable pieces. At least with Violette, she knew she'd had a happy childhood. All that money could buy along with Lucien's devotion. It almost felt as if Marguerette was her penance for choosing to give up her babies.

She blinked back tears, trying to concentrate as Coralina stroked black mascara onto her eyelashes with a fragile wand before digging into the bottom of the pot to rescue the last flakes. 'The other girls think she's gone off with a man, but...' She flashed her a worried look. 'She wasn't interested. Six months and she never accepted a date from anyone, and that wasn't for want of them asking.' She laughed briefly, a far from happy sound. 'They come for the show and think we're included in the price, but that's not how it works. We date who we want and when we want. Mostly, we can't be bothered with them. We have boyfriends of our own, in some cases husbands and children, and we need to eat. This is a job like any other.'

Flora picked up Carolina's discarded glove, smoothing out the intricate crocheted garment, her creative brain trying and failing to work out how the maker had worked the delicate stitches.

'What do you think could have happened?' she said, placing the glove back with its pair, and turning slightly only to find a transformed Coralina in front of her. She'd been beautiful before. Now she was stunning. 'No one seems to know anything or, if they do, they're not saying.'

'I'd hazard a guess that her fancy couturier father knows something.'

Flora stilled, her attention on where Coralina was quickly lining her lips in vermilion red. 'You know who her...?'

'Monsieur Lumineau.' She leant in, her voice low. 'Only I know, and now you, but I think you knew before, eh, mama. You're too alike to be anything else.' She picked up her gloves, holding one up briefly before tucking them inside her beret. 'Marguerette is both beautiful and talented. These gloves are my most treasured possession.'

'She made them?'

'Bien sur. Of course. And the dress she sang in.'

'Coralina, I must insist,' the dresser bellowed out across the room. 'Five minutes and you're on.'

'Coming.' Coralina stood quickly and, rummaging through the dressing table, finally found what she was looking for before thrusting it into Flora's hands. 'Why not come backstage and watch? I have the first song. There's plenty of time before curfew.'

Flora nodded, intent on the thin, mass-produced programme, an image of the windmill on the cover. Turning it over, she saw a photograph on the back.

It was like looking at a reflection of herself in the mirror. Similar to Tomas's photograph but also very different. A glamorous version in a slinky crocheted dress, which skimmed from neck to feet. The only parts visible were Marguerette's face and hands, and yet Flora had never seen anything more sensual in her life.

A bell rang and, lifting her head, she watched as Coralina raced out, her gown shimmering in the light. When she followed shortly after, her footsteps were slow and deliberate, her vision distorted by a haze of sudden tears.

'You Flora? Coralina told me to look after you, as if I don't have enough to do.' The man was dressed in a sharp suit with satin trim, his kindly smile belying his grumbles. 'Stand there.' He grabbed her shoulders, moving her further back into the folds of a dusty red curtain, his breath smelling of garlic. 'No. There. Don't move and don't speak.'

A clatter of heels behind her before Coralina appeared, her hands adjusting the strap of her dress before checking the line of her skirt. 'What are they like, tonight, André?'

'Noisy as hell and it's only going to get worse.' The sound of stamping feet had him hurrying onto the stage, his voice raised to a shout.

'Bonsoir, gentlemen.' Flora saw him take a deep bow, his arms spread. 'Welcome to Le Moulin Rouge, where all your dreams come true. This evening, we're going to start with a ballad from the beautiful Coralina. It's called "Alone Tonight", for all of you apart from your beloved wives and girlfriends.'

Within seconds he was back, his voice lowered to a whisper. 'Over to you. You'll find the microphone further back from the stage. We can't have a repeat of yesterday's events.'

'Thank you, chéri.' Coralina dropped a kiss against his cheek before walking towards the stage, a wide smile planted on her vermilion lips.

Flora hazarded a step closer, her eyes adjusting to the bright lights beaming across the stage, the audience in darkness, but not in silence, the occasional shout and guttural roar filling the air.

The band started up and soon the sweet smoky notes of the song were all she heard, the anthem to a lost love causing her breath to hitch. Not a lost love. Two lost loves, which she was more determined than ever to find.

She waited for Coralina to leave the stage to rapturous clapping and more stamping feet, having to press back against the curtain as the dancers raced past, their gowns billowing around them, but she didn't stay. She'd seen and heard enough. Instead, she retraced her steps down to the sewing room, remembering to tuck the cube of beeswax in the bottom of her bag before covering it with a handful of rags.

SIXTEEN

The Librairie Universelle bookshop was situated along the Rue de la Pompe and only a short walk from Madame Billy's.

The door creaked when she pushed it open, the little bell above her head heralding her arrival with a sharp jingle. The shop was empty apart from a dark-haired woman in her late thirties, her expression set into a worried frown as she worked on a ledger, a pen in her hand.

Flora breathed in the musty scent of old books vying for position among newer tomes. The shop was dark and a little dingy with an old, scarred wooden counter running along the left wall. A curtain separated the back of the shop from what lay beyond. Probably stairs, she thought, her attention shifting to the round table in the centre with a circular arrangement of books. There was a ladder too. One of those tall ones to reach the highest shelves. She'd always fancied climbing one.

Turning back, she approached the counter. 'Bonjour, madame. I'm looking for a first edition of Victor Hugo's *Les Misérables*.'

The woman's dark eyes sparkled with amusement, her finger tapping lightly on the set of five volumes beside her, the name

Victor Hugo stamped on the spines. 'Alas, all I have are these. A bargain at two francs.' She strode from behind the counter, her hand outstretched in greeting. 'You can only be Flora. I'm Marianne.'

Tomas had dictated her use of first names when he'd got her to memorise the coded message. All she knew about the bookshop owner was that she was called Marianne and that she was sympathetic to the resistance. She hadn't questioned him, though she would have liked to know more. The less she knew about what went on in the French networks the better.

'Bonjour, Marianne. I have a delivery for our mutual friend along with a message.' She removed the cube of beeswax from her bag, placing it in Marianne's outstretched hand before watching it disappear into her pocket. 'Sunday evening will be ideal as they're out for dinner.'

'Of course. You're sure that...'

The bell jangled behind them, bringing in an influx of cold air and the sharp sound of boots clanking against the wooden flooring.

She noticed the way Marianne's face slipped back into its entrenched frown lines before smoothing into something blander.

Flora forced herself not to turn, a smile of sorts on her lips as she continued to look ahead. A few days in France and she'd forgotten this was no longer the Paris of her birth. Fear took hold, rooting her to the spot.

Breathe, Flora. They don't know you. They can't. Act normally. You're in a bookshop. Buy a book!

'I'll take them. If you could wrap them for me, please. They're a present.'

'Of course, madame.' Marianne nodded at someone behind her, standing so close that she got a fleeting smell of heavy cologne. 'I'll be with you in a moment, Herr Standartenführer Reiner.'

The sound of heels clicking filled the air and then he was beside her, watching as Marianne folded brown paper around the books before tying them with string. He was also watching Flora, but she refused to make eye contact. She stole a quick glance, taking in his peaked hat and SS uniform. What interest would the SS have in a bookshop?

With the bill paid and the parcel tucked under her arm, she made for the door, the bell again chiming its tune. Reaching behind for the handle, she took her time in pulling it closed behind her, long enough for her to hear the officer speak.

'Who is that woman? I recognise her.' The words were sharp. Barked out like an order.

'A stranger to me, Herr Reiner.'

Their exchange was enough to quicken her feet as she hurried to the Metro station, her parcel clutched in her hands.

Luckily, she didn't have long to wait for a train and, with the morning rush-hour out of the way, she was able to find a seat for the half hour journey. By the time she exited the station, a feeling of lethargy had replaced the adrenaline surge of earlier, her body drained as she crossed the road towards the red beacon of Le Moulin Rouge in front of her.

She paused outside the door, swapping her package between hands as she went to turn the handle, only to stop dead, the hairs on the back of her neck standing to attention for the second time that morning. Something was wrong and she didn't need a crystal ball to know what. Turning slightly, she scanned the street only to lock eyes with the SS officer from the bookshop.

SEVENTEEN

Le Moulin Rouge, 10.30 am

'Bonjour, Flora.' Odile glanced up from her work, only to pause, a look of concern flashing across her face. 'What is it? You're as white as a ghost. Amantine, run upstairs and ask the manager for a drop of brandy. It's an emergency.'

'Of course.'

Flora heard the sound of chair legs scraping against the floor and footsteps hurrying across the room before the thump of feet on the stairs. The smell of Juliette's light perfume followed as she leant over, pressing her handkerchief into Flora's clenched fists.

'It's clean.'

Flora sank into the nearest chair, her legs giving way beneath her, the handkerchief pressed to her face, surprised at how weak she felt. She was also surprised by the kindness she'd found in the small room in the basement of the dance hall, which only made it harder to swallow back her tears.

'Here.' Odile took one of her hands and wrapped it around a square glass. 'Now drink.'

'I... I can't.'

'You can and you will, Flora. I'm the boss here and you do as I say.'

She'd put on her stern voice, the same tone she'd used on Flora's first day when she'd interviewed her for the job, but it didn't work. Flora had quickly realised that, underneath, Odile was as soft as the satins and silks she worked with.

'Thank you.' She sniffed, then swallowed before wiping her eyes one last time. 'I don't know what's come over me. I'm not normally like this.'

'Which means something must have happened.' Odile settled on the chair opposite, while Amantine and Juliette hovered off to one side, the table littered with their half-finished dresses, the machines silent, when they were never silent.

'I popped into a bookshop on the way here, the little one on the Rue de la Pompe opposite the school.'

Glancing around, she spotted where she must have placed her bag and her parcel of books on the shelf by the door, although she had no memory of it.

'There was a German who came in while I was there.' She lifted her head, her chin tilted, her eyes direct. 'An SS officer. He followed me here, right to the entrance.'

A single beat before Juliette reared up like a lion. 'Filthy boche. What I'd like to do to them if I had the chance.' She slammed her fist on the table, the noise loud in the otherwise quiet room. 'Killing our men and terrorising our women. When will it end!'

'Calm down, Juliette. That sort of talk won't get us anywhere. It will end when one side wins and not before.' Odile pressed her hand on Flora's shoulder, squeezing gently. 'I'll have a word with André. Would you recognise the man again?'

I'll never forget him, she thought, the image of the grey-haired man filling her vision, his square face dominated by a florid, drinker's nose.

'Tall and solid. Grey hair. Intense gaze. Bulbous nose.'

'Which could be any of *them* of a certain age.'

Flora took a sip from the glass, her face screwing up at the taste.

At this rate she'd be an alcoholic before she knew it. With the glass back on the table, she started removing her hat and her coat, resolved to push the German to the back of her mind. There was work to do. Lots of repairs by the number of dresses on the rail. She'd sink herself into the job and, after, she'd sink herself into making quilts. It wasn't much, but it was something.

She was halfway through the day, her scissors in her hand as she snipped away at the bodice she'd been repairing, when she stopped, her scissors aloft, her cheeks warming to red hot.

It made no sense for Reiner to recognise her, none whatsoever. She'd never met him. It wasn't as if she would have forgotten his glacial expression and dead-fish stare, and there were no images of her that she knew of in France. How could there be?

She placed the scissors carefully back on the table, her heart giving a quick thump in her chest, her mind in ribbons.

What about Marguerette?

Her daughter who was meant to be the image of her. Even Coralina had mistaken her for the much younger woman.

Plucking up the scissors, she forced herself to finish cutting out the ripped section, her mind in a loop. There was nothing she could do about any of it until Saturday, her next day off. She'd arranged to meet Lucien, but that wasn't until the evening, which still left the rest of the day free.

With one last snip, she removed the panel and placed it on a new piece of fabric as a template before starting the laborious process of cutting and tacking it in place. It was a task she'd carried out so many time before that she had no need to concentrate. Instead, her mind was busy making plans.

The Champagne region of France was only a two-hour train journey from Paris. It was time to do something for herself for once.

EIGHTEEN

Saturday 5 December – Épernay train station, 11 am

Flora gripped onto her bag, before loosening her fingers and slowing her breathing, her eyes glued to the soldier standing by the barrier up ahead.

'Heil Hitler. Your documents.'

Delving into her bag, she handed them over, forcing herself to meet his gaze, the sound of the steam train pulling out of the station reminding her that it was too late to turn back.

'And the reason for your visit?'

'Family.' She nodded to where she'd placed her ticket inside her ID card. 'I'll be returning this afternoon.'

'A short visit?'

'A birthday,' she lied, the date of the twins' birthday, one she'd never forget.

He stared at her before dropping his gaze to study the photograph on the card, looking for so long that Flora began to worry. She felt dizzy, waiting for his reply. Waiting for the possibility of being outed as an enemy of the state.

'Enjoy your celebrations.'

Once outside, she looked left then right, wondering what to do next. The street was empty apart from a horse and cart. Hardly surprising. She'd been the only one to alight from the train. Shrugging her coat more firmly around her shoulders against the bitter wind, she wandered over to the horse, patting the animal's nut-brown head. The chateau was meant to be a short walk from the station, but in which direction.

'Bonjour, madame. You look lost. May I be of assistance?'

The man walking over to the horse and cart was no more than a youth.

'I'm looking for Chateau Beau Marin. Is it far?'

'About half an hour or so walk, or ten minutes with Olive at the helm.' He nodded at the brown horse before patting the seat beside him. 'Jump in. I'm heading in that direction.'

'You are? You're sure it's not out of your way?'

'I said so, didn't I?'

'That's unbelievably kind, thank you.' Flora accepted his help up the step before settling on the bench and arranging her coat over her knees.

'Not unbelievable if, like me, you happen to work there.' He grinned. 'Just been dropping off the post to the train. They usually tell me when there's someone who needs picking up?'

'Yes, well, it was all very last minute.'

'So you're not here for a job then?'

Flora fiddled with her gloves, unsure of what to say. It was obvious by her simple clothes that she wouldn't be visiting to purchase champagne so the guess about a job interview was a good one, except that it was a Saturday.

Instead of replying she decided to ask a question.

'You don't happen to know Violette Lumineau, do you?'

'Whoa.' He pulled the horse to a stop and turned to face her. 'The boss's daughter. Course I know her. We all do.'

'We?' she said weakly, her stomach still trying to recover from the sudden stop.

'My parents and I. Papa is manager while Maman queens it in the kitchen.' He belatedly held out his hand. 'I'm Yves Delamaire.'

Flora hesitated briefly before coming up with an alias. 'Marie Martin, a friend of Violette's father's.'

'Funny they never told me to expect you.' He shrugged, picking up the reins.

'I thought it could be a surprise. I haven't seen Violette for such a long time. I probably won't even recognise her.'

'Oh, you'll recognise her alright. Could hardly miss her.' His voice dropped and he coughed to clear it, his cheeks stained cherry red.

Flora hid a smile, remembering how beautiful Violette had looked in Tomas's photograph. 'I hope she's nice as well.'

He darted her a look, the pink starting to fade. 'She's nice.'

'What about her mother?'

'You certainly like to ask questions, don't you?'

'I'm not here to cause trouble. Promise.'

'My papa has a couple of shotguns if you do.' The words were said with a laugh, but the underlying meaning was clear. *Don't mess with me.* 'We don't see Madame Lumineau from one year to the next, but Monsieur Lucien is a regular visitor. A real gentleman.'

'That's good to hear. I'll be sure to tell him when I see him.'

The roads were empty, the wheels of the cart soporific, Fields of bare vines, like twigs, filled either side of the dirt track with nothing to break the monotony except the sight of a black horse and rider cantering in the distance. She wanted to ask more. To ask everything she could about Violette, but it wouldn't be fair and the risk too great.

'How much longer?' she asked, starting to feel the hardness of the wooden bench through her coat and dress, the landscape unchanging for what looked like miles ahead.

'We've been on the chateau's land the last mile back. See that lane up ahead on the left? Down there for another mile or so.'

Once they'd turned, she lifted her hand to her eyes, shielding her face from the low winter sun, her gaze riveted to the horizon. It was a long time since she'd seen a chateau. It was a long time since she'd seen her daughter too...

They rounded another corner and the chateau was right in front of them.

Flora caught her breath, her eyes widening in delight.

Turreted grey stone surrounded by a sweeping driveway with tall trees and too many windows to count. That something so breathtakingly beautiful was also a working vineyard was astonishing. That Violette was somewhere up ahead had her skin tingle with anticipation.

Yves veered to the right of the building, overtaking a large black car parked on the bend. 'I'm going to drop you around the back. Olive needs a rest before I head back to the station with Monsieur Rives. Don't worry, my mother will look after you while you're waiting for Violette.'

'Tomas Rives, from Paris?'

'You know the wine merchant?' Yves turned to face her, the reins looped around his wrist. 'You should have said. One or other of the wine merchants from the city is here most weeks trying to negotiate terms with the weinfurters. They steal our land and now they're intent on stealing our grapes.'

Flora closed her eyes, a brief respite.

'We've met once or twice,' she finally managed through gritted teeth, her heart like a stone in the bottom of her chest, all the blood squeezed out. Why hadn't he told her, she thought, glancing around the courtyard in alarm.

'They're probably in the kitchen.' He pulled Olive to a halt before jumping down and proffering his hand. 'I'll show you where and then find out about Violette. She's usually somewhere around the stables.'

Flora nodded, knowing she didn't have an option. It was meet Tomas or brave the threat of Yves's father's shotgun. Reaching into the cart to collect her bag, she stopped halfway, her ears picking up the muted sounds of voices coming from the chateau beyond.

'Good to see you again, Rives. Thank you for doing business

with us. Heil Hitler.' She stayed where she was, listening to the sound of boots stomping across the courtyard before the car engine started up and revved down the drive.

She wouldn't believe that Tomas was in cahoots with the enemy, but it certainly sounded like something suspicious was going on.

She slowly eased backwards out of the cart, using the horse as a shield, her bag forgotten, knowing she was trapped.

Tomas suddenly appeared around Olive, his face draining of colour. 'What are you doing here?'

Yves glanced between them before unhitching Olive from the cart and hurrying her into the stables.

'Hello, Tomas.' Flora watched as he scrubbed his hand along his jaw in that telltale movement she was beginning to recognise. A sure sign that he was feeling both awkward and uncomfortable.

Good. She wasn't feeling that great herself. Her excitement and anticipation at seeing Violette had disappeared, only to be replaced by a dull ache. What had possessed her to visit the chateau?

'I've come to see Violette.' She made a point of turning full circle. The stables up ahead, the chateau to the right. Stone barns to the left. The vineyard peeling away behind them. 'You haven't seen her, have you?'

'Flora… I…'

'It's Marie,' she replied, lowering her voice as she darted a quick look towards the barn. 'It's alright, Tomas. Yves has gone to find out where she is.'

He reached her side, his hands thrust deep in his pockets, his mouth pulled into a thin line. 'She's not here, *Marie*. I'm sorry.'

She stared at him, trying to read his expression and failing.

'That's not what Yves said.'

'I saw her not half an hour ago saddle up her horse and head across the fields. It's likely she'll be gone hours.'

Flora remembered the horse in the distance and knew he must be telling the truth.

• • •

'This is ridiculous. You must speak to me.'

'I don't have to do anything, Tomas. You could have easily told me about your business at the chateau and meeting Violette, and yet you chose not to.'

Flora placed her patchwork on her lap, favouring the view of the River Marne running parallel to the train, her fingers needing a rest. For the first hour of their return journey, they'd sat in silence, the busy carriage no place to discuss anything. She'd resorted to working on her quilt, the sight of her needle flashing through the fabric preferable to the sight of Tomas's stony expression opposite. Now the carriage was empty, everyone having alighted at the pretty town of Meaux. She'd watched them collecting their bags and baskets, her anger wearing away to intense disappointment. Disappointment at not seeing Violette and disappointment in him.

'I know I should have told you, Flora.' He stood from his seat, taking the one beside her instead. 'There are a lot of things I should have done differently, but I knew you'd be upset.'

'You don't know me well enough to make that call,' she hissed. 'And I can tell you that I'm far more upset at being kept in the dark than if you'd told me from the start.' She puffed out her cheeks, trying to ease her emotions back inside where they belonged. Losing her temper wouldn't help either of them. 'It makes complete sense that you would have visited the chateau on business and that you'd get to see her.'

'Only in passing.'

'I don't care about that. All I care about is that you couldn't trust me enough to tell me what you were up to. What exactly were you doing there, Tomas, or is that on a need-to-know basis like everything else with you?'

'Oh, for heaven's sake.' He pulled out his cigarettes and worked on lighting one.

He only spoke after the second puff. 'Working as a wine merchant is my job but also my cover. I've never kept that from you, or that I travel. I travel all around the country seven days a week trying to help vineyards, learning what I can about the inner workings of the weinfurters as I do before sharing the information to those in the west. I also seem to remember telling you about the Lyon silk industry and Lucien's part in it.' He dropped his barely smoked cigarette, stubbing it into the floor with his boot before picking it up and flicking it out of the window, darting her a quick look in the process. 'It didn't seem relevant at the time to mention that I only happened upon this little nugget by chance during a visit to a Beaujolais chateau just north of the city. And as for Violette. I've never met her, but I have seen her in the distance. That's all. I promise.'

Flora raised her hand to stop him, feeling a fool. Of course Tomas wasn't tied up with the Germans. One look at his hunched shoulders and beleaguered expression spoke more than a hundred denials. She'd jumped to conclusions with little or no evidence. Not only that. If the German had spotted her...

She felt sick to her stomach.

Picking up his packet of cigarettes, she withdrew two, afraid that he'd tear them out of her fingers. Instead, he took the one offered, the smell of burning tobacco quickly filling the carriage and easing the situation.

'I've made a complete mess of things, haven't I?' She shook her head at her stupidity.

'Flora...'

She placed her hand on his arm, feeling his strength under her fingers. 'No, let me finish. Not only does Violette not know about me, but when Yves tells his parents, she's bound to contact Lucien.'

'That's not the end of the world though. He must realise that you'd want to see her.'

'I'll have to make him understand. A mother's love getting the better of me. After all, it's the truth.' She managed a smile, one he returned. 'Despite all this, Tomas, despite making a complete mess of everything, it was worth going to see her. I did see her.' She laughed. 'Astride a horse no less and I've met Yves. Are his parents as nice?'

'They're good people. Lumineau, for all his faults, made the right decision in sending her there.'

'I'm glad.' She tilted her head back to release a stream of smoke. 'He's not the same, you know. Less arrogant. Whatever you think we're going to find, I hope it's not long drawn out. I don't think I could bear it. We need to visit his showroom and quickly.'

'I'm just waiting for the locksmith to get back to me.' He glanced out of the window at the sight of Paris up ahead, the white domes of the Basilique du Sacre-Coeur visible in the distance. 'In fact, if there's no hold ups, I might be able to catch him before he shuts for the night.'

He reached for her hand, smoothing his thumb over her skin, so near that she could count the grey in his hair and see the emotion flickering in the back of his eyes.

'Still friends, Flora?' he said softly.

She stared at him, unable to look away.

'Still friends, Tomas.'

NINETEEN

L'Etoile de Kleber, 6 pm

'One won't hurt, ma chérie.' Edith waved the bottle of calvados in front of her, her mouth arranged into a pout. 'The only evening I have off this week and you're deserting me.'

'Only a small drop then please,' Flora replied, watching in dismay as she poured out a large measure. She already had the start of a headache from sewing in the poorly lit train carriage. Alcohol would only make it worse.

After leaving Tomas, she'd spent an hour on her quilt before hurrying to get ready for her evening with Lucien. She'd added ten squares, which had calmed her mind and soothed her mood. She'd made a mistake in visiting the chateau, but it hadn't been irredeemable and a lesson had been learnt: to think before jumping to conclusions.

Staring down at the amber liquid, her gaze shifted to her hand. She could almost feel the faint touch of Tomas's thumb, just as she could smell the woody scent of his shampoo.

She took a quick sip of the bitter liquid to break the image before setting the glass on the nearest surface. No good could come of it.

'Sorry, I can't manage more. I'm meeting Lucien and I need to keep a clear head.'

Edith's eyes sharpened, her knees pressing together as she leant forward on the bed. 'As in Lucien Lumineau, of Maison Lumineau? The same Lucien who keeps Madame Billy company in her salon every second Tuesday?'

'Yes, that's the one. Marguerette's father.'

'Hah, I suspected as much.' Edith reached for the bottle and topped up her glass. 'I saw him collecting Marguerette from the bottom of the hill once. She didn't speak about him afterwards, but it was easy to see she was upset about something.'

Flora glanced at her. Why would she have been upset? Lucien hadn't said much about Marguerette. She remembered how he'd shut down the conversation when her name had cropped up. What was there to hide?

'And she didn't tell you more?' she probed.

Edith toyed with her glass, her eyes huge in her gamine face. 'She never took me into her confidence, Flora, and I'm not surprised. Remember, the gap between eighteen and twenty-six is as wide as it is treacherous. All I know is the little Marguerette told me about being a twin and her parents having to flee the country.' She knocked back her drink, a trace of lipstick smearing the rim of the glass. 'One day she was twirling around the room in one of her delightful, crocheted creations, checking to see what I thought about her wearing it to go out to dinner with her father, and the next.' Edith's mouth drooped, and suddenly she looked incredibly young and forlorn. 'She must have packed during the night. Her room was empty in the morning. The only thing left behind was an upset sparrow pecking at her window.'

Flora took Lucien's arm as they walked from the car to the entrance of his apartment block. 'When you said you lived near, I didn't quite realise that it was only round the corner.'

'You really expected me to make you walk? How quaint,' he

said, distaste reflected in his voice. 'I don't walk anywhere if I don't have to.' He held the front door open for her. 'Come. We're on the third floor.'

Flora followed him across the marbled lobby to the lift beyond, unsure of what to say. She'd never been in this position before. She wasn't about to start an affair. An affair was the last thing she wanted after what Brian had done. She was only here to search Lucien's personal possessions and papers for anything that might link him to the enemy. She felt her headache escalate a notch. There was also her trip to the chateau...

'Welcome to my home, Flora.'

She walked past him into the spacious apartment, not knowing what to expect, but not the plain white walls strung with a plethora of mirrors polished to a high sheen. Polished by the maid, no doubt. Someone able to feed information back to Sabine.

Flora knew she was being bitchy. The trouble was, her dislike of the woman had little to do with what had happened to Marguerette. Was she jealous? She ruthlessly shoved the thought aside.

'Let me take your coat, and don't worry. When Sabine's away I often give the staff the time off to spend with their families.'

Flora didn't reply as she slipped off her navy wool coat before unwrapping the knitted scarf underneath, suddenly embarrassed by the plainness of her dress. She'd made a good job of matching the fabric and style to what women in 1940s Paris were wearing, but nothing could disguise the cheapness of the cloth. It was little consolation that she was playing a part. It only made it worse when she remembered who he was married to.

'Charming.' Lucien walked around her, his head tilted as he examined the cut and the box pleat she'd hidden in the back seam, the knife-edged tucks giving her room to stride.

'Easier to walk and it only uses up a little more fabric.'

'I can see that.' His eyes lingered on her legs a beat longer than necessary. 'I've clearly got competition.'

'Hardly.' She lifted her hand to his face briefly. 'Remember,

I've seen what you can do with a scrap of charcoal. I hope you know how good your designs are, Lucien. Your clothes make women fall in love with their bodies again. It's not about looking our best. It's about feeling it.'

'Flora...'

She blinked up at him, realising her mistake. While she'd meant every word, the intensity of his gaze told her she'd have been wiser to keep her thoughts to herself.

Instead of replying, she slipped her hand through his arm and pulled him towards the nearest door.

I'm playing a part. Find the evidence and get out.

'What about you show me around. I'd love a tour.'

'Of course. It's more Sabine's than mine.'

He stepped back, allowing her to enter the room first, her attention immediately drawn to the wide expanse of windows covered with blackout blinds. Turning, she took in the white sofas and chairs before staring at the gilt-edged mirrors filling the walls. Rectangular, square and round with ostentatious frames, her reflection caught in a confusing array of angles, making her squirm. There was no room for bookshelves. No books. No photographs or artwork. It could have been a furniture showroom for all the soul it had.

'It's not to your taste?' she finally hazarded.

'I loathe it. You talk about beauty being about feeling your best. In a room full of mirrors there's nowhere to hide.' He smiled briefly, turning to the door. 'I'm rarely here unless she's hosting one of her interminable parties. Come on. I'll show you Violette's room.'

Violette's bedroom was at the end of the corridor. Still white walls, but the fabrics and bed linens were in hues of purple. There was a pile of cushions on the head of the bed and a pile of books on the nightstand as if she'd only walked out of the room instead of being bundled out of Paris in a rush.

Flora sank on the edge of the bed, her hands spread over the satin quilt embroidered with tiny white flowers. Violette's quilt.

Violette's bed in Violette's room. Her eyes started to fill despite Lucien propping up the door jamb, waiting.

She sniffed, pressing back tears. 'I'm sorry. It's just...'

One second, he was by the door, the next he was beside her, taking her hand in his. 'She's a lovely girl. A credit to you. To us,' he amended.

'Lucien... there's something you should know,' she said, her voice low. 'I did something foolish, very foolish earlier. I took a train to Épernay.'

'Did you indeed?' He smiled. 'I'm not surprised. I probably would have done the same in your position.'

'Would you?'

'Absolutely I would. To be kept away.' He stopped, his voice choked. 'What I did. I hope, sometime in the future, that you'll be able to forgive me.'

His expression was full of anguish. She squeezed his hand gently. It seemed as if she wasn't the only one suffering. That a decision made so long ago could still be causing ripples across so many lives...

'It's not about forgiveness, Lucien. You've given her a good life. Made her happy. For that I'm truly thankful. I didn't get to meet her even though it's my dearest wish.'

He hugged her close, pressing a kiss on the side of her head. 'You silly thing. Of course you must meet her.' He leant away, tapping his chin with his forefinger. 'To arrange a meeting might be a little precipitous but, perhaps, a letter? Violette loves receiving letters and she'll be delighted to learn that Sabine isn't her mother. There's no love lost between them.'

'Really?'

'Absolutely true, dearest. It's about time I sorted out the mess I made.'

'I was worried you'd be cross.'

'With you! Never.'

'What about Sabine? I thought the chateau was hers?'

'She hasn't set foot in the place in years. The manager deals only with me. I haven't heard from him yet – no doubt I will, but don't worry about it.'

She smiled weakly, her headache lessening a notch. 'What's our daughter like, Lucien? Yves said she's nice?'

He threw back his head and laughed. 'Yves would. Puppy love since the first time he laid his eyes on her, and why not. She's a delight.' He concentrated on playing with her fingers. 'Beautiful to look at but that's a given.' He dropped her hand in favour of her hair, where a long strand had come adrift. 'The staff both here and at the showroom adore her. Nothing is ever too much trouble.'

'I'm pleased she makes friends easily,' she said, feeling his nearness, but reluctant to move in case he stopped speaking.

'And stray pets.' He shook his head. 'If it wasn't for Sabine's strict no pet policy, the place would be overrun with cats and dogs. Even the odd horse. She loves horses.'

Flora smiled, remembering the horse rider.

'She's talented too, just like her darling maman.' He pushed away from the bed and made for the armoire next to the door, pulling open the bottom drawer. 'I made this for her when she was fourteen, only she thought it a little dull.' He sounded amused at the criticism as he lifted out an exquisite taffeta dress. The fabric rustled as he shook out the folds, the embroidery running along the skirt causing her to gasp in delight.

Flora rose to her feet.

Silken threaded animals danced along the hem, their limbs festooned with a riot of flowers, from pansies, daffodils and roses. Running her fingers over the skirt, she could barely breathe at the quality of the embroidery, enthralled at the way the light bounced off the design, bringing it to life. She'd never seen finer work.

'She did this?' Flora raised her eyes to his, offering a watery smile.

'No one else. Sabine can't thread a needle let alone sew on a button and you know how useless I am at that side of the business. That's what I pay others for,' he added, attempting his wife's honeyed drawl.

Flora would have laughed, but the way his jaw tensed into firm lines told her that it wouldn't be appreciated. Instead, she replaced the dress back in the drawer and followed him out of the room.

He stopped in front of the next door, pulling his keys out of his pocket, his gaze assessing before relaxing into a smile. 'My study. Where the magic happens. And mirrors are banned,' he added bleakly, but with a glimmer in the back of his eyes. 'Make yourself at home. I'll be back shortly.'

Flora watched as he walked down the hall, with a spring in his step. A complex man, far more complex than she'd thought when she'd first met him. Then he'd been the handsome atelier with more charm than was good for any woman. Now she didn't know what to think. If Tomas was to be believed, he was a traitor. All she'd seen so far was a man whose greatest success wasn't his business.

It was his daughters.

The study was a world away from the rest of the apartment. A mirror-free zone full of the old-fashioned charm and architectural detailing that was missing elsewhere. The focal point was a large fireplace with a sofa angled off to one side, the red leather cracked with age. There was even a fern plant taking up place in the middle of the side table, offering a refreshing dose of greenery. Nothing was new. Even the lighting was old-fashioned – wall sconces, which looked to have been converted from gas. The room smelt of woodsmoke, and warm leather, with an undertone of old books and the base notes of Lucien's subtle aftershave.

This was the type of room that shared its secrets, unlike the rest of the apartment. She wanted to know what part he played and why he'd chosen to side with the enemy. The desk drawers would be a good place to start. She frowned. Lucien would be the last man to want her rummaging through his things, which meant she needed him busy elsewhere.

She turned to study an easel positioned off to one side of the window, presumably to catch the light, a bin for discarded sketches underneath. There was also a pot containing charcoal and pencils

– the tools of his trade. Before her better judgement got the upper hand, she flipped over the cover to find a drawing of a wedding dress. The most perfect wedding dress imaginable.

Cut on the bias, the ivory silk gown skimmed the wearer from neck to ankle, bringing with it a sense of Hollywood glamour. The top was a blouson bodice gently gathered at the high neck. There were no sleeves. There was no other embellishment. Some might think the dress plain, but not Flora. It might appear simple, but the dress relied solely on the cut of the pattern and the skill of the seamstress to carry it off. The fabric was important too. A light-weight plain silk or satin. No beading, embroidery or lacework. Nothing to detract from the perfect craftsmanship. Lucien was a genius, but she knew that it would take someone with a rare talent to translate this image into reality.

She flipped the cover back in place and turned to the books, the picture of the dress tucked away in the back of her mind.

The shelves were packed, books squeezed in, some resting horizontally on top. Fashion had a shelf to itself but not just haute couture, design and dressmaking. There were sections on knitting, crochet and embroidery as well as the history of clothes from the dark ages and beyond. She was flicking through a practical guide on costume design when the sound of his voice had her hurrying across the room, the book discarded on the nearest chair.

'Here, help me with these.' Lucien elbowed open the door, before shutting it with the underside of his foot, his hands full of a large tray brimming with dishes and drinks.

'Of course.' Flora rescued the bottle of champagne and two glasses, her gaze on the little bowls of hors d'oeuvres containing olives, slices of chevre and cubes of dried meats. There was even a bowl of crackers. The man had thought of everything. 'I thought you didn't know your way around the kitchen?'

'I left my cook instructions to leave a few things.' He deposited the tray on the side table beside the sofa and busied himself with the cork, laughing as frothy bubbles cascaded over the top. Handing her a glass, he toasted her gently, his hair almost white in the glow from the fire. 'Here's to us, darling. I can't change the past, but I can try and make up for lost time.'

Flora managed a smile, her thoughts elsewhere. The study seemed the most likely place to uncover his secrets, but it would be a mammoth task and take time she didn't have, unless...

She only hoped she had the acting skills required to pull it off.

TWENTY

Flora settled back on the sofa, and crossed her legs, the brief respite providing the valuable time needed to plan what she was going to say next. 'My intention was always to return to Paris at some point, you know, but the war got in the way. The offer of a job at Le Moulin Rouge through a friend of a friend felt like fate.' She spread her hands. 'It's good to be back.'

'It certainly is. For both of us. Never a day has gone by without me thinking of you and dreaming that one day you'd decide to return to me.' He topped up his glass before joining her on the sofa.

Flora masked her expression as he pulled her close. They'd finished off the hors d'oeuvres along with the first bottle of champagne, or she'd finished them while Lucien had concentrated on his drink, and they were now well on their way to finishing their second. She took a small sip, only wetting her lips, her thoughts with the fern plant and how it was faring after being doused with vintage bubbles. Hopefully it would recover but, as Lucien draped his hand across her leg, she realised she had far more important things to think about. Up to now, she'd managed to divert him with her life story since leaving Paris, sticking to the truth as much as she dared. Her work as a seamstress and her marriage to Brian. It had all being going well until he'd started probing about the war years with a distinct gleam in his eye, one she had to handle carefully. There were many things she would do to help rid her beautiful homeland of the enemy but sleeping with him wasn't one of them. She'd done that and still had the scars to prove it.

'You're so beautiful, ma chérie.' He lifted his hand to her hair and started removing the pins. 'I have never forgotten the colour. Living fire.' He raised a lock to his lips in reverence. 'So many times I've tried and failed to replicate it in my work. There's never been a fabric designed to match it. That I let you slip through my fingers in favour of...'

She stroked the side of his face, the faint trace of stubble a rasp against her palm. 'You say the most perfect things. You always did.'

'Oh, my dear.' He drew her to him and she let him, his hands iron bands around her waist as he dropped his mouth to hers. Flora kept her eyes open while he plundered her lips with the finesse of a teenager on his first date, wondering what she'd ever seen in him. At one point she'd have given her life for him. When she'd discovered she was pregnant, she nearly did. It all felt impossibly sad and murky in the cold light after their hot storm of emotion. Their beautiful daughters were the only good thing to come out of it.

Now he was back and wanting more. She had nothing left to give him apart from her pity and that wasn't going to be enough.

Easing back a little, she studied his florid cheeks and excited expression. A combination of alcohol and lust. She'd have to make her move or it would be too late to stop him.

'How about I go and tidy myself up while you go in search of more champagne.' She tapped the end of his straight nose gently with her fingertip, her voice set to a honeyed sweetness. 'In case we get thirsty later.'

He took her hand briefly, kissing her fingertips before staggering to his feet. 'Don't be long.'

Lucien had pointed out Sabine's bathroom earlier, his mouth curled in disdain at the white walls and carpet. The thought of stepping into the white chamber terrified her. What if she spilt something? But Sabine wasn't here, and she had far more important concerns like how long it would take Lucien to fumble his way back from the kitchen.

The bathroom was lined in wall-to-wall mirrors. Rows of nail polish in all the colours imaginable fighting for space among jars of creams, powders and paints. There were ointments for her neck and her eyelids as well as her hands and her feet, more than Flora had ever seen in one place before. Certainly, more variety than in their local chemist back in Carrickfergus.

She forced herself to concentrate, her hands sifting through the contents for what she was looking for, annoyed she hadn't thought of it earlier.

Find something to dampen Lucien's ardour.

The bottom shelf contained bottles and boxes. Sachets of indigestion powder. A carton of aspirin and an amber-coloured brown bottle with a cork stopper, the label written in a lopsided script.

Sleeping draft. One teaspoon before bed.

With the bottle in her pocket, she hurried back to his study and quickly poured most of it into the bottom of his glass before topping it up with the rest of her champagne. A quick stir with the end of a knife and she didn't think he'd notice, apart from the taste. Her nose wrinkled as she gave it a gentle sniff. It certainly smelt medicinal.

'I'm back.'

She started, her nerves unravelling as she pretended to take a small sip before setting the glass down with an embarrassed laugh.

'Oh good. I hope you don't mind that I took a sip of your drink.'

He glanced from his glass and back to her, his eyes glazing, his speech slurred. 'What's mine is yours, although I do think I need to extract payment.'

'And I think I need some of that lovely champagne first, mon chéri, After, we can negotiate terms,' she purred, dropping onto the sofa, her long legs stretched out in front of her, her skirt hitched to just above her knees, his gaze travelling the short distance and staying there.

It was easy to read his mind as he popped the cork and refilled her glass. Her only worry was the length of time it would take for the sleeping draft to work.

Longer than she wanted, but sooner than she'd expected. She allowed him to take a few liberties on the sofa, but only after he'd finished his champagne and started on the next glass. With his movements starting to slow, she rearranged the neck of her dress and, easing to standing, held out her hand.

'Your sofa is all very well, but how about we see if your bed is as comfortable as it looks?' She pushed against him, careful to avoid his hands when he went to drag her close.

'Darling.'

She allowed herself to be drawn into the bedroom, her hand on his arm when he went to switch on the light.

'Let's not, mon chéri. It's much cosier this way.' She lifted her hair over her shoulder, angling her back to him so he could unzip her dress. The fabric quickly pooled in a circle around her feet, leaving her still wearing her camisole and her slip.

'My turn, Lucien,' she said, when he reached for her shoulder strap. 'It's not fair that you have all the fun.' She stepped closer, starting on his buttons.

'I think you'll have to.' He tried to hide a yawn. 'That champagne must have gone to my head.' He managed a wicked twinkle, pulling his shoulders back when she started on his belt buckle. 'I'll be alright shortly. More than alright.'

'I can't wait.'

It didn't take long to undress him and help him into bed. Leaning down, she kissed him briefly on the lips, saying, 'I'm just going to the bathroom. Back shortly.'

'Wear my robe. You don't want to catch cold. It's behind the door and don't be too long.' He yawned again, this time not trying to hide it, his eyelids drooping closed.

TWENTY-ONE

Flora waited in the shadow of the bathroom, almost too scared to breathe. Minutes passed before she ventured across to the bed to stare down at the shape huddled under the covers. There was no sound, not even the trace of a snore and no movement that she could see in the dimly lit room. The bedroom door was nearly shut, with only a thin thread of light spooling across the floor and she certainly had no plans of opening it further.

How much sedative did I give him? How much is too much?

The thought jumped out, causing her pulse to skip. Flora wanted him asleep, not dead. It didn't matter about the past or even what he was up to in occupied France. Lucien was still the father of her children. There was also the fact that there was only one way out of the building, which was past the concierge in the lobby downstairs.

She was in a quandary as to what to do until she placed her hand gently on top of the blanket and waited. The infinitesimal shift as air expanded his lungs had her closing her eyes in relief. She waited for another couple of breaths to be sure. After, she crossed to the door and slipped through, pulling it gently behind her.

Back in the study, she switched on the lights before hurrying to the table and collecting the glasses. Whatever followed, she couldn't leave any trace of what had happened in the room. Her first job was to rinse out the crystal and return the brown bottle to Sabine's bathroom cabinet, having first topped it up with water. A couple of sleepless nights was just what the woman deserved.

The desk came next. A large antique piece, with an inlaid top and ornate legs. The surface was free from clutter. A box to hold fountain pens, with an inkwell off to one side and a leather-bound blotter, which appeared to be new. There was also a silver letter opener next to the telephone. The desk diary was another leather-bound affair and, turning the pages, full of appointments. The barber and manicurist. His tailor. Luncheon and dinner dates, but no names, only initials, times and venues. Le Moulin Rouge snagged her attention, and she concentrated harder, her finger tracing the entries.

12th September
MT dinner at Café de la Rotonde.
19th September
MT no contact. Send letter.
9th October
MT 5 pm pick up MB
13th October
MT 6 pm pick up Le Moulin Rouge.
14th October
Cancel lunchtime appointment, in case MT needs me.

MT and MB must be Marguerette Toussaint and Madame Billy, but why would Marguerette need him?

Flora hurriedly flicked through the remaining pages, but there was no further mention of MT or MB. In desperation she turned to today's date. It had been left blank.

Closing the book, she focused on the drawers underneath.

Pens and pencils. A sharpener and a ruler. Spare blotting paper. Headed notepaper and envelopes. A box of paper clips along with one of rubber bands. A small bunch of keys. A bottle of ink and, pushed to the back, a photograph of Sabine and Lucien on their wedding day.

Flora stared down at the black and white image of the couple, wondering what had made him shove it into a drawer in a locked room. If he disliked it so much, he could have got rid of it and no one would have even noticed.

She examined his face, the years rolling back to the Lucien she remembered. A dapper-looking man dressed in a formal grey suit and a chic tie, a top hat in his hand. Sabine was wearing an elegant woollen dress, with a matching floor-length cape, the hood pulled back to reveal sleeked back hair, which only emphasised the shape of her eyes and the angle of her cheekbones.

They looked idyllic together – made for each other, which in no way explained what had happened for him to shove the frame in the back of the drawer.

She couldn't help twisting her lips at what might have been if only he'd asked her to be his wife.

Instead of pursuing the thought, she flipped the frame over only to stop. The back was black velvet, the fabric faded and worn, especially where the clips pressed into the pile. Before she realised it, she'd removed the back to reveal a second photograph hidden beneath. An image she'd never seen before. The convent garden and the tree, with her standing beneath, the twins in her arms.

Her eyes roamed the picture, her hand clutching onto the frame as she drank in Violette and Marguerette's faces. Her babies on one of the last times she'd held them. She'd lived with the memory for eighteen years, their images frozen in the amber of her mind. She remembered Lucien getting a photographer to visit the convent. It had been hot, one of those blisteringly humid Parisian days shortly after she'd given birth. Too hot to go out of doors, but the photographer had encouraged her with bribes of the shade under the tree and the threat that his job might be at stake if he disobeyed Lucien's demands. It hadn't taken long, seconds, before she'd whisked the babies back inside. And, in the harrowing days that followed, she'd forgotten all about it.

The wall clock chimed the hour. She had to get a move on. It was with a great deal of regret that she reassembled the frame before positioning it back where she'd found it.

Where would a man like Lucien hide what was important?

Her gaze landed on the artwork, only to pause on each one. Seven vibrant paintings of things she recognised. People, flowers, a bowl of fruit and all with that muted patina, which suggested age. Flora wasn't an expert, but she knew what she liked and she loved these. Moving closer, she wasted precious seconds squinting in the corners to see a signature before stepping back and tracing the brushstrokes with her eyes. One of the paintings, an oil of a man on a horse, was slightly askew. Only by a fraction but it was out of keeping with the rest of the room.

Removing it was easy, withholding the gasp that followed at the sight of the safe was far more difficult.

A grey steel door, embedded into the wall, the edges carefully blending into the wood panelling. There was a central dial, with a keyhole underneath, which had Flora returning to the desk and rummaging through the top drawer to find the small bunch of keys. The first key turned with a slight click. The combination however was going to be almost impossible to guess. The desk diary held no clues. No random number sequences scribbled on the back pages. She tried his birthday, a date she'd never been able to forget. Nothing.

Then it was back to the desk diary scrabbling through the pages, her attention flitting to the wall of books and back again. It was an impossible task. Sabine's birthday, maybe? Hopeless as she didn't know it. She snapped the book closed, unwilling to admit defeat and yet knowing that was exactly what she was about to do. The likelihood was that any proof was going to be locked away from prying eyes.

She stared at the dial, a splurge of hope building at the thought of Marguerette and Violette. His daughters? Why not. Their birthday was a good enough way as any for remembering random numbers.

No click.

What else? She looked around the room desperate to find an answer. The books. The paintings. The desk. There was nothing. She thought of Tomas then. What he'd do in this situation. The one thing he wouldn't do was give up.

Think, Flora.

She eyed the door, the key in the lock. Lucien was so security conscious. Obsessively so, but he had a lot to lose if a design was stolen by one of his competitors. The combination must be something that Sabine wouldn't easily remember either, otherwise why lock the door?

A memorable date. It had to be. The first day they'd met? Even she couldn't remember that, but what about the day she'd handed over the twins. Lucien's expression when he'd first held his daughters was something she'd never forget.

Flora made a face, recalling that Sabine hadn't bothered to turn up. It had only been Lucien and the nanny who'd arrived to collect Violette and Marguerette on that faithful day. Perhaps another reason for him choosing it. She could only hope.

The 30th August, 1924.

300824

There was a faint click before the door swung on its hinges, causing her to stumble back in amazement, her thoughts on the man taking another detour, the pendulum between sinner and saint veering a little further to the right.

Inside there were two ledgers on top of each other, a wodge of cash and a large, old leather jewellery box, the red leather patchy in places.

The Cartier box was inlaid with velvet, the diamond choker dazzling in its brilliance. There was a slim diamond bracelet to match and impressive pendant earrings. Flora couldn't imagine wearing something so perfect, or expensive. There'd never been money left over for jewellery. She'd never had an engagement ring, only a second-hand wedding band, worn thin with age.

She closed the box, losing interest. This wasn't her life and she wouldn't want it to be. All the jewels in the world couldn't improve how a person behaved. The opposite was probably true.

The ledgers were about the business. The first was a detailed inventory of the garments. When he'd designed them. The fabrics and trimmings used. The raw cost and the mark up. There were even some sketches. Beautiful drawings filling the pages with colour, bringing the designs to life. She imagined him working on the book late into the night, while Sabine was off out somewhere. A complex, lonely man despite his talent, successful business and all the trappings of wealth that went with it.

She closed the book with a snap, shutting down her thoughts.

The next ledger was the same, but very different. The kind of information an accountant might need to balance the books. Money in and money out. It looked as if business was booming, despite the war, but Flora had never had a head for figures outside of managing the housekeeping and trying to squirrel away a few shillings for herself. Instinct told her that it wasn't what Tomas was looking for.

With the safe closed, she forced herself to turn to the shelves, her eyes gritty and her senses dull with fatigue.

Books and more books. If she hadn't been in a hurry and falling asleep on her feet, she'd have loved immersing herself in between their covers. The one thing missing was the evidence they needed that Lucien was anything other than an overworked couturier. That didn't mean he wasn't guilty. Only that they'd have to work harder to prove it.

The clock chimed a soft one o'clock when she slid a random book back where it belonged. She'd found nothing incriminating. Either Lucien was highly organised and aware of the risks he was taking, or he'd decided to keep anything incriminating back at his salon.

There was a third option, of course.

That the network had got it wrong, and Lucien was innocent.

Walking into the bedroom, she hurried over to the bed to check that he was still breathing, before turning to the bedside cabinet and easing the drawer open.

A watch. A few coins. What felt like a pair of cufflinks and a small book. She pocketed it and slipped out of the room, careful to close the door fully behind her before switching on any lights.

Back in the hall, she sank onto the floor and opened the notebook, turning to the first page.

1st January

New year, new beginnings, but not so you'd notice. No sign of Sabine after last night's party. It looks as if today's plans are cancelled. Will go for a drive out to Chateau Beau Marin to see Violette instead.

8th March

Sabine insisted on bringing Reiner to church. The priest and the nuns nearly had apoplexy. How she can bear to associate with the man is beyond me, but I suppose I have to make allowances. He's been good to

He'd scored through a word that Flora couldn't quite make out. A name beginning with L.

Reiner, Flora froze, remembering the German SS officer in the bookshop. She carried on reading.

Although I know what she sees in him, more fool her. More fool me for putting up with it.

The same man who'd followed her to Le Moulin Rouge. Sabine was having an affair with a German officer.

Hurrying now, she flipped through the pages, trying to tally the entries in his desk diary about MT.

There wasn't a next page. She'd reached the end of the diary. Picking it up again, she examined the telltale raggedy, torn sliver of pages close to the binding.

There had been more pages, but they'd been ripped out.

Glancing around the hall, she knew she wasn't going to find them in his bedroom. A room that wasn't locked.

Back to his study then.

Probably burnt.

She rushed down the hall, her bare feet soundless against the white carpet.

The fire had died to embers. The skuttle beside piled with wood.

The bin under the easel.

She groaned at her stupidity, but she'd thought it full of discarded drawings. It probably was.

The paper on top was screwed into a tight ball, the sheets lined in the same way the diary had been.

Spreading the pages out, she started to read.

8th September

Met Pablo for lunch at Café de la Paix. Surprised to see Cancale oysters back on the menu. He told me about a singer at Le Moulin with a voice like an angel. Can't abide the place, but I've promised I'll accompany him on Friday – most likely a wild goose chase.

10th September

I should have had some premonition, but nothing could have prepared me. So like her mother I could have cried, and as for her voice. I hope I managed to disguise my thoughts from Pablo although, as my friend, he knows

*most of it. I have to meet her. If only she'll agree. What
to do!!!*

Flora pressed her hand to her face, her eyes narrowing as she
continued reading.

> *14th September*
> *Took her to the café. I'm not sure what I expected,
> but not so much bitterness. Hatred even. At the war, at
> what had happened to the Langs but also at us. She
> wasn't interested in me or her mother. All she wanted to
> know about was her sister. I've suggested meeting up later
> in the week. Hope I haven't bungled it. I'm beginning to
> realise what a dreadful mistake we made all those
> years ago.*
>
> *9th October*
> *Such a relief when she got in touch. I picked her up in
> the car and we drove to Bois de Boulogne for some fresh
> air. She said she's been ill and it's true she doesn't look
> quite like she did the last time. There's a fragility about
> her as if she'll break if I press too hard. I'm determined
> to discover what's wrong and help if I'm able. I can't let
> her down again, like I did her mother.*

Her precious Marguerette was ill.

'Morning, darling. I've made us coffee,' she said, hurrying over to
the blackout blinds. The darkness created an intimacy she didn't
want. It was far more difficult to be romantic with daylight

streaming in through the high windows. Or at least that's what she hoped.

Lucien groaned, poking his head out from the nest of blankets. 'I feel like death.'

'You'll be better after a nice cup of coffee. It was that second bottle of champagne.' She giggled. 'Or maybe the third. I can't remember. You do know it's nine o'clock. I'll have to think about leaving soon if I'm going to make church.'

He looked astounded at that, and a little disbelieving until he checked his watch. 'I never sleep in,' he ground out, his voice a gravel of sound.

'Unless you're brewing something, darling.' She leant down, placing a cool hand against his forehead. 'I've heard there's flu going around.'

'I'm also never sick.' He grabbed her hand, his eyes twin pinpricks in his pale face. 'Yesterday was wonderful.'

She allowed him to draw her close, wondering how much he remembered. They hadn't done anything, and they certainly weren't going to do anything now either. 'It certainly was, but...' She slid gently out of his grasp and made for her clothes. 'Now it's today and I really do have to get on or I'll miss church. Are you okay if I use the bathroom first?'

He waved her on, leaning back against the pillows, his hands behind his head. Her last impression as she closed the bathroom door behind her, gently securing the bolt in place, was the thick frown across his brow. It was difficult to tell whether he suspected something, or if he was simply trying to negotiate his hangover. She hoped the latter, but she had to remember that Lucien was an intelligent man. It was likely he'd have his doubts.

With the wine glasses washed and put away, he'd have difficulty in proving it.

TWENTY-TWO

Church had been an excuse.

She'd arranged to meet Tomas. After yesterday she wasn't going to let him down.

He was waiting for her in the garden, his hands tucked in his pockets, his hat pulled low against the biting wind. He looked good. No. He looked great, she amended, managing a smile.

A night with Lucien hadn't stopped her thinking about Tomas. A ridiculous state of affairs. She had no plans of swapping one husband for another. She'd had the same thought lying in bed listening to Lucien's snores.

A bed she'd just left. By his sour expression, he realised it.

'Hello there. Been waiting long?' She adjusted her bag on her arm.

'Madame Billy invited me for breakfast. She's kept you back something.'

Which means you've been waiting for me for a good hour or so.

Flora settled on the bench beside him.

'I'm not hungry.'

She had been positively starving right up until she'd walked through the gate and seen the disappointment etched on his face.

What did he expect?

'Did you manage to catch the locksmith?'

He patted his pocket briefly. 'I was thinking I might take a look tonight.'

'Good idea. I'll come too.'

'I don't think...'

'Well, I do, Tomas,' she interrupted smoothly. 'I used to work there so I know the layout. Lucien mentioned something about meeting friends for dinner so it will be perfect timing, especially as I didn't find anything of importance in his apartment.' She crossed her legs, watching as he dug out his cigarettes.

'Smoke?'

'Please.'

He offered her the packet before fumbling to light a match, the sudden flame highlighting the shadows and grooves of his face. While his voice might sound composed, his expression told a different story. There were lines as deep as craters. Was he unhappy with her and what she might have been up to last night, or something else entirely? The fact that she was starting to care what he thought about her was a sharp reminder that she couldn't and shouldn't. She mustn't lose sight of her priorities.

Leaning forward, she took a deep drag, enjoying the feel of smoke fill her lungs. She should really cut down, but not yet. She enjoyed it too much. Something to do with her hands, she thought, stretching back her neck to watch the thin trail of smoke hovering above her head. Something to focus on.

'You say you didn't find anything?'

She flicked her ash, concentrating on the glowing tip as she remembered the photograph and the diary. 'Nothing of use to the cause, if that's what you mean. He had a safe, which I managed to crack...'

'You what!' he exploded, stamping his cigarette into the ground before turning to stare at her in astonishment.

'Don't look so surprised. It wasn't that difficult to work out the combination and it's not as if there was anything much in it. It's where he keeps Sabine's jewels and the ledgers for his business.' She waved her hand in the air. 'I went through them all and there was nothing. I also went through his desk and his desk diary. The only interesting thing about the whole evening was mention of someone called Reiner.'

She watched him as she announced the name, noting the way his fingers curled into a fist, her heart ricocheting off her ribs at the sight.

'I take it you know who that is?'

'Commander of the security police.' A muscle flicked in his cheek. 'I've heard from Marianne that he's been hanging around the bookshop. Visits most weeks. Up to now we've been safe, but it won't last. The man has a knack for sniffing out resistance fighters and has no mercy when he finds them.'

'He followed me from the bookshop too, Tomas,' she said, her voice deathly quiet, her cigarette joining his half-finished one on the grass. 'Right to the dance hall.'

'Did he indeed? Probably routine.' But she could see by his expression she'd shocked him, which made her own worry escalate. If Tomas was worried, then she was terrified.

'Well, for what it's worth I've read Lucien's diary. He specifically mentions that Reiner keeps company with Sabine and, if that's the case, what about the traitor being his wife and not him?'

'Hmm. It's certainly worth thinking about. We've been tailing Lumineau for months now, but he rarely breaks the pattern of home, visiting a few friends, Madame Billy's and work. Perhaps we need to stick a tail on her too.'

Flora didn't reply. If they were tailing Lucien then he'd already know she'd spent the night. Why hadn't he come right out and said so?

'You've done extremely well in finding out that much.' He focused on his shoes, clearly taking time to choose his words. 'I'm not sure how you managed to...'

'I drugged him,' she said simply, not proud of the fact. After all, she might have killed him. It had been a large measure. 'He'd staged the seduction scene beautifully, from the champagne to getting rid of the servants, and he could barely keep his eyes open.'

He laughed, his eyes crinkling up in amusement. 'Remind me to never underestimate you, Flora. I can see I'm in the presence of a serious spy.'

'Non, mon chéri.' Her voice was off hand. 'Only someone desperate to find out what's happened to Marguerette. At least I've seen where Violette is and know that she's relatively safe. But Marguerette...'

She bit her lower lip, her narrow little world falling around her. She'd always considered herself strong, probably something to do with her upbringing. Always moving forward and never looking back, except when it came to her daughters. In her messy life, they were all she had left, even if they decided they didn't want anything to do with her. She loved them unconditionally while, if Lucien's diary was to be believed, Marguerette hated her and Violette didn't know anything about her.

'Are you alright?' There was a light touch on her arm, so fleeting that she might have missed it if her gaze hadn't caught the brief movement of his hand.

I'm far from alright. But he wouldn't want to hear that. She wasn't important, only in what she could do to help the cause. He'd been conniving enough to use the one thing that would make her come back to war-riddled France. Toying with her feelings for his own ends. Tomas wasn't interested in her as a person, or her daughters, only in the cause. Best she remembered that.

'There was something else in his diary. Nothing to do with the mission,' she added quickly, thinking about yesterday and what a fool she'd been to go to the chateau. 'To do with Marguerette and her illness.'

Instead of replying immediately, she watched as he selected a fresh cigarette, his fingers steady, his expression impassive apart from a firming of his chin.

'Marguerette had some surgery,' he said eventually. 'I only know because of something Madame Billy said when I dropped off the last order of wine. It's something Lucien mentioned to her. I know I should have told you straight away, but after yesterday...' Instead of lighting the cigarette, he removed it from his mouth and returned it to the packet. 'I've checked with the hospital and it's true she was admitted, but no one seems to know where she went after. Her records appear to have been mislaid.'

TWENTY-THREE
LUCIEN

Lucien left his tie draped over the end of the bed and made for the kitchen in search of coffee. He normally didn't suffer from champagne hangovers, but it felt like there was a hammer clawing through his head. Cheap red wine, the kind his friend, Pablo, served up by the bucketload, was a different matter, but he knew enough by now to take a precautionary aspirin and a gallon of water beforehand. Good champagne, and he never drank anything else, usually fused with his blood only leaving an invisible seam of grape juice behind.

Pausing in the doorway, he looked back at the room. The left-hand side of the bed remade, the pillow plumped. No telltale clues that he'd had company. He didn't remember much about the evening, only feeling incredibly tired, which was strange. Completely out of character.

Turning, he stopped then made his way over to his bedside cabinet. The drawer was nearly closed, but not quite when he was always particular about such matters. Pulling it open, there was nothing to see. A few coins. His favourite cufflinks. His diary, exactly where he'd left it.

Lifting it out, he held it up to his nose, feeling slightly foolish.

Flora wouldn't have reason to rummage through his personal possessions. That was more Sabine's style. He took a gentle sniff. Paper and ink. Nothing more and, turning the pages, nothing untoward.

Tucking the notebook under his arm, he made for the study, his steps slow. The door was ajar. He frowned. He couldn't remember locking it but, without Sabine around there'd been no need.

The room felt musty, so he yanked back the blackout blinds and opened the shutters and then the window. The Eiffel Tower was visible in the distance. Everything in the room looked the same and yet felt different. He couldn't explain it. He didn't want to. There were no signs of their impromptu feast, which was both reassuring and worrying. A guest that cleared up after themselves had him wondering why.

The bin next to his easel still held the scrunched up pages from the diary. Bending, he scooped them out, annoyed that he hadn't thought of it before. If Sabine found them... His fingers flexed, the knuckles gleaming white.

His wife was as determined to make his life miserable as he was of stopping her.

There was a stove in the kitchen. He eyed the notebook and the pages with regret. They were better burnt to a crisp and after, he'd head into Maison Lumineau.

Instead of going to Maison Lumineau, Lucien spent the day wandering around Paris as if he'd never seen it before. He strolled through the Tuileries Gardens before stopping at a small café for lunch. They'd move somewhere quiet. A small house on the coast to live a simple life with their daughters visiting whenever they could.

Sabine launched herself at him as soon as he returned to the apartment.

'Lucien, at last. We're due to leave in ten minutes.'

'Good evening, dearest.' He pressed his lips to her smooth cheek, a smile still lingering as he remembered his day. 'I had some urgent work to finish. The countess, you know...'

Sabine pouted, her expression relaxing. He didn't even have to mention them by name. Their title was usually enough to stop one of her onslaughts.

'I forgive you but do hurry. You know how I hate being last to arrive.'

He nodded, knowing no such thing. Sabine always liked to be late. It made it much easier to be the centre of attention when everyone else was there first.

'I'd like you to wear your navy, with a red kerchief.' She smoothed a hand over his lapel, her talons painted blood red to match her lipstick. 'It will be the perfect foil for my red dress.'

As if I have a choice.

'Have Pablo and Dora been invited?'

She pursed her lips. 'That man. I don't know why you insist on his presence. He doesn't add anything and as for that woman. Poor dear Olga...'

'Pablo and Olga have been separated for years. The sooner you accept that the better.'

There were many things he'd give way on, including having Reiner sleep in his wife's bed, but not this. He'd met Pablo during his early days in Paris. They'd spent many an hour in Café de la Rotonde swapping yarns and speaking about how, sometime in the future, they'd be the toast of the city. Idle talk powered by booze but, in his friend's case, true. Pablo had always been destined for great things.

They arrived at the hotel thirty minutes later, bright smiles pinned in place. He crossed the room to join his friend as soon as he could.

'Sabine is looking particularly lovely this evening.' Pablo pulled on his cigarette, before blowing out the smoke and picking up his glass, swirling the liquid around to catch the light.

Lucien was amused. Pablo was always threatening to paint his wife, one day he'd let him. She'd be outraged. Sabine didn't understand modern art, dismissing it as worthless. That the man standing beside him rejected fashionable clothes, instead choosing outdated pleated trousers and an ugly polka dot tie, topped off with one of his famed berets, was insult enough.

'Indeed.' He slapped Pablo on the back, before tipping his glass against his. All the guests had arrived, including Reiner, who was lounging on one of the sofas with a long cheroot, his hawk eyes veering around the room. When they landed on him, he turned away, unable to prevent a stab of pain in his chest. The debt that he could never repay. The name he had chosen to forget.

With a shake of his head and a determined set to his shoulders, he forced himself to concentrate on his friend.

'I have a favour to ask, if I may?'

Pablo caught his eye, his glass paused on his lip but only briefly. Appearances were everything. 'I'm listening.'

'I need to hide some... things from my dear wife. Things she doesn't need to know about.'

'Meet me tomorrow. My studio. Ten o'clock,' Pablo whispered on his way to stub out his cigarette in the ashtray beside him. When he straightened, he started a rambling conversation about his latest piece. 'I'm thinking of calling it the bull's head, simply because that's what it is.'

Lucien laughed, playing along, the hairs on the back of his neck sweeping to attention. 'Sounds intriguing. Now, I must circulate or Sabine will...'

He turned to find Reiner hovering over his shoulder.

For a large man, Reiner had the ability to cross a room at speed. He was also renowned for always catching his prey. Lucien took a step back before correcting the movement, disgusted with himself for displaying any weakness in front of the man.

Reiner's eyes gleamed, his lips parting in a thin victory smile.

The smile of a man who knew all your secrets, even the ones you couldn't bear to think about.

Lucien managed to regroup by feigning a surprise he wasn't

feeling; he felt nothing but alarm and dread. A bead of sweat appeared on his brow out of nowhere and tracked down his cheek.

'Oh, Otto. Where did you come from? Please excuse me. I need to circulate. You know my dear friend, Pablo Picasso?'

TWENTY-FOUR

Flora's footsteps slowed as they approached the Elysees Palace, only a few doors away from Maison Lumineau. She didn't need to be here. She could be back in her attic bedroom adding patches to her latest quilt instead of walking past the German sentries guarding the palace gates, rifles casually slung over their shoulders. There was nothing for her at Maison Lumineau that was worth risking arrest.

Tomas held her arm, a bag looped over his shoulder. A couple going for an evening stroll. That his arm was as rigid as hers told her he wasn't as relaxed as he'd led her to believe.

Maison Lumineau was situated nearly directly opposite the Hôtel de Castiglione where Lucien had told her he was dining with friends, which made the thought of breaking into his fashion house worse somehow. What if he decided to drop in on his way past?

'Ready?' Walking up to the door, Tomas increased the light pressure on her arm to accompany the word. They'd agreed on a little playacting in case someone was watching.

'Ready.'

'I won't be long, darling.' He worked the key in the lock with a little jiggle. 'If I don't finish these drawings by tomorrow, Lumineau is going to sack me.' The sound of the sharp click was one of the best noises she'd heard all day. 'Do you want to come in? I'll only be a minute?'

'I'll wait in the hallway out of the cold, mon chéri.'

Tomas closed the door, checking the handle before pulling a couple of torches out of his bag and handing her one, suddenly all business. 'Where to first?'

'If there's anything, it's going to be in the office on the second floor. That is, if they haven't changed the layout. Come on, follow me.' She hurried up the stairs in the thin pool of light cast by the beam of her torch. Now she was here, she was keen to leave as quickly as possible.

Lucien's office was closed, which caused a second of worry until the handle turned with ease.

Flora watched him head for the desk and start on the drawers.

'I'll check the other rooms. See if there's anything of interest.'

Retracing her steps, she entered the shop on the ground floor. A plush room with gilt chairs and floor-to-ceiling mirrors and curtains, which reminded her of Sabine. Apart from three well-dressed mannequins there was nothing of interest. No cupboards or drawers. No shelves. Nowhere to hide any secrets.

The next floor was given over to their fashion shows. A large salon that spanned the width of the building. Ornate golden chairs, reminiscent of Madame Billy's drawing room, placed evenly around a stretch of ocean blue carpet, with curtains at one end, which hid the business end of the room: a small space for the models to change. There was a chaise longue with a coffee table in front. Somewhere for Lucien to chat to customers. Stupid women who'd queue up to greet him, while they parted with their husbands' money.

She only gave the salon a cursory glance, keen to keep moving through the building.

The third floor had once been her domain, but not anymore.

For staff only. The plush cream carpet stopped abruptly, leaving bare floorboards and rendered walls, instead of brilliant white.

The sealed windows, now covered with blackout fabric. The rows of tables, holding the tools of her trade. Scissors, rulers, tailor's chalk, pins, sewing machines. The covered racks, which housed the half-finished garments.

She gripped the back of the nearest chair, lingering a moment. She'd loved her job here. Being trusted with the silks, satins and wools. The work had been hard and demanding, but it was in this room that she'd finally learnt how to be a dressmaker. To follow a set of measurements and transcribe them onto the brown paper they used to build their patterns. A dart here, a pleat there. A tuck. Pulling and pooling the fabric to shape and complement. Every garment was as unique as the wearer. It had been part of her responsibility to help interpret Lucien's one-dimensional drawings into a masterpiece of movement and form. The senior dressmaker had quickly identified that Flora, the most junior member of the team, had a flair for turning Lucien's designs into reality. Those few months under her tutelage had been the best of her life. She'd never forgotten the lessons she'd learnt in that room, just as she'd never forgotten the lessons she'd learnt in Lucien's bedroom. But, as the cold of the room infiltrated her coat, she knew that given the choice she'd change none of it. She could never regret having her daughters.

Back in the office, Flora couldn't believe that forty minutes had passed. 'We really do have to leave.'

Tomas moved quickly to the door before pulling it closed behind him. 'Just finished. There's nothing.'

'Perhaps because there was nothing to find. Remember what I said about Sabine?'

'You might be onto something. Either he's been incredibly cunning and destroyed everything or...' He scrubbed his hand over his jaw. 'What we need is definitive proof.'

Flora remembered the diary and the ripped pages at the back. The pages she'd found in the bin – but there might have been others. Tomas was right. Guesswork couldn't come into it. They needed more. Lives depended on it.

The torch slipped through her fingers and clattered to the floor, the light extinguished in an instant.

'Blast!' They both stooped to pick it up, only to clash heads on the way up.

'Well, that wasn't meant to happen. You alright?'

'I'll live.' She managed a laugh, her hand massaging her temple, the other clutching onto the defunct torch. 'What an idiot.'

'Oh, I wouldn't say that exactly.' He smiled down at her, his eyes gleaming in the weak light cast from the one surviving torch.

The small space between them appeared to shrink, the air turning heavy. His softening expression. A warmth spreading across her chest, one she recognised. Tomas was a man she liked for a multitude of reasons, none of which had anything to do with their covert mission.

'Tomas, I...'

'Flora.' He lifted his hand to cradle her face, his eyes flicking to her mouth, his head lowering to hers.

The sound of the front door opening then slamming shut caused them to jump back.

Tomas switched off the torch, his finger to her lips.

Flora took a second to process what was happening, the feeling of warmth replaced by ice-cold fear clutching at her chest and shortening her breath.

Who could it be at this time of night? Lucien coming to collect something? He must be going to his office or the workrooms one floor above instead of the empty salon below. They had to move now and hope they were quick enough not to get caught on the stairs.

Flora grabbed onto Tomas's arm and pulled him down the short flight, aware that the footsteps were drawing nearer.

Once inside the salon, she negotiated the table and chaise longue from memory before reaching the relative sanctuary of the curtained off area at the back. With a quick tug, she checked the curtains met in the middle before lowering herself onto the floor, her back pressed against the wall, her legs too weak to support her.

Tomas crouched down beside her, reaching for her hand, panic spreading across his face.

Flora's head started to pound as she imagined being arrested by the SS. Lucien must have realised the trick she'd pulled with the sleeping draft and reported her to the authorities.

Time trickled by. A minute. Two minutes before the sound of feet stopping outside told them they were about to have company.

'I was sure I'd find his diary upstairs. I've searched the apartment from top to bottom. I need to know what he's up to.'

'And I need you, Sabine. Now. Come here.'

'Really, Otto. There's no time. What if...?'

'We're alone and ten minutes won't matter.'

'You're a very naughty man, mon chéri.'

Flora's eyes widened, the curtains filling her vision. Her imagination provided a cinematic quality of images to match the sound of zips being pulled and shoes flung across the room instead of the plush ocean-coloured drapes.

No, surely not. They couldn't be about to... to make love in the salon?

She blinked, the unmistakeable sound of panting and groaning making a mockery of the thought. That was exactly what they were doing.

If they're not careful they'll damage the pile of the carpet.

Flora felt a wave of hysteria rise. She'd always viewed herself the most mild-mannered of women, but she'd never found herself in such a position. Fifteen minutes that felt like fifteen hours before the sounds seemed to be reversed along with her growing conviction that they might escape without being spotted.

'Where has my blasted shoe gone?'

'Perhaps behind the curtain, Liebling?'

Flora clenched Tomas's hand tight, the room suddenly deficit of the air she needed.

'No, I see it. Under the table. Stupid thing.'

'But they make your legs look extraordinary.'

'You say the nicest things, Otto, but if you don't get me back across the road to the party, Lucien will smell a great, big, German rat.'

'Hah.' He chortled. 'Not a lot he can do about it.'

'But he has his uses, darling. Providing me with an excuse to see you for one.'

'You still think you need an excuse? We own Paris.'

'You might own it, but not everyone in it, yet. Lucien offers respectability so for the moment he's useful. And anyway, he's no trouble, not since we closed his little messaging racket in the south. Since the arrest, he's been like a lamb. Spends his time drinking and working.'

'Oh, I'm not so sure about that.' There was the sharp sound of a lighter clicking before the acrid smell of cigarette smoke filled the air. 'I've heard that Flora Toussaint is back in Paris.'

Flora clamped her hand across her mouth, unable to quite believe what she was hearing. That Reiner was discussing her after what he'd just done.

'You can't mean it?'

'I never say anything I don't mean, Sabine.' His voice was stiletto thin, a warning hidden between the words.

'No, of course not, chéri,' she said, backpedalling. 'It's just a shock to hear her name after all these years. I was hoping she was dead. The best thing that could happen to her for all concerned.'

Flora turned to Tomas, her anxious expression mirrored in his own. It was all very well Sabine knowing about her, it made sense that Lucien would have told her about the mother of his daughters, but where and how did Reiner fit in?

'My thoughts exactly, meine Liebe. I'm tempted to arrest her. It wouldn't take much. We know she's associating with a person of interest in one of the local bookshops. We must think of the girls. If it ever got out...'

The room was plunged into darkness as Sabine and Otto left

the room, their voices fading as they walked down the stairs, closely followed by the sound of the front door slamming behind them.

Flora went to stand, only to realise that Tomas was still holding her hand. He pulled her back, whispering, 'Let's wait a few minutes, just to be sure.'

She sank down, letting out a long, slow breath, her eyes closed. Sabine and Otto having an affair was one thing. For Otto to know about their daughters was something else entirely.

Otto Reiner. The man who'd recognised her at the bookshop and had subsequently followed her to the dance hall.

He'd recognised her because of her similarity to Marguerette.

It was something she'd suspected. Now she knew.

'That should be long enough.' Tomas jumped up and was at the door before she'd got to her feet, her legs heavy with exhaustion.

She met him at the top of the stairs.

'They've definitely gone, but we've missed curfew. We're going to be stuck here until five at the earliest.'

Flora's heart tripped before common sense kicked in. 'Well, it's relatively warm and I can probably rummage up some food from somewhere.'

He walked past her back into the salon, his hands thrust in his pockets, his shoulders hunched.

'It's not what's for supper that I'm worried about.' He turned to face her. 'It's knowing that the commander of the security police wants you arrested.'

TWENTY-FIVE

'I think we should get you out of Paris as quickly as possible, Flora. Now we know that it's Sabine and not Lumineau betraying their country, the need for you to stay doesn't exist,' Tomas said, picking up the conversation baton as soon as they were settled.

They were sitting behind the curtain. It would only take Otto, Sabine, or even Lucien to turn up for them to be discovered. They knew they couldn't rely on luck saving them a second time. Flora had pulled some silk scatter cushions from the chairs onto the floor. There weren't any blankets. Instead, she'd helped herself to a neatly folded pile of dressing gowns that were offered to customers attending fittings. After, she'd found a box of madeleines in the kitchen along with a jug for water. It was easy to assume some of the staff might take a couple of cakes, but not Lucien's best champagne, which he kept for his most important clientele.

'And what if I don't want to go? I know where Violette is. Seeing the chateau. Even meeting Yves. Knowing she's safe, but Marguerette? I can't leave until I know where she is. I won't leave.'

'We can continue looking for her without putting you in danger. The one man in France you can't afford to mess with is Otto Reiner.' He clicked his fingers. 'He can make someone disappear just like that and we'd never know what had happened to them.'

'You think I don't know that, but it doesn't change things.'

'You'll be safe enough back in London,' he carried on, obviously not listening. 'Miss Maxse is bound to offer you a job and somewhere to live until you get yourself sorted.'

She turned to face him, suddenly aware of how close they were. 'I've decided to stay in France when all this is over. There's nothing for me back home. This is my home,' she amended. 'And I don't know anyone in London.'

'Are you sure that's a good idea? Reiner isn't going away any time soon. I know your daughters are important to you but...'

'My daughters are everything, Tomas,' she snapped. 'The reason I came to France.'

'I know.' His voice faltered. 'But I worry I'm not going to be able to protect you.'

'I'm not your responsibility, Tomas.'

'Aren't you? I feel as if you are.'

An awkward silence fell between them, which he finally broke. 'What about Lucien, now you know he's innocent?'

Flora wasn't sure where Tomas was going with this. She suspected, but that wasn't the same as knowing. 'As in?'

'Am I wrong in thinking that the man is besotted with you? Wining and dining. Asking you back to his place when the risk of Sabine finding out must be huge.'

'I can't help that and, by the look of things, the secret is out, or it will be shortly. Sabine isn't the type of woman to let something like that go.' Flora picked at a stray thread on the dressing gown, giving it a little tug. 'It's naïve to assume that Lucien never told her the full story behind the twins' birth. If I'd been in her place, I'd have demanded it.'

'Which only adds to my belief that your time in Paris must come to an end. You certainly can't go back to working at Le Moulin Rouge. And it won't be long before Reiner discovers that you're staying at Madame Billy's.'

'I'm not leaving Paris until I know what's happened to Marguerette,' Flora replied sharply. 'I'm convinced Lucien knows where she is.'

Tomas grunted. 'You're not in love with him?'

'What kind of question is that?' She ignored the thread, instead turning to watch him. 'I was only doing a job, a job I might remind you that you asked me to do. Nothing more. Nothing less. I'll admit that my relationship with Lucien is complex, but then it's going to be.'

'Which still doesn't answer my question.'

Flora was at a loss as to what he wanted from her. Her emotions had gone through a wringer since she'd returned to Paris and there wasn't the hope of a resolution in sight. The collapse of her marriage closely followed by the news of Marguerette and Violette was too much to absorb. He wanted more than she was prepared to give.

'I'd answer if I thought it was fair. I have no intention of rekindling anything with him, if that's what you're asking, but I'm not going to repeat my mistakes if I can help it. Knowing that he's innocent of any traitor charges doesn't change that.' Reaching down, she yanked at the thread, aware she'd ruined the dressing gown and she didn't care. 'Instead of talking about him we should be talking about Sabine. What do you intend to do about her?'

He nodded, accepting the change in conversation with a small smile.

'Follow her. Find out what she's up to. Make her disappear, if it's true.'

'Make her disappear.' She whispered the words. 'You'd do that?'

'We'd have to. You must realise that in war it's either them or us. I'm sorry if I've shocked you.'

Flora wasn't shocked for Sabine's sake. The woman was capable of anything. She was shocked by the finality of it all. No arrest. No trial, but how could there be?

'Do you need me to follow her?'

'Flora.' He picked up her hand in the same way Lucien had yesterday, threading his fingers through hers. 'I need you to be safe. Only that. We have men and women trained to blend into the background. That's not you, my dear.'

My dear.

She stared at him, knowing they'd been heading in this direction for quite a while now. 'You're not married, are you, Tomas?'

'Hah. Where did that come from? No, I'd be sitting on the opposite side of the room if I was.' He shifted, increasing the distance between them. Letting her hand go. 'Why don't you get some sleep? I'll keep watch.'

She knew what he was trying to do and she didn't try to stop him. It was better this way. There'd be time enough for them once all this was over.

'Goodnight, Tomas.'

'Goodnight, my dear.'

Flora settled beside him without moving, the floor starting to bite into her hip and her shoulder.

Trucks rumbling past. The odd shout. The heat draining from the building as evening shrank into night. Her muscles started to relax and her breathing to slow but, with her mind full, there was little chance of sleep.

A small sound from Tomas next to her. She opened her eyes a fraction to look at him, taking a moment to adjust to the lack of light. The set of his mouth and hunch in his shoulders portrayed a vulnerability she hadn't expected. Shifting slightly, she stretched across the distance and took his hand. The slight pressure and comfortable warmth had her slipping into a deep, dreamless sleep.

TWENTY-SIX

L'Etoile de Kleber, 5 am

Curfew ended at five. By one minute past they were hurrying out of the front door, pulling it gently behind them. Flora looked left then right, half expecting Reiner to be waiting for them, but the street was empty apart from a couple of early pigeons pecking in the gutter.

'Are you sure you'll be alright?'

They stopped by the garden gate, Tomas's face barely visible in the dense black of pre-dawn. It was the first thing he'd said during the walk across town. When she'd woken at four, she was lying on her back, both hands tucked under one of the towelling robes. A restless sleeper normally, she was certain that he'd been the one to place them there.

'I'll be fine.'

'If I hear anything about Reiner, I'll let you know. You can always contact me at my shop.' He stepped a little closer, his expression guarded, his movements slow as if trying to find his way to the next move, his eyes seeking hers. Flora stood motionless, unable to drop her gaze, and suddenly he was drawing her towards him. The feel of his arms holding her tight followed by a light kiss pressed onto her mouth. 'I... want to tell you that...'

A couple of seconds passed before he dropped his arms and moved back, his face disappearing into the shadows. 'I'll get a message to Odile that you won't be in for a few days.'

She knew that wasn't what he'd been about to say but she let it go. Instead of replying, she hurried through the gate, dashing a rogue tear from her cheek with the back of her hand.

Wandering into the hall, she started for the stairs, her movements slow as she worked on what had just happened between them.

Nothing really and yet everything.

Pushing her bedroom door open, she hesitated. Should she follow him? A tap on the window drew her to the glass and the sight of the little sparrow staring back.

'Hello there. Just in time to prevent me from making a fool of myself.' She unlatched the casement and, with her hand in her pocket, pulled out her handkerchief before scattering the few crumbs she'd saved from her madeleine. 'Lucky for you I remembered your breakfast.'

She watched the sparrow devour his impromptu feast before it flew away.

A sharp knock. 'Bonjour, Flora. Hello.'

Flora blinked in relief as she hurried to the door, dropping her hat and coat on the end of the bed on the way.

'Edith.'

'Hello, ma chérie. Can I come in?'

'Of course.' Flora held the door open, her face breaking into a smile. Edith brought a trailing scarf and a new hairdo. Black instead of the red she'd grown used to.

'Your hair!'

She lifted her hand to her head with a laugh, tucking the ends behind her ears. 'I know. Too much? Too dark? I wanted blonde, but the hairdresser absolutely refused to bleach it. Mon Dieu, whatever is the world coming to when the hairdressers are in charge.'

'Well, there must have been a reason.' Flora glanced down at her watch, noting the time. The one thing about Edith was the hours she kept. She went to bed late and got up late. 'You're up early?'

'Haven't been to bed yet,' she said on a laugh, pulling out her cigarettes and, without asking, lit two before passing one over. 'Busy, you know how it is. Too many clubs want too much of me, but it's money and that I like.' She leant back, resting her head against the chair, concentrating on blowing smoke out through her nostrils. 'When you're brought up with nothing then something becomes very important indeed.'

'I know exactly what that feels like.' Flora studied Edith through a veil of smoke. She noted the pallor of her skin and the dark circles, too dark for someone only in their twenties, but she didn't say anything. It wasn't her place.

'And what about you, ma chérie?' Edith's eyes narrowed with concern. 'I'm guessing not so good? Monsieur Lumineau treating you well?'

'That obvious?' Flora didn't know what to say. If she listened to Tomas, she'd say nothing. Edith was a huge unknown. Living at the same address was no guarantee that the woman wasn't a collaborator. *Where would she find the time?* Her instincts told her that Edith was interested primarily in her music.

Mostly everything else passed her by. And, if that was the case then Flora knew she could trust her. The one thing she needed right now was someone to confide in. Someone she didn't have burgeoning feelings for, like Tomas, and someone she didn't have a complex relationship with, like Lucien. There wasn't anyone else. That Edith knew Marguerette was the final push she needed for her story to come tumbling out.

'Lucien's wife has found out that I'm here and isn't happy about it. In fact, I think she's about to set the Germans on me.' She turned her head away, ostensibly to stub out her cigarette, but she was really hiding her distress. Her voice had dropped a notch, but there was nothing she could do about that. She could see Edith out of the corner of her eye, seemingly absorbed in the yellowed ceiling above her head. The normalcy of it gave her the courage to continue. 'There's this German. An SS officer high up. Sabine is in a relationship with him and, for some reason, he knows about me.' She pressed her arm against her forehead, trying to control her breathing and failing miserably. 'He followed me to Le Moulin Rouge so I can't go back and it's only a matter of time before he tracks me down here.' She looked up then, her eyes flooding with tears. 'All I've ever wanted, Edith, is to find my girls and try to atone for deserting them.'

Before she knew it, Edith had joined her on the bed, placing her hand on her forearm, leaning in, the smell of lavender and cigarette smoke filling the air between them. 'It sounds as if you need to leave Paris for your own safety.'

'You don't understand.' Flora sniffed, rummaging up her sleeve for her handkerchief. 'I won't leave without knowing about Marguerette. It might be my only chance.'

'She'll understand, mon amie.' She squeezed her arm before retreating to the chair opposite. 'Remember, I know Marguerette, and that's not a criticism. I'm the last person to criticise how others live lest they decide to turn their attentions on me.' She busied herself with tucking the ends of her hair behind her ears again. 'She's beautiful and clever and talented. All the things a parent wants for their child, not realising that none of those things matter. She's also troubled. I'm not sure why, but I think the rot started when her foster parents had to flee the country. Sixteen and let loose in a world that was changing by the day.'

Flora watched as Edith paused to pick a strand of tobacco from the corner of her mouth, willing her to hurry up while at the same time not wanting to hear another word. No wonder Marguerette had become ill.

'She told me that her father, her real father, was horrified when he learnt about the Langs leaving, especially as it was two years after the event,' Edith continued. 'He was angry too. Furious. The nuns would have got to see another side of the flamboyant couturier for keeping that little nugget to themselves.' Edith shrugged, the fine bones of her shoulders rippling under her thin black jumper. 'Madame Billy and I took her in hand when she moved out of the pension. She had to do quite a bit of growing up in a short space of time, but she managed. In fact, she was doing brilliantly until...'

'She disappeared.'

Edith pushed to standing, her gaze flashing briefly. 'I don't think disappeared is quite the right word. It's not as if someone magicked her away. Madame Billy let slip that she had a hospital appointment, but that's all I know.' She paused to stub out her cigarette, hovering from foot to foot. 'I'm going next door to give you some peace and I suggest you use it to sleep. If you don't mind me saying, you look dead on your feet. Rest and we'll talk later. If we put our heads together, I'm sure we can find her.'

TWENTY-SEVEN

Monday 7 December – National Bank for Trade and Industry,
9 am

Walking into the National Bank for Trade and Industry was akin to walking into another world. Lucien had little reason to veer off his usual stamping ground, but the Boulevard des Italiens held the one thing necessary for his current happiness. A way of securing the future for Flora and his daughters.

Pablo strode on ahead, a leather satchel looped across his back, as if he owned the place. Perhaps he did. Lucien's attention was fixed on the marble walls and flooring set around a central domed ceiling fit for a king. It certainly appeared to be a prosperous place, although the sight of a German soldier lounging near the door gave him a stab of worry. The last thing he needed right now was for news to get back to Reiner, and by association, Sabine.

He followed Pablo to one of the desks, where an immaculately dressed man with a large moustache rose to his feet, his hand extended in greeting. 'Monsieur Picasso, what can I do for you today?'

'I need access to my vault and I'll trouble you to provide the greatest assistance to my friend while we're at it.'

'Of course.' The man turned towards him, his expression one of enquiry.

'I'm in need of a safety deposit box,' Lucien said, dropping his voice to a murmur.

'Certainly, monsieur. I'll need your full name, address, occupation, date of birth and identity card.' He rattled off the list from memory, placing a form in front of him. 'The box will be renewed annually for a sum of 250 francs a year.'

Lucien withdrew his pen from his breast pocket before working his way through the document, aware that Pablo had decided to stay by his side. When he came to the last section, he paused slightly, the nib of the pen hovering over the paper.

The clerk escorted them down in the ornate lift; a cage that rattled the bones in his body and the teeth in his head.

'Your safety deposit box, Monsieur Lumineau.' He produced two small, slim brass keys from his pocket.

Small enough to lose. Small enough to conceal.

'You'll need your key to gain access. Two keys, we keep one.'

Pablo followed a step behind, and Lucien was happy to let him. There could be no secrets between them, not now he needed his help.

The safety deposit box was shoebox size in depth, but about twice as long. The clerk placed it on the desk before backing out with a curt nod. 'I'll wait outside.'

'It's all very cloak and dagger, isn't it?' Lucien said, removing a thick envelope from under his coat, his fingers gripping onto the side of the expensive vellum.

'It has to be, mon ami.' Pablo paced the small room, the sound of his footsteps reverberating around the chamber. 'You're sure this is the best way? If Sabine finds out, she's not going to be happy.'

'She'll only find out if something happens to me and by then it will be too late. I must ensure that they are provided for.'

'As you wish. You know I will do whatever I can if it's in my power to do so.' Pablo undid his satchel and pulled out a rolled-up canvas. 'This has always been yours, my friend. You might as well have it now instead of waiting until my death.'

Lucien laughed, an awkward sound to dispel his embarrassment. He had struggled to make close friends. Too much to hide. No one apart from Pablo and Violette. He hoped to add Flora and Marguerette to that list soon, but he couldn't be sure of anything anymore.

'I think you're destined to live to a ripe old age, but I'm not going to refuse.'

Lucien unrolled the canvas, his breath caught as the rainbow of colours revealed themselves in stages. Blue, red, green and yellow. The canvas was small, about forty by thirty centimetres. A portrait and one he recognised.

The Weeping Woman, and yet not. It had the same shape and form, but with inconsistencies that marked it out as different. Lucien knew that his friend often did many versions of the same work until he was happy. This must be one of them, he thought, his throat starting to ache. Picasso would have a weeping man on his hands if he couldn't pull himself together.

'I don't know what to say. It's...'

'Unconventional? Unique? Disturbing? Tortured?'

Lucien pulled out his handkerchief from his pocket and wiped his eyes, needing a second to compose himself.

'It's all of those things and more, but primarily it's passionate, Pablo. It shines with all the things you care about the most.'

Pablo slapped him on the back before hugging him briefly, his eyes glittering with emotion. 'This bloody war. All bloody wars. Let's finish up here and go for a drink.'

Lucien had been drinking a lot over the last few days, mostly to forget his troubles. It hadn't made a jot of difference, but there'd be Sabine at home and most likely Reiner too...

He clutched the canvas to his chest briefly before picking up the envelope. He'd do what Pablo suggested. Drink wine and forget that he was meant to be at work, but first he needed to ask Pablo for one more favour.

TWENTY-EIGHT

Maison Lumineau, 1 pm

Lucien plucked a sheet of notepaper from the pile and, with his favourite pen between his fingers, started composing a reply to Violette's last letter. It would cheer them both up. There was no point in moaning about the state of his marriage, instead he should continue pursuing a way to end it.

'Bonjour Monsieur Lumineau.'

The countess didn't knock, she never knocked. She was in the office and halfway across the room by the time he'd processed her arrival.

'Dear lady, what a pleasure it is to see you.' He turned the half-finished letter over before pushing away from the desk and striding across the room. A kiss against both rouged and powdered cheeks before stepping back, his expression schooled into its habitual blandness.

The Countess de Valcroix was short and wide, with a bull neck and no middle. It was always a challenge to dress her, but one he was unable to refuse. Her parties had been the talk of Paris before the war.

And will be again, he added silently. *Just as soon as we can get rid of the enemy.*

'I've come for my fitting.' She wagged her finger at him as if he was a naughty schoolboy. 'My spies tell me that you've come up with the most amazing dress for me.'

Lucien frowned at her word choice. No one wanted to think in terms of spies. That he thought it likely he had one in his home was unnerving. All his hard work in helping transport messages and documents had come to an end with Otto's arrival in his life. That he owed him a debt of duty was abhorrent and something Otto played on whenever he had the chance.

'Of course. Let me take your coat before I escort you downstairs. Coffee? Champagne?'

She tittered. 'Champagne so early in the morning is decadent, but if you insist then how can I refuse?'

The showroom was empty apart from one of the women busying herself behind the desk.

'Ah, Clotilde. The countess is here for her fitting.'

'Bonjour, Countess. And how are you today?' Clotilde switched on the easy charm as she approached, which was one of the reasons he'd employed her. She had an extra level of human connection that made her indispensable to the business. The customers adored her. Sabine couldn't stand her, which only added to the woman's allure.

'Your scarf. Such a delightful choice, Countess,' she continued. 'Matches your skin colour beautifully.'

Lucien suppressed a smile at the sight of the countess lapping up the compliment, his gaze on the pig-pink scarf that was a speciality of one of his rivals. He'd have to think about giving Clotilde a Christmas bonus – a large one.

It didn't take long for the countess to be standing before him in his creation. The black was a good choice, the only one. It softened her complexion as well as the lines and curves of her body. But it didn't matter what he thought, he remembered. A lesson learnt at the hand of the master – Paul Poiret. The customer was always right, even if she was wrong. It was his job to ensure that the two opposing views between designer and customer met somewhere in the middle. His reputation and therefore his livelihood depended upon it.

'Pins, if you please.'

Slipping off his jacket, he knelt on the floor and started to work. Designing a garment was only the start of the process. Choosing the right fabric was closely followed by the skill of the pattern maker, then the skill of the seamstress. After came the fittings. The trying-on of the garment to ensure the design was tailored to the client's unique set of measurements. The final piece in a jigsaw that often took weeks. To the untutored gaze, the dress was lovely. Long and flowing and with the high waist he'd planned. It didn't require much. A couple of darts to add a hint of shape. A tweak in the line of the hem. The cap sleeves were perfect, the length just long enough to disguise the top of her arms.

After, he pushed himself to standing, feeling a twinge in his lower back and remembering that he wasn't as young as he used to be. Fifty-one next birthday.

He spread his arms, gesturing to the mirror in front of them.

'There. What do you think?'

The brief silence said it all. When she finally spoke, her words were choked with tears. 'Thank you, Lucien. Your greatest triumph.'

He gave a little bow. The countess was a dragon, but with a heart full of gold under her bluff and bluster. She also paid her bills on time and was always kindly to the shop girls, if a little patronising, but that wasn't her fault. She'd been raised that way.

Lucien offered one of his special smiles, a rare event, but appropriate as it might very well be the last time he dealt with her. She'd be unlikely to search him out once he left Maison Lumineau. He couldn't very well take the fashion house with him.

'If you'll excuse me. Clotilde will attend to you. I have something important to see to.'

Clotilde sent him a searching glance, which he ignored.

He strode out of the room and, running up the stairs, made for his office. This situation with Sabine had to come to an end. He'd go and see Marguerette and after, he'd go and see his lawyer.

Lucien hated hospitals. He'd always been that way ever since his darling maman had entered one when he was a small boy, only for him never to see her again. He'd been around six or seven, but he remembered it like it was yesterday. What he most remembered though was what had happened after. The dark depression that had fallen upon his father. Absinthe had been his choice of drink and it had been his undoing in the end. Within a year, his hands had become too unsteady to continue as a lamplighter, within two he'd been admitted to the same pauper's hospital as his wife. Lucien had sworn then that he'd never treat his children in the same way, which was partly the reason he was here. He sat in his car, staring through the wrought-iron arch at the red brick of the building beyond, willing himself to continue instead of turning back.

The private hospital was situated in Villejuif, a small suburb south of Paris. A specialist clinic, but his daughter deserved the very best. When he'd first suspected she was ill, he remembered a recent conversation he'd had at one of Sabine's interminable parties about an innovative young surgeon. This would be the first time he'd plucked up the courage to see her after whisking her out of the municipal hospital in the centre of Paris. It wasn't the first time he'd made the half hour journey to the hospital, but on each occasion, he'd lost his nerve.

Lucien had decided to dismiss his chauffeur and drive himself. The fewer people who knew where he was going and what he was up to the better. He wouldn't put it past Sabine to bribe the staff to spy on him. There were things she seemed to know that she shouldn't, like most of his movements. The truth was he hadn't cared until Flora had arrived back in his life. He had very few secrets – mostly to do with his precious pieces of artwork that were now squirrelled away in the bank. He was convinced that Sabine didn't know about them.

The Café de la Rotonde had been a hive of artists in the 1920s, the tables crowded with more talent than all the streets in Montmartre combined. For the price of a few drinks, he'd managed to collect a decent collection of mostly unfinished sketches. Some sheets torn from artists notebooks. Even some napkin scribbles. Worthless to the untutored eye except for one element; the artist's signature. Sabine wasn't into art, but she knew the value of things right down to the last centime. The few paintings he kept in his study were itemised for insurance purposes and therefore part of any divorce package. Until he'd taken out a safety deposit box, he'd kept his personal collection in a hollowed-out book on byzantine art, which lived in full sight on a shelf in his office at Maison Lumineau. The sum total of his life's work after Sabine had stripped it of any value.

He climbed out of the car, remembering to pick up the bunch of flowers on the passenger seat before making the short distance to the entrance. He could no longer stay married to the woman. It would mean leaving the business, but he couldn't think about that now. The war had been disastrous for the haute couture industry with many of the designers leaving Paris altogether. Apart from a few diehard customers like the countess and the wives of Germans, who he hated dealing with, his showroom was only that. For show. Behind the scenes, he was making some money, but not enough to keep them in the lifestyle Sabine demanded. They had the vineyard for that.

Leaving the marriage would mean he'd leave with nothing. He didn't mind, not really. If only he'd chosen Flora over Sabine. His life would have been far simpler, but much happier.

The inside of the hospital had that clinical smell that caused his throat to close and his eyes to smart. He approached the desk, his long overcoat swaying around his calves, his hat tilted just so. He might not want to be here, but he was still Lucien Lumineau, one of the top ateliers in Paris. People recognised him from the newspapers and society pages and expected a certain style, which he was happy to give them. He might be breaking inside at the thought of meeting Marguerette again, but his smile was broad and his greeting effusive for the receptionist.

'Bonjour, madame. I'm here to see Mademoiselle Marguerette Toussaint.'

Within minutes he was being led down a brightly lit corridor to the room at the end.

Marguerette's room was in darkness, the curtains closed against the fading afternoon.

'I'll turn on the light...' The nurse went to the switch, but his soft words stopped her.

'No, leave it,' he whispered, watching his daughter sleeping peacefully. 'I can see perfectly well. If you wouldn't mine putting these in water?' He passed her the flowers before settling in the chair.

No one knew she was here. It hadn't been his stipulation when he'd rescued her from the municipal hospital, far from it. It had been hers. He'd have preferred it if she'd had her friends to support her, but she hadn't listened.

Just like Violette.

His mind drifted to tomorrow. Another party invitation that he'd been forced to accept simply because Sabine wanted to take Reiner. The thought filled him with dread.

He'd been sitting in the room for a couple of minutes when he noticed an uneven pattern to her breathing.

She wasn't asleep, only feigning it.

'Hello there, my dear,' he said gently, pulling his chair a little closer. 'I know you're probably not in the mood for visitors and that's fine, but I couldn't not come and check on you. If you'd like me to go, I will, but I'd really like to stay for a bit with your permission.'

The silence extended from a second, two seconds into ten or more. He was starting to think she wasn't going to answer and that he should leave.

'Thank you for coming. It was good of you.'

The words were little more than a whisper of air, but the relief they brought was storm force.

It took him a moment to catch his breath, his eyes brimming with sudden tears. 'I'd like to ask how you are but I'm too scared,' he finally said, stretching out his hand and placing it on where hers rested on top of the blanket.

'I've felt better, but not as bad as I did yesterday or the day before.' She pushed up the bed, her auburn hair the exact shade as her mother's tumbling over the pillow, the large bandage under her chin swallowing her neck whole. 'And for that I have you to thank...'

'You don't have to thank me for anything, Marguerette,' he interrupted, his voice fierce. 'I've spent most of your life letting you down. This is minor in comparison.'

'I don't think saving my life is minor, Lucien. I think it's huge.'

He knew she was being dramatic, but he let her. It was the same with Violette. Always inflating the situation. He'd show her Violette's letter before he left. It would be lovely if he was able to reunite them, but he needed to tell her about Flora first.

'I have lots of news if you'd like to hear it?'

'That sounds ominous. Why wouldn't I?'

'Because it's about your mother, Marguerette. Your birth mother,' he elaborated, noting her sharp intake of breath with a sigh. She wasn't going to make it easy for him, but he couldn't expect anything else. It was time to try and make amends for what he'd allowed happen to their daughters.

'Flora is in Paris and would like to meet you.'

TWENTY-NINE

Flora didn't know what had woken her. One second she was asleep, the next she was sitting up in bed blinking at the darkened room. She swept her hair back in annoyance. The day had disappeared, along with any plans she'd had to tackle Lucien on his way home from work. She was more determined than ever to seek his help in contacting Marguerette. With Reiner and Sabine aware that she was back, the situation had become urgent. She also had to think about where she was going to sleep tonight. If she stayed, she'd be putting everyone at the brothel at risk. Edith would probably be able to put her up temporarily with one of her friends, but she couldn't ask her. Her audience in the singing clubs was primarily German. A sniff of something out of place and she'd be arrested.

There was only one person left.

Sister Maria Clara.

The convent wasn't far, but the streets were busy with workers making their way home. The streetlamps offered just enough of a glow to light the way, but not enough to display faces.

She let out a sigh at the sight of the convent up ahead, easing her way into the thought that coming here was exactly the right thing to do. The nuns had helped her once before. While she didn't want to put upon their kindness, she was sure they'd help her again.

The stout wooden door was firmly closed now the evening was drawing in, but that didn't stop her progress. A little further on there was a narrow lane that skirted the convent garden, which took her to another door. A door that was always left open.

The garden was in darkness, but there was enough light to see the hulking shape of the beech tree beyond. The sight of the tree dragged her straight back into the past. It was the day she remembered the most. The texture and feel of the warm air filled with the scent of lavender. She even remembered the ache in her chest from breasts heavy with milk. But mostly she remembered the pain and sadness of the day. The day she'd handed over the twins to Lucien because he hadn't given her a choice.

Flora shook her head as she hurried to the door, knowing she'd have to pass the same tree on the way out. Confront the same memory. There was no getting away from the mistake she'd made. Lucien hadn't been entirely to blame. In Paris she'd recognised that there'd always been a choice, even if no one had pointed it out at the time. The past was over, so why did hers refuse to let go?

Walking into the hall, she was dismayed to see the Mother Superior bearing down on her. She remembered her as an old woman, now she was positively ancient. Her face was a road map of wrinkles, her eyes a glint of blue almost buried between the thick folds of skin, but it was her expression that hurt the most. The careful assessment before her mask slipped into place, but not before Flora had seen the dislike etched clear. She'd never quite worked out why the nun disliked her so.

Flora straightened her shoulders. It didn't matter what the woman thought.

'Bonsoir, Révérende Mère. I'd like to see Sister Maria Clara if I may?'

She was examined like some unsavoury creature that had

dared to creep into her path. 'Sister Maria Clara is in the kitchen. Don't keep her long, if you please.' And, with a swish of her skirts, she stalked along the corridor, her spine ramrod straight.

Flora turned towards the kitchen, only feeling sadness.

'Flora!' Sister Maria Clara pushed back from the table in alarm, her palms flat against the surface as if to steady herself.

'No, stay where you are.' Flora joined her at the table and started removing her coat. The room wasn't warm, but the simple action gave her precious seconds to compose her features and marshal her thoughts. It had only been two weeks, but the deterioration in the nun was clear to see. She'd lost more weight when she'd only been skin coating bones to begin with, but it was in her face that the greatest change had occurred. The black shadows under her eyes as if she hadn't slept a wink since she'd last seen her. She looked troubled, her hands almost too frail to hold her glass of water as she took a small sip, her tremoring fingers causing a dangerous ripple across the surface.

Had her return to Paris in some way caused the gentle nun distress? A flash of memory slid into her mind. Flora, at fourteen, returning to the city after her foster mother had slashed her back to ribbons with her broom handle. Sister Maria Clara had been her only friend then. They'd spent hours together in the garden, talking about all sorts of things, including how a German nun had ended up in a French convent.

She dropped her gaze, aware of the growing silence between them.

'I'm sorry for interrupting your evening. I promise I won't be long. I've met with Monsieur Lumineau and he's told me how wonderful Violette is.' She watched as Sister Maria Clara's mouth softened into a smile. 'I think I have you to thank for that, Maria Clara. He says that you have always been kind to her, showing her the right path.'

She saw the nun relax, which was exactly what she'd planned. She wasn't there to cause her distress, only to find the truth. 'I know she's safe at the chateau and, for now, that has to be enough.'

'I'm so glad. She's a lovely child. I would do anything for her.' Sister Maria Clara patted Flora's hand briefly before returning to her water.

'And Marguerette too,' Flora continued carefully, remembering she'd attended the same church until she was sixteen.

'It was such a joy to see her every Sunday. That young woman lights up any room she's in.' Sister Maria Clara's eyes shone. 'You really have been blessed with your two daughters.'

Flora's throat ached, but she tried to swallow it away.

She stared across at the nun. Both Lucien and Sister Maria Clara knew something that they weren't telling her. Lucien had promised her everything, but had offered little information in return. She'd learnt what she knew from the diary in his bedside cabinet, the one with the pages torn out.

The room started to spin along with her thoughts. She hadn't eaten since the couple of madeleines in the showroom at Maison Lumineau, but she knew that wasn't the main reason.

'Are you alright? Can I get you anything.' She felt a light touch as the nun laid a hand on her arm.

Sister Maria Clara, the keeper of secrets. What wasn't she telling her and why?

Flora focused on the plain, wooden crucifix hanging above the door opposite but, instead of the iconic figure all she saw was the entry in Lucien's diary. The one that had confused her. The one where he'd mentioned Reiner being good to L.

Another thought flashed, a much more recent one from only a few seconds before.

You really have been blessed with your two daughters.

Why hadn't she called them twins? Why hadn't Lucien? No one ever called them twins except her.

She blinked, sliding her eyes from the crucifix and back to the nun's worried expression.

'Sister Maria Clara, tell me about L?'

Flora watched, transfixed as the glass tumbled out of the nun's hand and onto the floor, crashing against the tiles with a bang and fragmenting into a hail of shards. Her heart stopped before juddering back into action at the sight of a ribbon of blood trailing along Sister Maria Clara's arm.

'You're hurt. Let me...'

'It's nothing.'

'It's not nothing.' Her voice was firm as she went to the sink and filled a basin with water and carried it back to the table along with a clean tea towel. 'I'm going to bandage your arm and you're going to let me, Sister Maria Clara, just like you helped me with my back all those years ago,' she continued, her voice softening. 'Glass cuts can be nasty. We don't want it to get infected.'

With the wound clean, she wrapped a fresh tea towel tight around the nun's arm, keeping her thoughts in check.

Maria Clara is my friend. Whatever might have happened in the past, it would have happened with the best of intentions. Please let that be true.

'There, that should do. No doubt you'll be using one of your special concoctions to aid healing.'

Flora returned the bowl to the sink, before washing it out and leaving it to drain, all the while continuing a stream of inconsequential chatter to bridge the gap between what had just happened and what must come next.

Sister Maria Clara's face had collapsed into a bleak parody of her usual benign expression. She hadn't said more than the two words since dropping the glass. It almost felt as if she couldn't, as if she'd lost the power of speech.

Flora retook her seat, watching as the nun opened her mouth before closing it again. It took three attempts for her throat and lips to gather enough momentum to speak.

'We named your daughter Lili, not thinking that she could survive. The last of your babies and so small.'

'No, that's not right.' Flora attempted a laugh, which came out as a strangled croak. There was nothing funny about what was happening. 'You're getting muddled. Marguerette is the youngest by twenty minutes...'

'I'm sorry, truly.' The nun took Flora's hand, her eyes shimmering, her cheeks the colour of old parchment. 'You had three daughters,' she continued firmly. 'Violette, Marguerette and finally, Lili.'

Flora stared at their clasped hands before sliding her gaze back to the nun's face, unable to move, disbelief filling every corner. There were no words. She'd have to feel something, anything apart from the heavy weight of disappointment and loss that was threatening to drown her.

A third daughter. Why hadn't they told her?

The sound of Sister Maria Clara's renewed coughing finally broke through her thoughts and, for all the sudden hatred filling her veins, she knew that it wouldn't have been her friend's fault. She could believe many things, but not that Sister Maria Clara would have been intentionally cruel. She didn't have it in her.

Back at the sink, she filled a fresh tumbler with water, placing it in front of the nun to sip.

'Better now?'

'I'll never be better, Flora. I think you realise that. You're a good girl, you always were no matter what the others might have said.'

'I don't understand. Why didn't you tell me? Did Lucien know?' She blinked, remembering his diary.

Of course he knew.

'Triplets, Flora. It was unheard of in the 1920s. That you managed to survive was down to a miracle. That you're all still thriving is a gift from God.'

Flora closed her eyes, pressing her hands to her face, struggling to push back the veil of time. The hard mattress, nuns floating about, their lips muttering prayers. The stabbing pain strong enough to wrench her in two. Nothing more. No sign of Lucien.

'I don't remember.'

'You wouldn't.' Sister Maria Clara brought her back to the present with a jolt. 'You were delirious with pain, and we had nothing to give you.'

'I only remember waking and you placing two babies in my arms.'

'You were lucky to have two. If it hadn't been for...' She stopped abruptly, air easing into her lungs as she lifted the glass and sipped from the edge.

'If it hadn't been for...?' Flora prompted, a cold shiver of dread snaking up her spine.

'If it hadn't been for my brother dropping in to see me that evening, it's likely that none of you would have made it. As a doctor, he was just what you and your babies needed the most. Lili though... we didn't think she could survive. A poor little scrap, hardly bigger than my hand. My brother decided to take her to the nearest hospital. Monsieur Lucien was beside himself with grief at the thought of losing her. He loved you all so very much. When we learnt she'd survived...' She coughed again and this time when she removed her handkerchief it was stained with blood. 'It was too late then. You'd gone and poor Marguerette had been returned to us, while Monsieur Lumineau was a doting dad to Violette. Révérende Mère felt it best not to interfere further.'

'You mean your brother...?'

'My brother and his wife had two boys, but not the girl they craved. He offered Lili a good home back in Germany and Révérende Mère decided to accept. You have to remember we knew that Monsieur Lumineau wouldn't have been able to take her, not after returning Marguerette to us.' She shrugged. 'At the time, we thought it the best option. She was a sickly little thing, and he was a doctor.'

Flora was still reeling from the thought that she'd managed to give birth to triplets. How? And that they'd all survived. Her stomach flipped. They had survived, hadn't they? That's what the diary entry must have meant when it mentioned L.

She lifted her head to look at Sister Maria Clara.

The nun was fiddling with her handkerchief, balling it in her tight fist, her face averted. There was more to this than she was telling. Flora had known almost from the beginning that the nun had come from Germany as a novice and had decided to stay. The convent had a reputation for helping the poor. She wondered if that extended to helping the resistance and how that worked with a German in their midst?

It suddenly felt as if Flora's time in France had been leading to this moment. Lucien's ties with the resistance and fears over him being a traitor had been irretrievably enmeshed with her search for her twin daughters. Tomas had only decided to use her because of this link.

She stared down at her left hand and her wedding band. Had he known that she'd had triplets? He seemed to know everything else about her life. She felt something crack deep inside. Nothing noticeable, like the broken glass she'd swept into the bin, but as painful as the cut on Sister Maria Clara's arm. Her mess of a life was of her own making but, at thirty-six, she'd hoped she'd finally found the right man in Tomas Rives. Clearly she'd been mistaken. The only person she could depend upon was herself and that started now.

A frown materialised as she tried to rearrange the facts into a workable order. There were things that still puzzled her. Missing links in the chain of events, like Reiner's words to Sabine at the fashion house. *We have to think of the girls,* when he wouldn't have had any reason to be interested in Marguerette. And then there was Lucien's diary entry about making allowances because Reiner had been good to L, the rest of the word scribbled through.

Flora took a steadying breath as the missing links materialised in a chain of clarity. All she needed was confirmation.

'Maria Clara, before you became a nun, what was your name? Your family name,' she elaborated, in case she hadn't made herself clear.

Sister Maria Clara tipped her head, her expression relaxing. It almost looked as if she was relieved that Flora was moving the conversation away from Lili and onto something less emotionally charged. Flora decided to keep it simple and not tell her where she was going with the question. There was only so much she could take before running out of the convent screaming. To have your life ruined so completely and only to discover the fact years later was going to take some adjustment.

'My brother is called Otto. Otto Reiner.' Her expression hardened. 'It was luck that he was in France visiting family at the time. His wife is French. I've only ever seen him once since then, but from a distance. Our paths travel in very different directions from the days of our childhood in Germany.' She shrugged. 'I can't agree with how he lives his life these days but my parents tell me that he's been a good father to Lili. He was always good with children when we were growing up.'

Flora felt the floor sway beneath her feet. It couldn't be true.

Lili Reiner, her daughter.

It didn't matter that she was German. There were plenty of good Germans out there, like Maria Clara. It only mattered that Lili had been brought up by someone like Reiner as her father.

Otto Reiner. She blinked then blinked again, remembering about his affair with Sabine. It was positively indecent.

The sound of footsteps outside reminded her of where she was.

Glancing at her watch, she couldn't quite believe that only an hour had passed since she'd left the safety of Madame Billy's. She felt like a different person to the one who'd brushed up the broken glass less than ten minutes before. It was only glass, when she'd lost a life. That's exactly what it felt like. At least she'd held Violette and Marguerette in her arms. She'd hugged them to her and thought them to be safe. She'd lost eighteen years of loving Lili. Eighteen years that she could never reclaim.

It was time to go to Lucien and this time she wouldn't accept any of his excuses.

The lies stopped here.

THIRTY-ONE

Flora burst out of the front door and hurried down the street, her handbag bundled under her arm. All she could think of was Lili, her third child. Her brain was as numb as her heart as she weaved through the busy streets. By the time she spotted Lucien's apartment block up ahead her breath was coming out in short gasps. The sudden stitch in her side had her panting for air. She pressed into a doorway, forcing herself to inhale and exhale slowly until the pain dwindled to a sharp ache.

The sixteenth arrondissement was still busy. She stayed in the doorway, partially hidden by the curve of the brickwork waiting for her pulse to slow. Acting on impulse was all very well but, with Reiner involved, she had to be careful. Glancing about her, she wished she'd planned things a little more carefully. A single woman hiding in a random doorway in one of the posher parts of Paris was asking for trouble. She was already getting searching looks from passers-by.

It was time to leave.

With her shoulders back, and the brim of her felt hat pulled over her face, she strolled over to the entrance of Lucien's apartment block.

'Bonsoir.' She smiled as brightly as she could, her bag open to reveal the top part of the quilt she'd been working on. 'If you could tell Monsieur Lumineau I'm here with the samples he requested,' she said.

'Certainly, madame.' The grey-suited and booted concierge moved his hand to the telephone. 'Your name?'

Flora hid her worry with brief smile. So much for being clever. If Sabine answered...

No. Sabine would never answer the phone. That's what servants were for.

'Madame Toussaint.'

Lucien met her at the door, a finger raised to his lips, his head tilted in the direction of the drawing room. He only spoke when they were safely ensconced in his study, the door locked behind them.

'Don't worry, it's only a safety precaution. It's the maid's night off and Sabine is secure in her room of mirrors.' He made a show of dropping the keys on the table before moving to the drinks cabinet. 'A whisky, I think.'

Flora placed her bag beside the bunch of keys, deciding to leave her coat and her hat, only removing her gloves and stuffing them in her pocket. She didn't intend on staying long. 'I don't want...'

'Have a drink, then you can tell me all about it.'

He handed her the glass and waited until she'd coughed and spluttered her way through the measure, the fiery liquid burning a trail right to her toes.

'There now, that's better. At least, you don't look as if you're ready to collapse.' He took her arm and led her to the sofa before sitting down beside her, his hand drifting from her back to her hands. 'Tell me what's wrong, and I'll see if I can fix it.'

She slid her gaze from their entwined fingers to his concerned face. There was nothing he could do to fix it. It was far too late for that. She couldn't even blame him for what had happened between them. She'd been an equal party, thinking herself in love with the suave couturier. That their relationship had resulted in three babies was something neither of them could have envisioned. The deceit had only occurred after, when it was too late to change things.

'First I need you to tell me about Lili and, after, I want to know where Marguerette is and to help me get a letter to Violette. You must, Lucien.' Her words were abrupt, unadorned but she couldn't help that. It was how she felt.

Lucien flinched, his fingers clenching hers before relaxing, his voice hesitant. 'I'm sorry. It was inevitable that you'd find out. I should have told you that day outside the convent, but I didn't know how. I'm a coward, mon amie. Always have been.'

Flora watched his carefully constructed demeanour collapse, his head bowed in shame. Lucien, the man she'd loved briefly before hating him with everything she had, was falling apart in front of her. If she wanted the truth, she was going to have to do something to change that.

'Don't say that, Lucien, dear. We can't alter what happened, but we have to find some way of dealing with it.'

'You're being too kind.'

'I'm not kind. I'm desperate, Lucien,' she said, her voice breaking. 'Desperate for news of our girls. And Lili. For all our girls. Did you meet her?'

'Only from a distance and not since the war.' He turned his head, his gaze flickering to the whisky decanter. 'There was a time in the thirties when I used to travel to Leipzig for the trade fair. It was easy enough to make a detour. Reiner would never have countenanced it, but his wife is made from a much more accommodating cloth.' He released her hands to pull out his handkerchief and blow his nose. His eyes were red-rimmed when he went to stuff it back in his pocket. 'And, to answer your second question, all you have to do is to look in a mirror.'

'I don't understand. I thought you said that Marguerette was like me?'

'She is. They both are. Identical twins. Shared the same egg or so I've been told. I don't really understand it, but Violette apparently had her own egg, which is the reason she takes after me, poor girl.'

Flora sat back, her hand raised to her face, not knowing what to say. No wonder Reiner had recognised her. He must have had a huge shock finding she was back in Paris.

'And where is she now?'

Lucien rose abruptly, pacing over to the fireplace before turning, his back to the grate. 'That's a good question. Rumour has it that Otto's wife has finally seen sense and left him, taking the girl back to France. Ingrid is French but...' He heaved his shoulders with an air of bewilderment that twisted like a blade deep inside her chest. 'He'll know, but secrecy is all part of the cat and mouse game he likes to play.' His chin jutted when he finally met her gaze. 'I can't ask him. I won't. It breaks my heart to even think of her, but Ingrid is a good mother. I have to believe that Lili is well and as happy as she can be in this blasted war.'

He looked sweaty and pale. Deeply unhappy, but there was nothing she could do about that. Flora knew she had to trace Ingrid Reiner to find Lili, which wouldn't be easy. A Frenchwoman could easily disappear back into the body of her family with no one the wiser, except the locals. She wouldn't know where to start.

'And Violette?'

'I posted a letter to her earlier today, mentioning that you're in Paris. She should receive it in the next couple of days.'

Flora moved to beside him, clutching at his arm, a feeling of lightness tinging her voice with a thread of hope. She was about to have part of her dearest wish fulfilled. 'Thank you. You don't know what it means. There's only little Marguerette now. Where is she, Lucien?'

The sound of a sharp laugh behind her made Flora jerk back in shock.

'Somewhere you'll never find her.'

THIRTY-TWO

'Sabine, how did you get in?'

Flora turned in horror. She hadn't heard the door open. She'd been too invested in Lucien to hear the key turn in the lock and the hinges engage. There might have been a noise. It was impossible to tell.

'With a key, Lucien.' Sabine dangled a small bunch in the air. 'I've always had a key.'

She looked magnificent framed in the open doorway, her hair a flow of curls draping one shoulder, her beautiful face picture-perfect. But it wasn't her beauty that had Flora's legs weaken and her heart thump. It was the woman's vitriolic expression, her eyes flashing with an undiluted hatred impossible to mistake.

'Hello, Flora. Long time no see as they say, although I'd rather you hadn't turned up on my doorstep. I'm fussy with who I invite into my home.'

'Now now, Sabine.' Lucien held his hands up, palms facing. 'There's no need to be like that. We're all grown-ups after all.'

'I'll say what I want, Lucien.' Sabine swivelled back to Flora, her hands in the pockets of her lacy gown. 'Don't think you'll get anything out of him. My home, my money,' she emphasised, her eyes glinting. 'The business would be broke, if I didn't encourage a few of my friends to buy his raggedy frocks.'

'I didn't come for money, Sabine.' Flora stretched her spine, suddenly pleased of the extra height it gave her over the shorter woman. She'd say what she had to and then she'd leave. It was time she told Lucien's wife what she thought of her. 'Returning Marguerette to the nuns was cruel and not telling me about Lili... I would never have agreed to Lucien's mad proposal if I'd known.'

Sabine rested her hip against the corner of the desk, her face completely immobile apart from her pout of a mouth. 'So, you've finally learnt the truth. Good. I hope it hurts. He was lucky that I accepted one of his bastards into my home let alone three.' She threw back her head and laughed, before stopping as quickly as she'd started, her eyes zoning in on Lucien, who hadn't said a word. By his dazed expression, Flora wondered if he hadn't heard. Like a fly trapped in Sabine's web. They were both trapped.

Flora's mouth dried and her heart thundered, her eyes shifting to the door. She'd been wrong to stay in the same room as her. There was something unstable in the twin spots of high colour in the woman's cheeks and the malicious gleam in her eyes.

It seemed as if Lucien was of the same opinion. 'Sabine, let's sit down and—'

'I think not, Lucien. I think it's time you said goodbye to your lover.'

'Yes.' Lucien turned, his face a pasty sheen of white. 'Flora, go now. I'll sort out...'

'That's not what I meant, beloved.'

The gun came out of nowhere. One second Sabine had both hands in her pockets as she languished against the desk, the next there was a small revolver clutched in her hand, her finger on the trigger as she lifted it and aimed it at Flora.

'No, Sabine. No!'

Lucien stepped in front of her, his hands spread wide like a shield.

The bang was far louder than their practice sessions in a field somewhere behind RAF Ringway. It took a second for Flora to register that the noise had come from the gun, the acrid smell of cordite blending with the sharper, heavier scent of Sabine's perfume. She was still processing the noise, her feet glued to the Persian rug, the sound of the shot ringing in her ears as she turned to Lucien.

'Lucien, we...'

'I... I...'

Moving sideways, she saw the surprise on his face, not understanding until she glanced down at the spreading red stain in the centre of his pristine, expertly pressed white poplin shirt, the soft ivory sheen from the mother-of-pearl buttons suddenly looking out of place among the mayhem.

'Lucien?'

She stepped back, her arms extending of their own volition as he crumpled against her.

With a little cry, she pressed her hand against his chest, powerless to stop the warm blood pumping through her fingers and gushing up her arm, her eyes riveted to the look of disbelief on his face. His breath was a gasp of sound in her ear as he struggled to bubble out some words.

'Tell the girls... I love them.'

'I will. Oh, my dear...'

Flora couldn't believe what had happened, but there was no denying Lucien's full weight starting to drag her over. She managed to ease him onto the floor before placing his head gently on her lap, the reflection cast from the flames leaping over the spreading stain. Stroking his hair, she whispered his name as his look of surprise slowly morphed into a death mask, his lungs expelling the last few bubbles of air, his heart thumping out its last beat.

Lucien was gone.

She tried to block out everything except him. It mattered but not as much as the weight of Lucien's head in her lap, the sheen of his white, blond hair, the faint smell of his aftershave. A last goodbye to the father of her children. Their children.

Lifting her hand, she closed his lids, knowing that the memory of his beautiful blue eyes would haunt her forever. With her hand on his cheek, she pressed the lightest of kisses against his forehead before resting his head back against the rug, her heart welling with sadness for the man she'd once loved so dearly.

'That will teach him to bring his whore into my home.'

Flora turned to look at Sabine in horror at her callousness, the words dragging her back into the room with a thump. She'd taken precious seconds with Lucien, seconds she could afford. After all, there was no way Sabine was going to let her escape. Not with a loaded gun in her hand.

Sabine had moved behind the desk, the gun still aimed in her general direction, but without the deadly intent she'd witnessed seconds before.

'Stay where you are.' She lifted the receiver and pressed it to her ear. 'Operator, get me Herr Reiner on 2299. It's urgent.'

Not death then. Arrest, which was worse. Much worse.

Flora shifted slightly, keeping her eyes on the gun, while desperately thinking of a means of escape. She had a gun too, she remembered, feeling a fool at the thought of it lying useless in the bottom of her bag. The door was wide open, but she wouldn't get very far, not with Sabine waving the gun around and, even if she did there was still the stairs to negotiate and the concierge in the foyer.

'Otto, darling. I've sorted out Violette and Lili's little problem.' Sabine's voice dripped with honey. 'It seems as if Flora broke into my apartment and murdered poor Lucien.' There was a brief pause before she spoke again. 'Yes, exactly. Two birds with one bullet. We'll have her arrested for his murder.' She half turned. 'In fact, it couldn't have worked out better. If the girls ever learn of what happened...'

It was in that instant that Flora saw her chance and took it. It wasn't much of one, but if she died, then so be it. With a suddenness that had Sabine shouting, she lunged for the door, only pausing a second to grab her bag and Lucien's keys.

She would have made it. She nearly did, but Sabine was a second too quick, her trigger finger snapping into action, her aim scarily accurate as Flora tried to shield her body with the door.

The sound of the gunshot streaked across the room, the noise so loud that a shriek filled the air. It was only after that she realised the scream had come from her.

THIRTY-THREE

There was a fleeting moment when Flora thought that Sabine might have missed, even though she knew she wouldn't. The woman had been too confident with the gun. Too accurate. When the pain finally arrived a microsecond later, it quickly crescendoed into something bone-shatteringly sharp. A brutal affirmation of what she already knew.

Sabine had shot Lucien in the heart. For Flora she'd chosen the head.

It was the kick start she needed to carry on through the door, pulling it closed behind her. If she stopped, she'd collapse where she stood, which wouldn't help anyone. She'd be arrested for Lucien's murder, which appeared to be Sabine's plan all along.

If she survived.

There was pain and blood. Too much blood. It smeared her cheek and dripped onto her hand as she clumsily tried to insert the key in the lock, her fingers slipping over the metal. Two keys, then three as her vision started to stretch and distort, the room pitching and rolling around her.

'Open the door. Help. HELP.'

Sabine's muffled screams came through the barrier of wood,

her fingers rattling the handle as she tried to wrench it open. Flora held firm until she managed to finally turn the key.

I have to get out of here.

She lifted her hand to her face only to let it fall to her neck, her hands shaking at the amount of thick, red blood. The sharp stabbing pain. The way her vision blurred in and out of focus, her legs threatening to give way.

She didn't need to look in one of Sabine's mirrors to know it was bad.

She unravelled her scarf before pulling it tight around her head, padding the wound with her clean handkerchief. Then she staggered towards the door, her hand bouncing off the wall as she struggled to maintain her balance, her fingers leaving a bloody trail on the pristine paintwork.

Just keep moving.

The corridor was empty. There was the lift and the stairs opposite, and most likely a German standing at the bottom, she thought, remembering Sabine's call to darling Otto. But she couldn't stay in the corridor.

Once in the stairwell she decided to go up instead of down, her hand clamped around the banister as she dragged herself along, one foot after the other. Three flights in total before she came to a metal door with a push bar across.

Fire Exit.

And if there was a fire exit there must be a fire escape.

The breeze on the roof was terrifying, a bracing wind that caused her legs to wobble. If she hung around, she wouldn't have to wait for the Germans to find her. She'd topple over the edge instead.

It was dark and bitterly cold, no moon in the sky. No sky, instead a shield of thick, low cloud. She staggered into the middle of the roof, waiting for her eyes to adjust. All it would need was for someone to burst through the door and she'd be dead.

Stumbling to the edge, she finally found what she was looking for.

A steep set of vertiginous iron steps pinned to the side of the building. With her head throbbing, she looped her arm around the railing and began to drag herself down. She had to get out before Reiner arrived.

By the time she reached the ground, she was gulping for air, her breath ragged.

The fire escape ended in a narrow lane at the back of the building, a row of bins buttressing the wall, a lone cat sniffing around in search of treats. Disorientated, she looked left then right, trying to work out which direction would lead her away from the front entrance. Hazarding a guess, she plunged away from the railing and lurched past the bins to the wall. At the end, she eased out of the lane, her eyes wide with fear as she set foot on the pavement.

Keep going, Flora. Don't stop.

She staggered along the street, one hand groping the wall to keep herself upright. Her head bowed against the wind, her mind refusing to shift from Lucien's study and the horrors within.

A fresh wave of pain exploded in her head, closely followed by a bolt of vomit hurtling up her neck. There was no warning, no opportunity to do anything other than brace her hand against the wall and avert her head as she retched in the street.

'Disgusting behaviour. You, madame, are a disgrace.' The man's angry words came to her as if he was speaking at the other end of a long tunnel, the voice distorted as he stormed past.

She pushed her hair back off her face, before wiping the back of her left hand across her mouth, careful not to dislodge the scarf. There was nothing she could or would do with her right hand until she'd had the opportunity to scrub Lucien's blood from her fingers.

She stifled a sob, as she side-stepped the vomit, instinctively moving back into the shadows away from prying eyes. The nagging ball of misery in the centre of her chest was only tempered by feeling more frightened than she'd ever been. Sabine and Reiner couldn't be far behind. Sabine would make sure of that. They'd decided to stitch her up for Lucien's murder. With Violette and Lili's parents gone, and Reiner separated from his wife, it would leave the way clear for the two of them to play at happy families.

Looking around, she was pleased to find that she wasn't alone. The disapproving man had rounded the corner out of sight, but there were other strangers hurrying along. Whatever happened next would be far more difficult in front of witnesses. Not impossible. Nothing was impossible as far as the Nazis were concerned. The thought drove her forward, increasing her step, her hand scraping the wall for balance. By the time she spotted the spire of the church up ahead, her breath was a sharp stab in her chest, her calves shooting balls of agony. But it was far more concerning that she couldn't feel one side of her head. There should be pain and lots of it. Instead, her face was completely numb.

Retracing her footsteps, she slipped down the lane at the back of the church, her energy reserves on empty. Once inside the convent, she sank onto the hard stone floor, her legs giving way, her world falling into darkness.

THIRTY-FOUR

11 December – Convent of Sainte-Marthe-des-Anges

'She can't stay here. Not with her image all over the newspapers. It puts everyone at risk.'

'You should have thought of that before handing her children out like missals at mass, Révérende Mère. We have a responsibility to the dear woman, which you can't deny.'

'How dare you speak to me like that, Sister Maria Clara. I will not allow you to...'

'I dare because no one else will tell you of the damage you've done, Révérende Mère. That poor woman is beside herself and you must take some of the blame.' There was a slight pause filled with the sound of chair legs scraping across tiles. 'I too must accept my burden of guilt. To allow my brother to take her daughter without her knowledge. Tell me, how many crimes did we commit, both in the eyes of the church and the state?'

'In the eyes of the Lord, we committed none and the state isn't interested in the likes of her. That woman, whom you seem so fond of, deserves none of your pity. She brought this upon herself.'

'Where is your forgiveness, Révérende Mère? Your piety? *Let him without sin cast the first stone.*'

Flora blinked at the sound of a door slamming shut then sweet, blessed silence. She rolled the words over in her mind, picking up strands of the conversation and trying to untangle them.

Lili. Her daughter.

The name floated in front of her, bringing another memory with it. Sitting in the convent with Sister Maria Clara. The broken glass. The truth.

Otto Reiner and the reverend mother conniving to keep her daughter from her.

Lucien lying in a pool of blood.

She gasped, struggling to sit. Her daughters. Where were they? And the nuns. It wasn't safe for them. What had they been thinking in allowing her to stay? If the police were to find out. If Reiner was... She'd never forgive herself if anything were to happen to them.

'Hush now.' A cooling hand on hers before she was assisted back against the pillow. 'You've been ill, very ill indeed. We don't want a relapse.'

Flora clutched at the nun's hand, drawing comfort from her familiar presence. The way that Sister Maria Clara had stuck up for her with the mother superior...

'You can't know what's happened. If they find me here, there's bound to be repercussions.'

'Don't you worry about that. We have you well hidden in one of our stores. The police have already been once and sent on their way and as for not knowing what's happened, you've made the front of all the newspapers. Not that we believe them.'

'I'm innocent, Maria Clara. I couldn't...'

'We know that, child.'

Flora flopped back against the pillows, too exhausted to move.

'That's right,' the nun comforted. 'You need to rest. This is the first time you've opened your eyes in three days.'

Three days! That couldn't be right. Flora scrunched up her face, feeling the skin pull in her cheek, a wispy memory fading in and out of focus before sharpening into full clarity.

A bullet whistling behind her.

'I was shot,' she said, suddenly remembering everything, from the stickiness of Lucien's blood between her fingers to the cat rummaging through the bins and the man's disgust straight after. The pain, the dizziness. The grief. She remembered it all.

She tried to sit again, and this time her friend let her.

'Shush now. Don't upset yourself so or you'll make it worse.' Sister Maria Clara perched on the bed beside her and, taking her hand between hers, gently directed it to her head.

Instead of her hair, she found a thick bandage swathing one side of her face.

'It's purely precautionary as we try and control the infection. The doctor doesn't think you'll suffer long term. You were very lucky, Flora.'

Lucky?

Flora stared back at her, trying to process the meaning behind the word and failing. She didn't feel lucky. Far from it. In fact, she felt the exact opposite. Yes, she was still alive but at what cost. Lucien was dead and she was in the frame for his murder. Where did luck come into it?

She braced herself as she asked the next question. 'And the bullet?'

'Entered the side of your head above your ear and exited at your cheek. A glancing blow only. It wouldn't have been a problem if it wasn't for the risk of infection. Bullet wounds are never clean.' Sister Maria Clara's voice was matter-of-fact and just what she needed. The unvarnished truth. 'I'll have you know that my stock of dried herbs is sorely depleted, but if the poultices have done their job...'

'Thank you, I mean that, and thank you for speaking up for me with Révérende Mère.'

'I'm sorry you had to hear. Don't think too harshly of her, Flora. She's from a different generation to us.'

'She won't take it out on you?'

'Her bark is far worse than her bite.' The nun's tone changed. 'Now, what about a drink, and I can bring you some soup?'

The very thought of food was enough for Flora's stomach to heave. She knew she hadn't eaten anything. There was an emptiness that she recognised, which sat alongside the knowledge that if she did, she'd see it again. 'Just a drink please.'

She let Sister Maria Clara help her before resting back against the pillow, her head throbbing with thoughts of unfinished business. Something that she needed the nun's help with. It would be risky, but not as risky as coming to Paris had proved to be. Everyone had been so kind at Madame Billy's and there was Tomas to think about. It wouldn't take Reiner long to work out where she'd been staying and who'd visited her. The stakes had raised to sky high now they were looking for an alleged murderer.

'I'll be back later. Anything else you want me to do for you before I go?'

Flora swallowed hard as she tried to find the words. It wasn't as if she could just blurt out that she needed the nun to deliver a message to a brothel.

THIRTY-FIVE

Friday 18 December – Convent Garden

Police issue description of wanted woman
Flora Toussaint, 36, is wanted in connection with the murder of Lucien
Lumineau, acclaimed couturier at Maison Lumineau

Flora folded the quilt, swapping it for the week-old newspaper that
was lying on the bench beside her.

The artist's image of her on the front page was a good likeli-
ness. Flattering. The way they'd arranged her hair in a coil emphasised her cheekbones. That she didn't look anything like the image
was both a blessing and burden. All of France was on the hunt for
Flora Toussaint, murderer of Lucien Lumineau. Not someone with
shorn hair and an angry scar splitting the side of her face in two.

A noise from the convent had her looking up to see Tomas
hurrying towards her, a shock which sent her emotions in a whirl
and her pulse into overdrive. She'd left a message for him care of
Madame Billy's a week ago. A week without news. She'd thought
him dead, then worse than dead. That he'd abandoned her to her
fate after the mess she'd made of things. After all, her contract
hadn't included murdering their prime suspect.

'Apologies. I would have come sooner. I've only heard about...' She watched as his gaze drifted to the side of her face before dropping to his shoes.

'You've been away.' It was more a statement than a question. She knew that he spent a lot of time travelling between France and Britain. It had been the one excuse she hadn't even thought of. The one that made sense. He'd been out of the country.

'Yes. I'm sorry. I should have...'

She struggled to her feet, suddenly restless, the blanket discarded on the bench behind her. 'No need to apologise, Tomas. You weren't to know.' She stopped abruptly a few feet away as an image of Lucien filled her mind, just like he filled her thoughts most of the time. The man she'd loved, then hated, then pitied only to learn to like when it was too late to do anything about it.

'Flora?'

She lifted her head, managing a smile.

'It's good to see you, Tomas. So good. How are Madame Billy, Mimi, Edith and the girls? How is Odile? Forgiven me yet?'

'Nothing to forgive. Distraught over what's happened. They know it's all lies, of course. You couldn't hit a target, even if it was right in front of you,' he added, taking her arm and escorting her around the empty flower beds.

'Charming!'

'But true, dear lady. Remember, I've seen you in possession of a gun. Scared me witless.' He stopped in front of the bench and, picking up the quilt, examined it briefly. 'Sabine?' he asked gently.

She nodded as she retook her seat, wrapping the blanket around her knees, her hands folded on top, her eyes locked with his. 'I went to ask him about Lili, and she walked in.'

'Lili?' He sat beside her, his head tilted in her direction with a look of enquiry.

'Lili Reiner, my daughter.'

'Lili who?'

Flora had spent the last week vacillating over Tomas's involvement and whether he'd known about her third daughter. Reiner's part had made complete sense, tying up the loose end of why he'd followed her from the bookshop. But Tomas? It took a quick glance at his confused expression to reject the notion as complete nonsense.

Shifting her hand, she curled it through his. 'You made a mistake in Carrickfergus, but it wasn't your fault.' She nodded in the direction of the convent, the windows hidden behind thick, wooden shutters. 'Instead of twins, there were triplets.' Her voice fractured but she continued anyway, her gaze determinedly fixed on the shutters and away from his face. 'Violette, Marguerette and Lili. Violette went to Lucien. Marguerette was fostered out to the Langs while Lili...' She bent her head, her face wet with sudden tears. 'While Lili was handed over to Otto Reiner and his wife to bring up as their own. It was a secret that was never meant to get out. Lucien knew and couldn't do anything about it, not with Sabine as his wife.'

'Oh, Flora.' She found herself pulled into his arms and she was happy to let him. The familiar smell of his shampoo and shaving soap, combined with a trace of his brand of cigarettes. It felt perfect. Like coming home, when it shouldn't. It couldn't. Not after everything she'd done. Not after Lucien giving his life. That meant something.

She eased away, fumbling in her pocket for her handkerchief.

'Here, take mine.'

After a moment of dabbing her eyes, she removed her hat, dropping it onto the bench beside her, determined to change the tempo of the conversation. It hurt too much to continue it.

'What do you think of my new hairstyle? A little too modern for 1940s Paris?' Lifting her hand, she smoothed her palm over her head, the hair patchy in places, bald in others. Sister Maria Clara had been adamant that the risk of infection was too great to leave it.

She turned her head, displaying the angry weal, the edges pulled together by a neat row of the tiniest stitches, her eyes defiant as they met his. 'I think it matches my face though. Very Boris Karloff, don't you think?'

A sharp intake of breath, which he couldn't disguise before saying, 'You do yourself a disservice, Flora. May I?'

'Of course.'

He lifted his hand to her chin, angling it to get a better look, his eyes squinting in concentration. 'Brave to stitch it with the risk of infection, but quite remarkable. It's one of the best jobs I've seen. You're very lucky.'

Flora shut her eyes briefly. There it was. That word again. Perhaps she should have it inscribed on her gravestone.

Here lies the body of Lucky Flora Toussaint.

She snapped them open.

Was this what madness felt like?

'You think so?' she finally said, reaching for her hat and tugging it back in place. 'I think it's the ugliest thing imaginable, but I mustn't moan. Better than the alternative.'

'Much.' He took her hand again and she let him. 'I take it one of the nuns...?'

'Sister Maria Clara. A talented herbalist. During the summer months the garden is full of more plants than I recognise or know the names of. I remember helping her pick and dry them in the racks in the kitchen before storing them in glass jars.'

The conversation was starting to lag. She didn't want Tomas to leave, but it seemed as if they were running out of things to say.

Be brave, Flora. There are things that must be said.

'It looks like I'm in a bit of a situation, Tomas. Ideally, I'd like to leave the convent. I'm only putting the nuns at risk by staying.' She looked at him, feeling her mouth tremble and unable to do a thing about it.

'And leave Paris?' His gaze slipped to her lips briefly. 'I know we talked about this before and you refused to go. If you really mean it then come back with me to Ancinnes. I have friends there who'll be happy to have you for as long as you want to stay. Actually, leaving Paris has been on my mind quite a lot recently,' he added, concentrating on the quilt. 'You're not the only one who's come to Reiner's attention. It's time I left too.' He smoothed his fingers over the patchwork. 'We might even be able to use this to alert them that we're on our way.'

She eyed the quilt briefly, remembering her excitement at coming up with the idea and Odile, Juliette and Amantine's enthusiasm. It all seemed so long ago. 'I'm sorry about that. Paris will miss you. Madame Billy will too. As for me, I don't feel I have a choice. I can't be responsible for any more deaths. Lucien's...' She ignored the sudden hoarseness in her voice. 'If I hadn't visited him then...'

He leant towards her, his tone urgent. 'You don't know that. No one does. Sabine might have been trying to get him out of the way for ages.'

'Which doesn't change the fact that I'm the one wanted for his murder.' She lifted the newspaper from the bench beside her and draped it across his lap. 'His funeral is tomorrow and I can't even go to say my last goodbyes, not with all of Paris after my neck on the nearest guillotine. Who's to say that Violette won't be there? The only chance I may ever get to meet her.'

They both turned at the faint sound of cups chinking against saucers and Sister Maria Clara bearing down on them with a tray of tea. Flora would have smiled if the sight hadn't plunged her straight back to the day she'd found Lucien waiting for her outside.

Would she ever be able to go through even ten minutes without thinking of him?

'Hello there. I heard you had a visitor. Some herbal tea is just the thing in this cold weather.'

'Here, let me take the tray.' Tomas jumped to his feet, gesturing for the nun to take his seat while he set the tray down on the table in front of them. 'You only brought two cups?'

'I've had mine.' She slipped her hands through the folds of her sleeve, her eyes inquisitive below her wimple and veil.

'This is Monsieur Rives, a friend. Tomas, Sister Maria Clara, my oldest and dearest of friends.'

'The good sister and I are already acquainted. Isn't that right, Sister Maria Clara?'

Flora watched a blush steal up the nun's cheeks, the first time she'd ever seen her look embarrassed.

Tomas passed her a cup of herbal tea, before picking up his own, absent-mindedly stirring it with a spoon. 'The sisters are helpful from time to time. They knew we were interested in Lumineau and when Marguerette showed up in a fluster about her father visiting her at the dance hall, they mentioned it.' He lifted his cup and took a brief sip, not quite able to hide his expression at the bitter taste.

Flora stared as one of the last pieces fell into place. How Marguerette had been recruited into the resistance when hardly anyone had known about her links to Lucien.

With his cup back on the tray, Tomas turned back to the nun.

'Sister Maria Clara. We have an additional problem, that I think you can help us with.'

'Yes, monsieur?'

'We need to move Flora to a place of safety. A place where she won't feel guilty about putting her friends at risk.' He shrugged. 'I know of such a place, but with her face all over the papers we need to camouflage her appearance.'

Sister Maria Clara nodded, going to stand. 'An outfit and an ID card should be sufficient.'

'An ID card?' Tomas's brow puckered. 'I can't imagine where...?'

She smiled briefly, giving nothing away. 'No one ever bothers to look twice at our cards, monsieur. We have one or two spare for such instances.'

THIRTY-SIX

Saturday 19 December – Église de la Sainte-Trinité, 2 pm

Flora wrung her hands in her lap, her fingers pulling and tugging on the rosary beads that Sister Maria Clara had lent her, along with a spare nun's habit. She shouldn't have insisted on attending Lucien's funeral. There was no sign of Violette and, with the church full, it looked like there wasn't going to be. She'd risked other people's lives for nothing.

'Stop fidgeting.'

'I can't help it,' she whispered out of the side of her mouth, trying to appear serene in front of the great and good of Paris settling on the pews around her.

A gentle hush ran from the back of the church to the front as the last of the mourners arrived. Heads turned at the sight of Sabine strolling down the aisle as if it was a catwalk, her hips gently swaying to some invisible beat, the brim of her hat hiding much of her face. She was wearing black, but not one of her husband's designs.

Flora lowered her head back to her beads, anxiety flaring at the thought that Sabine might recognise her. Instead of giving in to it, she started running through her encyclopaedic knowledge of the fashion industry that she'd once been a part of and had never been able to let go.

A long, slipper satin skirt topped off by a woollen square coat, with a fur collar, impressive buttons and the most wonderful sleeves. She suddenly knew that there was only one designer capable of putting together such a look.

Lucien's biggest rival in all things design. Cristobal Balenciaga.

That Sabine had chosen Balenciaga's label over her husband's was like hammering an extra nail in his coffin, although knowing Lucien, he'd probably have laughed.

The thought wasn't enough to prevent her hands squeezing tight around the worn beads.

'Alright?'

She nodded, casting a quick look over her shoulder at the last couple to enter, the door closing behind them with a dull thud.

She wasn't interested in the stocky man looking uncomfortable in a dark suit and polka dot bow tie. It was all about the woman by his side.

The outfit was also black. A plain black dress and coat, with none of the detailing found in the more expensive outfits on display. A dress worn out of respect and not for show, testament by the final touch of the traditional, lace mourning veil hiding her face.

'Who are they?' she whispered behind her hand, unable to stop herself from staring.

But she already knew who it was.

Violette.

It was there in her height and her shape. The length of her stride and angle of her head. Not a mirror image. More like looking at her reflection in water, the ripples distorting the resemblance. She wanted to laugh, then cry and, with a little gulp she realised that a couple of tears had broken free of their own accord.

Reaching for her handkerchief, she reminded herself that tears were fine. Everyone was allowed to cry at funerals, even nuns and those disguised as nuns. The invisible breed, as Tomas had taken pains to explain to her after he'd asked Sister Maria Clara to let Flora borrow a habit to wear.

Tomas bent his head closer on the pretext of tying his shoelace. 'Don't know about her but he's Pablo Picasso. A good friend of Lucien's.'

Picasso.

Lucien's friend from his early days in Paris. Who better to escort Lucien's beloved Violette than his best friend?

Flora watched as the couple positioned themselves in the pew behind Sabine. Picasso was clearly upset, the way he kept pressing a large handkerchief to his eyes. With her hand on his arm, it was now the woman comforting him.

Shifting position, Flora would have been tempted to slip away if the heavy door hadn't already shut behind them. She'd come to see Violette. There was nothing left for her here. No way of speaking to her with Sabine around. At least there was no sign of Otto Reiner, which had been Flora's greatest fear. But even someone like Sabine would have known that bringing her Nazi lover to her French husband's funeral was a step too far, not if she still wanted to continue enjoying Parisian life.

With a start, she realised that, with the pallbearers in position around Lucien's coffin, the funeral was drawing to a close.

Where had the hour gone?

'Stay where you are. We can slip out when everyone has left.'

Flora nodded, watching the fabric swathed coffin with its wreath of white flowers and the surge of people surrounding Sabine so that the only part visible was the peak of her hat. Picasso and Violette followed at a more leisurely pace.

Without thinking it through, Flora slipped out of the pew behind them, remembering to bend her head, her hands clasped piously in front of her.

'I thought I said to...' Tomas hissed in her ear.

'I forgot.'

She made for the door, only to change her mind and turn, but the aisle was blocked. Instead, she moved forward, keeping close to the line of pews, her head bowed.

There was no room on the steps outside, everyone milling about trying to capture a word with the widow holding court a few feet in front of her.

'Sabine, ma chérie. I'm truly devastated for you and Violette. What a thing to have happened. Have they caught the killer yet?'

'No, but it won't be long.'

'Someone who used to work for him at Maison Lumineau. I don't know what the world is coming to.'

So, that's the rumour they're spreading, Flora thought, glaring at the speaker's back. *Better than the truth, at least to them.* She went to move, aware that Tomas was hovering by her side, only to stop abruptly, her mouth opening in shock.

'And so tragic that Violette couldn't make it, dear Sabine. The funeral of her own dear father.'

'She's safer where she is. Lucien wouldn't have wanted to put her at any risk with a murderer still on the loose.'

Flora felt the blood drain to her feet at the words. She'd been certain it had been Violette. She couldn't have been wrong. Not in recognising her own child.

Lifting her head, she frantically searched through the crowds until she spotted what she was looking for. Picasso escorting the woman she'd thought Violette across the road. Before she knew it, she was hurrying down the steps, aware that Tomas, trapped in the milieu, was struggling to keep up with her, but she wouldn't lose them. She couldn't. Not until she knew the truth.

Flora caught up with them at the end of the street. She didn't know if Tomas had followed her and, in that moment, she didn't care. The road up ahead was empty, an opportunity she was determined to take. There'd be time to explain to him after.

'Monsieur Picasso?'

She watched him stop, his back rigid before glancing over his shoulder. The woman at his side didn't turn.

'Yes.' His expression changed from one of annoyance to confusion at the sight of her outfit.

With a deep breath, she relaxed her lips into a tight smile, her voice pitched to low.

'I was a friend of Lucien's too, monsieur.' Her eyes brimmed with sudden tears. 'More than a friend. My name is Flora Toussaint.'

'Mon Dieu,' Picasso cursed, only to apologise. 'Excuse me. I didn't know...'

'How could you when I'm dressed like this?' she said, plucking the fabric between her fingers. 'What I have to say won't take long.'

'Of course.'

She paused, her eyes shifting to where the woman in black had started moving down the road, her footsteps quickening as if she couldn't bear to hear another word. Flora felt the sting of her snub as sharp as a slap. If she was right, her daughter had chosen to walk away instead of hearing what she had to say. She couldn't blame her.

The sharpest sting of all was that she only had herself to blame.

'I... I want you to know that what they're saying about me isn't true,' she started, her words stumbling out in a rush. 'Yes, I was there when he died, but I didn't shoot him. I couldn't.' She swallowed, tracing the woman's movements as she disappeared around the bend in the road. 'Lucien was a part of me and one I never forgot. A good man who deserved far more than to be shot in cold blood.'

He reached out, placing his hand on her arm, his fingers curling around the black cloth. 'I'm guessing it was Sabine?'

Flora nodded slowly, her voice choked. 'I couldn't save him. I'm so sorry.'

'There's no need to apologise, Flora. Lucien suspected that she might do something like this.' His eyes softened under bushy brows. 'He told me what an amazing woman you are. The love of his life...'

'No, that's not true,' she replied, tears breaking free and running down her cheeks. 'He loved his girls more *than* life itself. In fact, his last words to me were *"Tell the girls I love them."*'

There was complete silence. The sort of silence that causes the world to fade and the air to still. A truck drove past, the sound of it backfiring filling the street. A match struck somewhere behind her. The faint scent of Tomas's soap combined with the smell of tobacco and he was beside her. She didn't deserve him. What must he have thought when she'd run away from the church? But the chance of seeing her daughter...

Picasso glanced between them, giving a short nod. 'Come to my studio, both of you. Hôtel d'Hercule, Rue des Grands-Augustins. Top floor. One hour.'

· · · ·

Rue des Grands-Augustins lived up to its pretentious name. A narrow street almost on the edge of the Seine, filled with grand seventeenth-century buildings with ornate balconies and carved balustrades. Instead of lingering, she barely afforded them a glance, not with the threat of arrest hovering.

Picasso had the whole of the attic of Hôtel d'Hercule. A cavernous space with a profusion of greenery, canvases stacked against the walls and an easel positioned just so to catch the light. There was also a table littered with a mix of paint tubes, a sofa and chairs, and an oriental screen. The sloping ceiling reminded her of L'Etoile de Kleber except for the heat, or lack of. She was thankful for the weight and thickness of her robe, as she tucked her hands up her sleeves and edged nearer to the stove in the corner, her eyes delving into all the dark corners for signs of the woman in black.

'Thank you for inviting us,' she finally said, turning to face him, trying to mask her disappointment with a smile.

'I couldn't not. A friend of dear Lucien's will always be a friend of mine.' He handed them a glass of wine each before gesturing for them to take a seat on the sofa, while he contented himself with the chair opposite.

'Your companion?' she asked, her voice hesitant.

'Resting. The funeral has taken its toll.'

'Of course.' She wanted to ask more, but it would have to wait. Her bravery was tissue-paper thin. Instead, she took a sip of wine which she didn't want. The clock was ticking on her time in Paris. She mustn't waste a second.

'A decent claret. Not easy to come by these days,' said Picasso, holding the glass to the light.

'You should speak to Tomas. He's a wine merchant.'

His eyes lit up. 'Always happy to add a wine merchant to my circle.' He sat back, crossing his legs, a cheroot in one hand, his glass in the other. 'I will miss Lucien greatly. A good man ruined by marriage to the wrong woman.'

Flora tightened her hand around her glass, knowing that she couldn't have put it better if she tried. Lucien wasn't perfect. Who was? He'd made the most of what life had thrown at him and had become very successful in the process. He'd also tried to be a good father to Violette and, latterly to Marguerette...

'It sounds as if you were close,' she finally said, feeling her way. She didn't know this man, only by reputation, which was legendary across France and beyond, but she couldn't let that keep her from her mission.

'It's difficult to forge friendships in such competitive professions as ours.' He placed his cigar on the edge of the ashtray. 'The artist and the atelier. It worked very well.'

Flora smiled, her eyes sparkling with genuine happiness at the thought that Lucien had formed such a close friendship. 'I'm delighted that he had such a good friend in you. It must have made a world of difference to him.'

'A world of difference to us both, madame,' he corrected.

'Please call me Flora.'

He nodded, thumbing the centre of his chest. 'Pablo.'

'We were wondering why Violette wasn't at his funeral, Pablo?' Tomas said, his expression hidden by the lengthening shadows as the afternoon slipped into evening. 'It's Flora's dearest wish to meet her daughters again. I don't know how much Lucien told you, but it's clear to me that the most important people in Flora's life are her children. Attending the funeral wasn't my idea. In fact, I was fervently opposed to it. She must leave Paris. It's too dangerous for her to stay.' He reached out and took Flora's hand and she let him, too stunned by his words to stop him. 'She also won't tell you that she was shot in the fracas that resulted in Lucien's death and nearly died as a result. The nun's outfit was the only disguise possible.'

Pablo took his time in replying, his gaze shrewd as he looked between them.

'It seems as if you have been lucky to find your own friend, Flora, which is as it should be.' He tilted his head at Tomas. 'And to answer your question, Sabine wouldn't have wanted Violette to steal the centre stage from her. There's a strong possibility that she might not even be aware of her father's death. I wouldn't put anything past that woman.' He turned back to Flora. 'You have to remember that Sabine's star is waning while your daughters are beautiful beyond words. All Lucien ever wanted was a woman by his side and what he got was a mannequin obsessed with her looks. The poor man couldn't breathe for mirrors. Work was always a performance for him, but he hated the fawning that went with it. After work, all he wanted was the comfort of his slippers and favourite velvet smoking jacket, not mirrors and sycophants.' He waved his hand around the bare space. 'He was happiest either here or in his study. Nowhere else.'

Flora was completely disarmed by his words. Pablo was a man who knew Lucien for the man he was and not for the flamboyant couturier everyone thought him to be. A man she hadn't really known at all.

'That's not quite true, Pablo. He was also happy when he was with me. I only wish I'd appreciated it at the time.'

They all turned as the woman from the funeral appeared from behind the screen.

THIRTY-EIGHT

This had to be Marguerette.

Flora couldn't stop looking at her. This wondrous woman replaced the only image she'd ever had – of her precious newborn daughter's face. For a second, Flora mourned the losses she'd had to endure over the years. Marguerette's first smile. Her first tooth. Her first steps. Her first day at school. Even her first boyfriend.

Pushing regret aside, instead she relished in the sight of the woman in front of her and not the baby she'd once been. Her mirror image before she'd met and fallen in love with Lucien. Before having her babies.

She couldn't look away. She didn't want to, but it was more than that. It was the near disbelief, and relief that she was finally with one of her daughters, despite the tragic circumstances surrounding their father's death.

We made a beautiful daughter, Lucien. Someone to be proud of.

The words whispered across her mind in the hope that somehow he'd hear them, wherever he was.

With the initial shock shifting to a sense of wonder, Flora started to notice things that she'd initially overlooked, things that added a thick layer of worry to her happiness. Marguerette was thin, too thin, the bones in her cheeks and chin only covered by the thinnest layer of skin. But it was her eyes that told the truth of her illness. Darkly shadowed and sunk into her head. Tomas had told her that she'd been ill but that she was better now. Instinctively she knew that to be wrong.

'Marguerette, ma petite.' Pablo took her arm, his words breaking the tense atmosphere. 'Come and join us. There.' He settled her into his chair before fussing over pouring her a drink. 'A toast, I think, to start with,' he said, raising his glass aloft. 'To my dear friend, Lucien, and also to Marguerette and Flora, two women he loved dearly. To Lucien.'

They all drank, a small sip in Flora's case as she needed to keep her mind clear. What was she meant to say to her, the baby she'd left in good faith, thinking she was giving her a better life, only to learn the truth? That she'd been betrayed. There was no apology large enough.

'Hello, Marguerette.'

Marguerette inclined her head, the mutinous line of her mouth telling Flora in all the ways possible that she wasn't going to make this meeting easy for her.

Flora dropped her gaze under such scrutiny, remembering just how badly she'd let her down.

'I hear you haven't been well,' she finally said, lifting her head, her eyes widening as she examined her face, her heart swelling in her chest.

My daughter.

'A lump in my neck. It's gone now.' Marguerette's voice was husky, hoarse even and so quiet as if speaking was difficult.

Dear God. A lump.

Flora closed her eyes, sending up a quick prayer to anyone who might be listening. *Please let it not be cancer.*

Opening them again, she noticed that Pablo and Tomas had drifted to the window, which made it easier somehow.

'I know it's probably too late, eighteen years too late but I need you to know that....' Flora placed her glass on the floor and pressed her hands to her face instead. A second. Two seconds before she finally managed to lower them. 'I've never forgotten you. What I did. The mistakes I made. I know I can never make it up to you, but I'd like to try.'

'I don't think...'

Flora forged ahead, knowing this was her one chance to get it right and when she had no idea of what to say.

'I loved Lucien so much when we first met. He was wonderful. So handsome and charming. A true gentleman too,' she rushed, leaving no room for Marguerette to interrupt. 'Nothing was ever too much trouble. He treated me like a princess, and then I fell pregnant. I want you to know that you were made with love. It was after, where we got it so wrong.' She fiddled with her plain grey gloves, Sister Maria Clara's gloves. 'I didn't tell him at first. I didn't tell anyone. I was too ashamed and at a loss. And when he found out he was ecstatic. The children he'd always wanted but not with me. You see, I couldn't give him what he needed, only what he wanted. A man like Lucien. Such talent required money. That's where Sabine came in when she agreed to bring up my child, our child,' she corrected. Reaching for her wine, she took a hefty sip, aware that the attic was silent, both men tuning in to what she had to say. 'And then there were... two.'

She stood abruptly, her hand under her nose as she searched around frantically for where she'd left her bag and her handkerchief, playing for time.

'Here, take mine.' Marguerette held out a lacy trifle.

'Sorry, thank you. I'm not sure where a nun is meant to keep such things with no pockets.' She wiped her eyes. 'Where was I?'

'And then there were two. Me and Violette.'

Flora managed a smile. 'You and your sister were adorable. My heart was so full, but children had always been Lucien's dearest wish and he was engaged to be married by then.' She dropped her gaze to her lap, unable to keep her head up. 'I was weak, Marguerette. I know that now. I could have managed, but back then I was sure they'd give you the best life possible. I thought that right up until I returned to Paris a few weeks ago...'

She stopped. There was nothing left to say. There was nothing else she could say.

Marguerette took her time in studying her. The black veil and greyish nun's habit. Her dusty black boots. Pausing on her tightly gripped hands before returning to what little was visible of her face.

Her eyes, nose and mouth and the small part of her cheeks not covered by the white wimple.

'Your hair?'

'The same colour as yours, Marguerette, or it will be when it grows back.'

Her eyes widened before relaxing again, her smile a tentative upward pull of her lips.

'Don't expect me to call you Maman.'

Pablo had stopped in front of an old chest of drawers, the top littered with a pile of newspapers.

'I have something for each of you. Lucien entrusted me with a letter for each of his daughters, and one for you, Flora.' He dug inside a large envelope before removing four smaller ones, flipping through them and handing them out. 'You see, he always knew that he couldn't trust Sabine to have his wishes followed. For Sabine, beauty and wealth have never been enough. She wanted to swallow him whole and spit out the remains, forgetting one important fact. Lucien was always far brighter than she was.' He stopped again, this time to press his forearm up to his eyes and inhale deeply, his words muffled. 'If only he'd realised how vicious she could really be. Something none of us could have guessed.'

He stumbled briefly on his way back across the room, before correcting himself, his chin lifting in an act of defiance. 'My most recent painting is over here, Tomas. You must see it before you go. I think you might like it.'

'I'm sure I will.'

Flora barely heard them. It wasn't difficult with the envelope in front of her.

Cream with the little L logo of Maison Lumineau in the

corner. She ran her fingertip over the embossed golden L and lifted the flap. Lucien was the last person to touch the paper, just as she'd been the last one to touch him before... Her fingers curled around the envelope before forcing them to open. She'd read this and after, she'd mourn.

My darling Flora,
There has never been a day since I first met you when you were not present in my thoughts. Time and distance did nothing to lessen my feelings, and seeing you again has only confirmed what I have always known. I lost my heart that day in the rain and I've never managed to find it again.
Please know our three darling girls are living proof of that love.
Find your happiness, wherever it may be. My only wish.
Yours,
Lucien.

She didn't notice the feather-light touch on her shoulder. The hand small, tentative. The perfume subtle instead of Tomas's familiar woody-scented soap. A woman's touch and a woman's scent. The words when they finally came were a mere whisper.

'Flora.'

She raised her head, her cheeks wet. 'My dear.' Flora held her breath, more nervous than she'd ever been as Marguerette knelt by her side.

'I'd like to accompany you, if I may, when you leave. We should get to know one another.'

'I'd love that too.' Flora managed a laugh. 'But I may not be the safest of travelling companions...'

'Actually, that's a good idea, Marguerette,' Tomas interrupted, striding across the room. 'With Flora's face splashed across the newspapers, getting you out of Paris until the furore has died down is very sensible.' He turned to Flora. 'Remember Octave from the parachute drop? His family in Ancinnes will be more than happy to put Marguerette up too.'

FORTY

Saturday 19 December – Ancinnes, North West France,
10.30 pm

They made an unusual trio as they left the security of the train after their five-hour journey from Paris to Ancinnes.

They'd travelled in silence, sitting near to but not next to each other, their stories plotted beforehand, the train crowded with soldiers. Flora breezed through the checkpoints, the soldiers barely glancing at her borrowed ID Card.

The invisible breed.

'This way.' Tomas led them through the deserted turnstile, the sound of the train chugging away into the distance, a belch of smoke filling the air with the stench of charred coal.

Flora shrugged further into her dress, the thick folds doing little against the biting wind, the scar on her cheek starting to ache in the cold. She'd give anything for a hot drink.

'How are you doing, Marguerette?' she said, glancing across at her daughter. A dim figure in the pale moonlight, her expression impossible to see behind her veil. To want to help in any way she could only to know that offers in that direction would probably be refused was a lesson in motherhood she could do without.

'A little fatigued,' Marguerette finally admitted, stumbling on a loose stone and struggling to regain her balance.

'Here, let me.' Flora plucked her bag from her arm, surprised by the heavy weight.

'No, you can't!'

'I can and I will, Marguerette.'

Flora lifted her head in relief at the sight of a familiar-looking lorry pulling up outside the station. It felt like four years since she'd landed in the field on the outskirts of Paris and not four weeks. That the truck had no suspension and no seats in the back was immaterial. It was one step closer to the comfort of a warm bed and putting an end to the day she'd said her goodbyes to Lucien and met her daughter. She couldn't cope with much more.

'Octave. It's good to see you.'

'And you, Flora.' He stooped, pressing the lightest of kisses against each cheek. 'I hear you've had an interesting time in Paris.'

'You could say that,' she replied, reluctant to speak about it. 'This is my daughter, Marguerette.' She drew her forward, her hand across her back. 'Marguerette, this is Octave le...'

'Just Octave will do,' he said, moving towards the truck. 'You'll find pillows, blankets and hot coffee in the back. I'll try and avoid the larger of the potholes. Alors, it's impossible to avoid them all. There are more potholes than there are roads these days. Twenty minutes and we'll be home.'

Home was a sprawling conglomeration of farm buildings lying between the Forêt de Perseigne and the village of Ancinnes, not that Flora saw any of it. She could barely walk when she finally climbed out of the back of the truck, relying heavily on Tomas to help her. Marguerette was in a similar state, with Octave having to half lift her inside.

She made a rudimentary toilette, which consisted of removing her outer clothes, before collapsing onto the bed in her underwear, Marguerette following suit in the twin bed next to her. Then it was as if someone switched off the lights in the room and her mind simultaneously until a cockerel heralded the arrival of another dawn.

Flora waited another hour before speaking, watching the sun squeezing around the edge of the badly fitted blackout curtain in hues of grey and liquid gold. She'd finished two cigarettes and was considering the wisdom of a third before deciding against it. Smoking wouldn't help.

'How can you sleep with that infernal racket?'

Marguerette rolled onto her back, her arm resting against her eyes to block out the light. 'To you it's a racket. To me it's a sound I grew up with.'

Flora sat up, wrapping her arms around her knees, trying to work out what to say next and how to say it. 'I thought the Langs were musicians?'

'You know about the Langs?'

'Not much, only what your father told me. He believed them to be good people.'

'They were.' A few seconds of silence. 'The very best. I would have gone with them if I'd been allowed. The risk would have been worth it.'

Flora felt the lump in the back of her throat solidify. They'd got so much wrong, but not in choosing good people to care for their daughter. 'Has there been news?'

'No, but no news is good news, or so I've heard.'

Flora toyed with her packet of cigarettes briefly before holding them out. 'Fancy a smoke?'

'I don't. Not anymore.'

'And I smoke too much.' She placed the packet on the bedside table, her gaze drifting to the narrow space between the beds and the sight of Marguerette's arms. So thin. 'This surgery you had?'

'I'm fine now.'

Flora bit down hard on her lower lip. *So fine that you don't want to speak about it, at least not to me.*

'Have you decided on what you're going to do next?' She

climbed out of bed and started smoothing out the coverlet, her head turned until she'd managed to compose herself.

'Continue with the war effort and find my sister.' She rolled on her side. 'It was a mistake coming here. The sooner I can get back the sooner I'll be of use.'

'Sisters?'

'What?'

Flora dropped onto the edge of the bed, her words slow and deliberate. 'Sister Maria Clara told me shortly before the shooting that there was a third baby. Lili. Triplets.' She looked up from where she was twisting the coverlet through her fingers, waiting for the explosion.

Instead, there was a heartfelt sigh.

'Why didn't you tell me? Why didn't Lucien?'

'I'm telling you now, dear. And, as for Lucien... He probably didn't know how.'

'Where is she?'

'That's the thing, Marguerette. Somewhere in France living with her mother. Tomas is trying to trace the family through his contacts, and the church, but it's not that simple. It's my dearest wish for you to be reunited but...'

She opened her mouth to tell her about Reiner's part in all of this before changing her mind. There'd be time for that later.

'It's Christmas in a few days. Will you at least stay until then?'

FORTY-ONE

Octave was waiting for them at the bottom of the stairs.

'Bonjour, Flora and Marguerette. I was just about to come up and get you. Come and meet my mother. We keep to one room now. Impossible to heat the rest.'

Flora followed him, wrapping her shawl around her, the cold quarry stone floor piercing the thin soles of her boots. The house was freezing in comparison to Madame Billy's. Even the convent had felt warmer, the thick walls keeping the heat in.

'Breakfast was at six, but we've kept you back something,' he added, pushing the door open to a long narrow room with a window at one end.

Octave's mother was sitting at the table peeling straggly carrots, a half empty hessian bag propped up against the table leg, the smell of chicory filling the air. A handsome woman with grey hair and kindly eyes.

'Take a seat. We don't stand on ceremony.'

Flora glanced at Marguerette to see how she was faring, before slipping into the chair opposite.

'Thank you for putting us up at such short notice, Mrs...'

'Call me Annick,' she interrupted, her gaze trained on where Flora had wrapped her head in a scarf, turban style, in an attempt to disguise her hair. 'There's bread and honey. Thank goodness for our bees. No butter. We save our milk for the children. If there's any left over we make cheese.' She fetched a plate of bread from the counter already cut into thin slices along with a small dish of honey, closely followed by a coffee pot and two additional cups.

Flora remembered the basket of croissants served up by Mimi every morning along with a dish of yellow butter. There'd never been talk of rationing. She'd handed over her ration card and forgotten all about it. The same had gone for the lunches she'd had at Le Moulin Rouge. Now she regretted every tainted mouthful.

Some people were eating like kings, while the rest of the country starved.

She scraped a thin layer of honey on the bread before passing the pot to Marguerette, knowing she was over dramatising the situation. There was food enough on the table and no doubt there'd be something to accompany the carrots later. Paris was different. She'd been playing a part.

The thought didn't lesson her guilt.

She finished her bread, watching as Marguerette barely touched hers. The smallest of bites and every swallow a struggle. Instead of saying something that wouldn't be appreciated, she cradled her cup and turned to Annick.

'Is there anything I can do to help while I'm here? Cooking, sewing. I'm at a bit of a disadvantage without being able to use my ration card.' She picked up a spoon and stirred her coffee, tempted to add a little honey to the bitter liquid. 'Tomas has told you that I'm a wanted woman?'

Annick nodded in the direction of a pile of old newspapers heaped at the side of the stove. 'I think the whole of France must know by now but, if Tomas believes in your innocence, that's good enough for us. The police rarely come out this way so there's little risk. And as for helping out...' She abandoned the carrots in favour of her cup. 'Tomas tells me you're an expert seamstress?' She shrugged. 'The problem we have is rationing. Our clothing coupons are useless when the shelves are empty. If you can find a way of creating clothes out of thin air then…' She tapped the table with her fingertip. 'We meet here every afternoon. You're welcome to join us.'

'You should, Flora.' Marguerette turned to her, her plate pushed away. 'And it will give me the opportunity to catch up on my beauty sleep.'

The group consisted of Annick and her two daughters-in-law along with a couple of toddlers playing with a pile of wooden bricks on the floor, their clothes of the make do and mend variety. There'd been no questions asked about who she was or what she was doing there, which meant that Annick had been talking, but Flora didn't mind. It made it easier. Less to dredge up.

She was quickly ensconced at the table, her quilt on her lap, enthralled by the stories her new friends were sharing.

'Octave arrived home wearing a German helmet, boasting a bottle of their Riesling under one arm and a freshly roasted chicken under the other. It was lucky we buried the bones deep, otherwise their dogs would have found them.'

'What about the wine?' Flora asked, not knowing what to believe.

'Have you ever tasted German wine?' Annick asked, leaning forward, her mouth feigning a sneer. 'We each had a sip before pouring it down the sink, although it did a good job of removing the rust stain from the bottom.'

Flora laughed, aware that she was being teased. Wine and food were in such short supply that she couldn't imagine any going to waste, despite the label. She snipped off the last thread and shook out the quilt. Her fifth and last unless she was able to procure more fabric scraps from somewhere, which she knew was unlikely in rural France. She'd made five, it would have to be enough.

With the quilt folded, she glanced around to see how everyone else was faring. Annick was working on what looked to be a boy's jacket in an indeterminate shade of faded brown while the other two women were unravelling garments, grey wool corkscrewing around them as they ripped back the rows before forming them into skeins, a pattern and knitting needles set out neatly in the middle.

'What are you up to?'

'Trying to kit these little darlings in clothes that will fit them.' Annick nodded at the jacket. 'And in between we recycle woollens to knit up for our countrymen. Hats, gloves, scarves. Whatever we can. It's cold in the camps.'

Her words were matter-of-fact, her head bent as she worked on pinning the edges of the new seam together. An everyday event of friends and family gathered around a table except that there was nothing everyday about their conversation.

Flora concentrated on the piece of paper set between the women. A pattern or so she'd thought.

Lines and dots instead of rows of knit and purl.

She smiled, suddenly feeling very much at home.

There was no fabric to work with. Instead, she'd learn to knit in code.

FORTY-TWO

'So, what's the plan, Tomas?'

'I'm not sure I follow?'

Flora glanced at him briefly before turning her attention to the uneven ground, careful where she placed her feet. The countryside was such a relief after Paris, a strange observation when Paris had always felt like home. But Paris was worry and loss. Here the only thing to worry her, outside of her daughters, was the surplus of cow pats and the insomniac cockerel whose piercing cock-a-doodle-doo was loud enough to wake the dead in the next parish, let alone this one. She could quite happily stay here, but she couldn't continue living with Octave's parents, relying on their kindness. Taking advantage of their food. She'd gladly knit with whatever wools she could find for the troops, but she also needed work. Something to pay the bills.

Looking at the cerulean sky and ocean of green fields in the distance, she needed to know where she fit into things. Marguerette would leave. She was already talking about it. What then?

'Then I'll put it another way.' She turned, lifting her face to the slight warmth from the weak, winter sun. 'I can't stay here. It's not fair on Octave and it's not fair on you.'

He stepped back, his expression one of panic. 'Why unfair on me?'

She flashed him a look, noticing that he was in need of a haircut. There was more grey in his hair too. Was that her doing? She liked the way he looked. The way he wore his hair. The way he shrugged into his jacket, before wrapping his scarf around his neck. She'd liked him from the first day, her heart doing that little flip when she'd stopped criticising his tailoring and concentrated on the man inside. Not that she'd let on. That would never do. She'd known he'd liked her during the drive back from the inn, but too much had happened between them to ever make that feel right.

'Because you're a bachelor and I'm a divorcee who's wanted by the police for murder. Octave is charming, as are his parents. It's lovely of them putting us up but I'm the scarlet woman in all of this.'

'Ha.' He lifted his head, chortling. 'No one who knew you would ever label you that and it's not as if I'm staying at the farm. I have a perfectly serviceable cottage of my own only a short walk from here. You and Marguerette must visit. In fact, I insist.'

'I'm not sure I can. I have a scarf to finish.'

'Hah. Annick has roped you in then? I thought she would. What are you working on?'

She tapped the side of her nose, her eyes alight with hidden laughter. 'Something top secret, on-a-need-to-know basis. I couldn't possibly divulge what.'

'You could always bring it with you?' He smiled down at her. 'I'm happy to help with a bit of code and a walk in the fresh air is just what Marguerette needs.'

She rested her hand on his arm, her expression faltering. 'You would tell me if it's bad? I know I have no rights as far as she's concerned, but I love her so very dearly.'

He covered her hand in his, looking as serious as she'd ever seen him. 'The honest truth is I don't know, but I think so. Bad enough for her to give up her job at Le Moulin Rouge, or that's what Madame Billy told me. She can't sing, Flora, when singing was her life.'

Flora stared at him, seeing his anguish and knowing it to be true. It wasn't something she'd even considered.

My poor dear girl.

The cottage was charming. Stone-built with faded, blue shutters and a black cat sitting on the top step.

'Come in. Welcome to my home.' He turned the handle, gesturing them through. 'No one locks their doors here. Long may it continue.'

Inside was sparsely furnished with a worn sofa and mismatched chairs and a table under the window. It was also warm, the fire banked up with logs.

'The kitchen's through there. Haven't got around to doing much with it yet.'

Flora slipped off her coat and removed her hat, patting her hair back in place. 'You've been far too busy.' What it lacked was a woman's touch, but she wasn't going to tell him that.

'I'll make the coffee while you have a wander. Two bedrooms upstairs in the eaves and a small bathroom downstairs on the other side of the kitchen.' He swept up their coats. 'Chicory do?'

Flora smiled sweetly. 'Perfect. Thank you.'

She followed Marguerette up the steep stairs, her hand on the banister, her eyes on her daughter's stick-thin ankles, which up to now had been concealed by the length of her skirt. So thin. Too thin. Was she even eating? Could she with the scarring on her neck?

There's no way you can ask.

The bedrooms were small, the countryside view out of the window stretching for miles in the distance.

'I could live here.'

'You should.'

Flora hadn't realised she'd spoken out loud until Marguerette replied. She watched as she dropped on the edge of the bed before resting back against the pillow, her feet dangling over the edge.

'I don't think...'

'Why not, Flora? Tomas is a good man and it's easy to see he cares. Good men are hard to come by. Lucien would have been the first to say that. He said it to me. If the right man comes along, grab onto him tight. His exact words, although who'd marry me. Not now.'

'You must know how beautiful you are.'

'You were always going to say that, seeing as we could be twins.'

'With this?' She fingered the scar on her cheek briefly. Mostly she forgot it was there until something or someone's startled expression reminded her.

'It's not that bad and your hair will grow, although wearing a turban suits you. Gives you a glamorous air.'

'If you say so.'

'Tomas loves you for yourself, Flora.'

Does he?

Flora stared out of the window, tracking the clouds scudding across the sky now the wind had picked up. Turning, she said, 'And what about you, Marguerette? The resistance?' She wanted to wrap her in the biggest hug, but it wasn't the right time. Their relationship hadn't progressed to that stage.

'All I'm good for is to pass on a few messages. Keep my eyes and ears open when it's required. At least I'll be doing something,' she said, only half managing to stifle a yawn.

She didn't mention her voice and Flora didn't press her.

'Why don't you have a nap? Tomas will understand.'

Back in the lounge, Tomas had set the table and included a baguette and a pot of honey, causing her to smile.

'Marguerette is having a nap. I said you wouldn't mind.'

'Of course not. Poor Marguerette. The last few weeks have been a trial for her, but she's young enough to bounce back.'

'I hope you're right.'

'I'm sure I am.'

'So, what are your plans now you're not travelling?'

'Still plenty I can do here.'

'Like blowing up a few bridges?'

His eyes twinkled. 'Well, now that you mention it. I might also take up knitting.'

'Can you knit, Tomas?'

'I'm sure if you were to teach me.'

She ignored that, instead waving her hand around the room. 'So, this will be home.'

'I know. It's not much but.'

'On the contrary, I think it's lovely. Perfect even. The only thing it needs is a...'

'Wife?' he replied.

She laughed. 'I was going to suggest a vase with a few bits of winter foliage along with a cat, but you already have one of those.'

'Which a wife could see to.'

'Tomas, I'm not sure that I'm the person you should be talking to.'

'Who else? You're the woman I love.'

She paused briefly, a smile blooming. One she squashed back down. 'But I'm tainted.'

'Tainted. A scarlet woman, a divorcee.' He counted them off on his fingers. 'Any more excuses you can think of as to why we can't be together? I know you like me and I certainly like you. I like you a lot. I would have shown you exactly how much if we hadn't been interrupted back at...'

'That's not the point.' She picked up her cup for something to do with her hands. There was always her knitting poking out the top of her bag, but somehow she didn't think he'd approve. 'It's too much too soon after Lucien and there's still Lili to consider. I need to find her. I must.'

He turned her to face him, his hands cradling her head, careful to avoid the scar. 'I know you must, darling girl, just as I know about the promise you made to Lucien, but what about you, Flora? What about us? What about the promise you could make to me? Marry me?' He dropped his head, planting the softest of kisses against her hesitant mouth.

'I can't. We can't. We hardly know each other.' She pulled away and he let her, dropping his arms to his side.

'I think we know each other more than most people do, Flora. We've even spent the night together, two if you count the trip over on the Halifax. How many couples can say that, or that they've jumped out of a plane together?'

She turned away, her gaze on the fireplace, where the logs were crackling and spitting sparks like diamonds. She could be happy here in the same country as her daughters, but she wouldn't marry him for location or convenience. That wouldn't be fair on either of them. And there was Lucien to consider.

She followed a log as it shifted, the bottom black and flaking into a thousand pieces of grey ash. Love was such a sneaky, complex emotion. It crept up on you unawares. A bit like sea water. Dipping your toe in and then your ankles. Before you knew it, you were out of your depth without a lifebelt in sight. She hadn't been in love with Lucien. Her infatuation had died almost as suddenly as it had started, but there had been so much to admire in him second-time-round that her hatred had turned to something akin to love. There was also the promise she'd made to him and that she was determined to honour.

And then there was Tomas. He was right in everything he said, including what had nearly happened outside of Lucien's office at Maison Lumineau. If they hadn't been interrupted...

So many ifs and buts, but she was weakening. It was there in the way she leant towards him, resting her head against his shoulder. She wouldn't marry him for convenience or for any of the other sensible reasons like hiding behind the security of his name.

But she could marry him for love.

She took his hand in hers, noticing the way he sighed right down to his bones, his eyes closed against what might be coming. A man who didn't see the scar or the shorn hair. A man who only saw her.

Dear Tomas. For better or worse, and they already knew what worse looked like. They had as good a chance as any other couple of making a go of it.

Looking back at the flames lashing against the dull brickwork, she turned her thoughts to the practicalities of marriage, or at least the wedding.

'I'll need a dress.'

There was a second's pause, just the one before he swung her off her feet, his head buried in her neck, his arms wrapped around her waist.

'You can have all the dresses I can find, my darling.'

She laughed, lifting her hand to his face in amazement at what she'd agreed to. 'Not just any dress.' She glanced towards the window and the fields beyond stretched out in a canopy of browns and greens. 'I'll make it myself. If only I can remember where I buried that parachute.'

FORTY-THREE

'I'd never have thought you could make a dress out of that. You're sure you'll have enough fabric?' Marguerette arched her eyebrow at the metres of parachute silk billowing off the edge of the table.

'More than enough,' Flora replied, reaching across and patting her arm. That her daughter was with her while she made the dress was like something out of a dream. She'd expected recriminations when she'd finally plucked up the courage to tell her and all she'd got was *About time. Anyone can see that you're made for each other.* After the pressures of recent weeks, Ancinnes was like stepping into another land. With only the occasional soldier passing through, it was easy to forget that she was still a wanted woman.

She'd commandeered Octave's parents' dining room almost as soon as the dishes from their Christmas dinner had been washed and put away. Octave's mother couldn't have been more helpful. She lent her a sewing machine and anything else she didn't have in her sewing kit. There was even a pencil and paper. Flora wasn't an artist, but she didn't need to be. She had a good eye and a good memory. Essential for her wedding dress.

'So, what's your plan then?'

Picking up the pencil, she hesitated briefly before sweeping the tip over the paper.

The final dress was a bit wonky, more than a bit, but it was the best she could do with Marguerette watching. She'd had a strong inkling at the time that Lucien's drawing in his study had been intended for her, but it wasn't a secret she intended to share. That Marguerette recognised his style was immediately apparent from the shocked silence that followed.

'It's absolutely perfect.' She picked up the sketch, running her finger over the lines and curves, her face softening into the hint of a smile. 'Papa really was that good at dress designing.'

Flora swallowed the sudden lump in her throat before coughing briefly.

She called you papa, Lucien.

'Your father was the best designer in Paris, quite possibly the world,' she said, busying herself with straightening the silk.

With a piece of chalk in one hand and the ruler in the other, she swiftly transferred the drawing onto the fabric. Front and back pieces for the bodice, including seam allowance and darts for shaping and four pieces for the skirt, all tailored to her unique body measurements, which hadn't changed in years. After, she swivelled the fabric around and worked on the facings before standing back and stretching, her hand pressed into her back.

'And it looks like you're as good with pattern making.'

Flora couldn't hide her smile of delight. 'Well, it's not that diff—'

'I beg to differ, Flora,' Marguerette interrupted, plucking at her A-line skirt. 'You forget that I make my own clothes, but not like this. You must have made a formidable team back in the day.'

'I was very junior when I worked at Maison Lumineau but I like to think that I knew where Lucien was going with his designs. The flair was all his though.' Flora waved a hand at the fabric. 'I would never have come up with this on my own.' She picked up the scissors and, with her heart in her mouth, started cutting the fabric. There could be no mistakes.

With the pieces lined up on the table and the rest of the fabric cast to one side, she sat on one of the chairs and started threading a needle.

'You're not going to pin it first? I was always taught to pin before tacking.' Marguerette sounded horrified as Flora started work on tacking the darts.

'I would normally, but I'd need silk pins for that.' She shrugged. 'I'm lucky to have found everything I need in Octave's mother's work basket including pins galore, but too thick for the fabric. Unsightly holes would ruin the look.'

'So, no mistakes?'

'I hope not.' Cutting the thread, Flora picked up the next piece. 'And anyway, I don't agree that you're not as talented. I've seen some of your crochet.' She glanced up briefly, catching her look of surprise. 'Coralina showed me. I could never make anything that intricate.'

Marguerette blushed, adding a much-needed colour to her pale cheeks. 'Time and patience, Flora. Working at the dance hall means long spells in cold corridors waiting my turn.'

'And it shows, ma chérie. I can honestly say that I've never seen finer crochet and Paris knows a thing or two about textiles. Lucien used to frequently commission pieces to insert into his designs, but nothing like your work.'

'Thank you.' Marguerette smiled and changed the subject. 'Have you thought about what you're going to wear on your head?'

Flora glanced at her before rethreading the needle and picking up the pieces of the skirt.

Marguerette avoided talking about herself. It was always the same. As soon as the conversation got personal, she shut it down and shut Flora out. It had hurt the first time it had happened until she remembered that it had taken Lucien a few attempts to reach her. He'd written about her bitterness in his diary. It was something she'd witnessed for herself but was helpless to know how to address. She knew Marguerette was softening towards her. She would have to be content with what her daughter was prepared to give.

'I haven't got that far. It's a bit of a problem, isn't it? Not a veil. Nothing to secure it to even if I had the fabric.' Flora sighed. Every woman wanted to look their best on their wedding day, even if it was second-time-round. It was a shame about her face and her hair. While her scar was continuing to heal, it was her hair that posed the biggest problem.

'What about a wide-brimmed hat? One of those floppy ones?' Marguerette said, picking up the discarded silk and running it through her fingers. 'I might be able to work some kind of embellishment out of thin strips of silk. The only problem would be in stiffening the fabric. It wouldn't hold shape as it stands.'

Flora sat back in her chair, a broad smile breaking, although she decided to hold back on the praise. It was obviously something Marguerette struggled with. 'I can tell you're not a milliner or a cook. Nevertheless, you've got yourself a hat-making job. You supply the talent, and I'll supply the fabric and the sheets of gelatine. Annick is bound to have some in the kitchen. She's fond of her jellies.'

FORTY-FOUR

Saturday 9 January – Pervenche Cottage, Ancinnes, 2 pm

The cold December morphed into one of the coldest Januarys on record with icicles at the windows and extra blankets on their beds.

Flora slipped into her wedding dress, bemoaning that she hadn't bothered with sleeves. Bare arms were for summer weddings, not ones with the sky tinged yellow, the threat of heavy snowfall on the horizon. That she wouldn't have had the heart to alter what might have been Lucien's last design was irrelevant.

Blinking, she pressed her hand under her nose, her handkerchief already tucked inside the little silk bag that Marguerette had sewn to match the amazing hat. She could always wrap a blanket over her shoulders during the ceremony if she was desperate.

'You alright, Flora?'

'I'm fine.' She twisted slightly, trying to see where Marguerette was fastening the buttons. 'How many left?'

'Only a couple. You did an excellent job covering them.'

'Thank you.'

She couldn't believe that she'd be married in an hour. That they were getting married at all was a surprise. An impossible event under normal circumstances, unless the mairie of Ancinnes also happened to be a close friend of Tomas's. Having grown up in the village, he seemed to know everyone. Documents that were meant to be lodged months before turned up in the bottom of the pile, while the banns had been waived. With Flora's name still in the newspapers, it was deemed prudent to omit it appearing on the noticeboard of the town hall for anyone and everyone to see.

It was also the reason that there were to be no guests. Only Marguerette, Octave, Annick and her husband as witnesses to the civil ceremony.

Flora stood in front of the mirror, smoothing her hand over the perfect silk dress and thinking of Lucien, when she should be thinking of Tomas.

If she hadn't guessed that Lucien had designed the gown for her then, she knew now. She'd never felt more beautiful, despite her face and her hair. But the dress made everything else insignificant. The scar would heal, and her hair would grow, but she'd never again be a bride wearing Lucien's gown.

'Ready?'

She closed her eyes briefly, trying to capture the memory. 'I think so.'

'Don't forget your hat.'

Flora twirled the stylish headpiece through her fingers, admiring the hours of work that had resulted in the most gorgeous trifle. The design was simple enough. A circle surrounded by a floppy brim. It was the crocheted silk flowers that added the touch of genius.

'Just like your papa.' The words slipped out before she could contain them.

The room fell silent.

Flora regretted that she'd had to go and ruin it, and they'd been getting on so well. Not like mother and daughter. More like friends.

'I think more like maman,' Marguerette replied. 'I can't see that Lucien was into floppy hats.'

•   •   •

'Hey. Why the tears? I thought brides were meant to cry after the wedding.'

'Brides can cry whenever they want,' she managed, giving Tomas a wan smile as she negotiated the final step.

Tomas pressed a kiss against her cheeks, careful not to dislodge the hat. 'You're stunning. Take my breath.'

'I had help. The hat...'

'Is perfect.' He stepped back, drawing Marguerette into the conversation with a kiss. 'Bonjour, Marguerette. You look charming.'

Marguerette touched the silk flower pinned to her dress that she'd made to complement the hat, a slight blush staining her cheeks.

'Now, no more tears or I'll have to... get a bigger handkerchief.' He grinned, escorting them outside to the waiting horse and trap.

'Pablo!' Marguerette saw him first, racing across the drive to fling herself at him.

'Well now. What a welcome. I couldn't not be here for this. Lucien would never have forgiven me.'

'How? Why? The risks.' Flora was delighted and worried in equal measure. She already knew that Pablo was under the watchful eye of the ever suspicious enemy, distrustful of anyone who wasn't German. The only thing stopping his arrest was his fame.

He waved her words away with a flick of his hand. 'I have a Nazi sculpture acquaintance who is keen to think that I'm his friend. It couldn't be further from the truth, but the man is useful on occasion. Enough of that.' He stepped back, his eyes wide as he examined her outfit. 'I can honestly say I've never seen such a beautiful bride. The... gown and hat are sublime.'

Flora smiled back as she slipped her arms into her boring jacket, thankful that he hadn't mentioned the designer. He easily could have. That he knew was enough.

The journey to the church was uneventful, as was the ceremony. A twenty-minute journey followed by a five-minute ceremony, where the signing of the register was meant to be the most important part. Flora would have felt cheated, but it wasn't about the ceremony. She had Tomas and she had one of her daughters by her side. She'd make that enough.

After a light lunch back at the farm, they returned to Tomas's cottage in the village.

Flora's new home.

'Champagne, I think.' Pablo busied himself with carrying in a succession of boxes from the car. There were enough bottles to belie that there was a war on. 'I know a few people. Called in a few favours.'

'You certainly did. I can't remember when I've seen so many bottles.' Flora had succumbed to adding a cardigan to her dress, her feet tucked into her slippers as she sipped on her champagne, Tomas sitting beside her, Marguerette and Pablo opposite. 'How is it in Paris?'

'I'm afraid not as good as it could be.' Pablo placed his cigar on the edge of the ashtray and loosened his tie. 'Your photograph is still in the papers most days, which makes me suspect Sabine and that Nazi boyfriend of hers have something to do with it.'

Flora's grip on her glass tightened briefly, the image of Sabine the last time she'd seen her making her hand shake. 'She hates me.'

'You're right, of course.' Pablo picked up his cigar from the ashtray. 'You had the one thing she didn't. Lucien's love.'

'And she has mine now. All this serious talk. It's meant to be a wedding. Anyone for a top up?' Tomas held the champagne bottle aloft.

'I shouldn't if I want to make Chartres by curfew, but I will.' Pablo held out his glass. 'Thank you, Tomas, and my sincerest apologies on your wedding day, but Sabine has been on my mind since last week. In fact, ever since my bank contacted me.'

Flora waited until Tomas sat down beside her. Tucking his hand in hers, she turned back to Pablo. 'What has Sabine got to do with your bank?'

'Nothing except that it's not just my bank. It's also where

Lucien had his safety deposit box.' He shook his head sadly. 'All my fault, I'm afraid. He entrusted me with helping him find a safe place in which to conceal your inheritance from Sabine's greedy clutches.'

'It's not your fault, Pablo,' Marguerette said, her voice soft. 'You're not to blame and anyway, the inheritance doesn't matter. That Lucien thought to leave us something is more than enough.'

'Hold on.' Tomas glanced at Marguerette briefly before turning to Pablo. 'I don't understand. Why would your bank contact you about Lucien's safety deposit box? Surely, it's nothing to do with you?'

'In the normal run of events, no.' Pablo stubbed out his cigar and picked up his glass, twirling the stem through his fingers. 'Safety deposit boxes are sacrosanct, the only people allowed to open them are the owner and their nominees. Unless you're dating someone high up in the German command, like, for instance Sabine,' he qualified, his expression souring in spite of the quality of the champagne label. 'I've heard on the grapevine that she was incandescent with rage when she couldn't find what she was looking for after Lucien's death. It didn't take long for her to discover about the box, or that I was with him when he set it up.' He placed his glass back on the table in favour of a triangle of cheese, a distinct gleam in his eye. 'When Sabine and Otto finally descended on the bank, along with a few of his Nazi henchmen for backup, unfortunately they found the box completely empty.'

'What!'

'I know, Flora. I'm as puzzled as the bank.' Pablo finished the cheese and started on a slice of baguette, his lips twitching into a smile. 'The bank have conducted a full-scale search for the envelope in question. It's a complete mystery.'

He brushed his hands together before pushing away from the table. 'Now, my dears, I have a little present for you and Marguerette, and Violette and Lili too. Don't get too excited, it's only something small. In fact, envelope-shaped.'

FORTY-FIVE

They huddled in the doorway to say goodbye to Pablo, the chill of the evening flooding the cottage, but Flora didn't mind that. It felt on some level that, with Pablo leaving, she was breaking her last ties with Paris, which wasn't as ridiculous as it seemed. With Otto still after her and suspicious of Tomas, their time in the city had come to an end until they won the war.

She wouldn't countenance any other outcome.

'You're sure you can't stay the night? We're happy to put you up.'

'Tut tut. On your wedding night, Flora.' Pablo drew her into a deep hug before kissing her cheeks. 'Remember, you always know where to find me, ma chérie. A friend of Lucien's is always going to be a friend of mine. Tomas, thank you for the hospitality.' He offered his hand before pulling him into a brief hug too. 'You're a very lucky man, my friend, but I'm sure you know that.'

Tomas draped his arm around Flora's shoulder. 'I certainly do. I hope you have a safe trip and the snow holds off.' They glanced up at the yellow sky, which had been hanging over them all day. 'And thank you for agreeing to walk Marguerette back to the farm.'

'A pleasure, as always. Come on, Marguerette, let's see if we can't beat the snow.'

Marguerette pressed a kiss against Tomas's smooth cheek. 'Look after her or you'll have me to deal with.'

Tomas smiled. 'Noted.'

'And the same goes for you, Flora.' Marguerette looked at her for a second before pulling her into a deep hug.

Their first hug, since their last one eighteen years previously.

Their bedroom was tucked under the eaves, the ceiling sloping on both sides over the bed, the chimney breast on the end wall. The bed was an old, wrought-iron bedstead, with a pretty patchwork coverlet smoothed over the top.

Flora placed her bag on the side and pulled out her nightdress, loving that Tomas had made room in the wardrobe and the chest of drawers for her few clothes. Walking over to the window, she stared at the blackout blind, keen to see the view out of the window. The way the temperature was dropping, there was a good chance that her next glimpse would be a snow-filled one.

The wedding dress was far more difficult to remove without Marguerette's help with the buttons. With her arms stretched over her shoulders, she finally managed to undo the top few before wriggling out of the garment, catching it before it pooled on the floor. Folding it gently, she placed it in the bottom of the chest of drawers, adding the hat on top and pushing it closed with a sharp snap.

All that work for something she'd never wear again, but it had been worth it. Every snip and stitch. A permanent record of the best day of her life, in the hope that there would be many more to follow.

The knock came out of nowhere.

'Ready?'

Flora hastily slipped her nightdress over her head, missing the weight of her hair on her neck, missing the warmth of the turban. Missing the confidence it gave.

'Ready.'

Tomas edged into the room, a bottle of champagne wedged

under his arm and a couple of glasses in his hand. 'I thought we could have a party of our own.'

Flora was glad that her nightdress was Edwardian in style unlike the undergarments she'd been asked to rustle up by some of her more adventurous brides. Slipping into bed, she was assured that the only parts of her visible were her head, neck and hands. She wouldn't admit to nerves, but she was feeling a little apprehensive. It had been a very long time since she'd shared a bed with a man that wasn't either her husband or in a drug-induced coma. She'd felt beautiful in Lucien's gown. Now all she could think about was her scar and her hair.

If Tomas noticed he didn't say. Instead, he busied himself with popping the cork and catching the fountain of champagne tumbling over the edge, much to Flora's amusement.

'Call yourself a wine merchant.'

'There's a big difference between a wine merchant and a sommelier, Flora.' He handed her a glass, his hand raised in toast, his soft gaze locked with hers.

'To my darling wife.'

FORTY-SIX

Friday 15 January 12.10 pm

Flora stood beside Tomas and Marguerette on the platform, her heart starting to ache. She'd always known she'd have to let Marguerette go before she was ready. The truth was she'd never be ready, not after losing the first eighteen years of her life. But this felt different. What if this time she lost her for good? Pablo had said the Germans and the police were still looking for her. Marguerette would be a stepping stone they wouldn't leave unturned. The horror stories of other broken lives and hearts flooded her mind. Loved ones who'd disappeared, never to be heard of again, but she was powerless. Marguerette was determined and there was nothing Flora could do or say to change that.

She reached for Tomas's hand, her eyes gritty from tears she refused to shed. 'You're sure you'll be alright?'

'I'll be fine. And you'll be fine too, Flora.' Marguerette tugged gently on her scarf, arranging it round her neck. 'Tomas is a good man. I'm sure Lucien would have approved. All he ever wanted was our happiness.'

Flora watched as their breath mingled in the cold air before turning to smoke, knowing it to be true. Poor Lucien. He'd made mistakes, they both had, but he hadn't deserved what had happened to him.

'Can I ask where you're going to stay?' she asked gently. 'I'd like to write.'

'I'd like that too, Flora. Madame Billy and Edith will find somewhere for me between them. Maybe back in my old room. Your old room too now.' The sound of her soft laughter rang out.

'There's this little sparrow who I've been feeding in your absence, Marguerette. He's quite partial to the end of my croissant.' Flora managed a smile, remembering the little sparrow. Remembering dear Edith.

'Darling maman. I should have known.' Marguerette pulled her into a deep hug, the warmth of her breath fanning her cheeks as she whispered in her ear. 'I also intend to find my sisters. They deserve to know the truth. There can't be that many Lili Reiners in France and I have my friends at Madame Billy's and Le Moulin Rouge to help me. We'll cast the net far and wide.'

'Marguerette, I…'

The train stopped with a screech, whipping her words away. The platform was suddenly filled with the sound of doors opening and slamming shut.

Flora froze. There was so much she wanted to say, but it was too late.

Marguerette tightened their hug briefly before moving across to Tomas and pressing a kiss on his cheeks, her face flushed.

'I must go. Love you, Maman, and you, Tomas.'

'I love you, Marguerette,' Flora whispered, her voice catching in her throat.

She watched as Marguerette boarded the train and settled in her seat, her hand lifted in a wave, and she continued watching, tears streaking her face as the train disappeared into the distance. She was unable to move, her gaze fixed on the end of the track and the plume of grey smoke slowly dispersing into the sky.

'Come on, darling. Time to go home.' Tomas took her hand and clasped it tightly.

They turned and slowly began walking to the waiting truck.

A LETTER FROM THE AUTHOR

Thank you for picking up a copy of *The Secret Dressmaker*.

If you'd like to join other readers in being the first to know about all future books I write, just click the link below for my email newsletter. I'd be delighted if you choose to sign up.

www.stormpublishing.co/jenny-obrien

I hope that you have enjoyed *The Secret Dressmaker* and if so, I would appreciate a review.

This is my first book where I managed to follow an outline, necessary as there are still Flora's daughters' stories to tell, but the plot still ran away with me. Lucien, a minor figure, quickly dominated to the extent that I realised I had to give him his own voice.

Towards the back, you'll find the *what's true and what's not* section. A detailed account of what inspired me to write *The Secret Dressmaker* and how the story developed, which also includes a playlist.

Thank you,

Jenny.

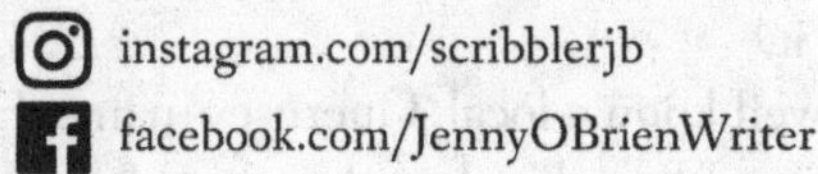

WHAT'S TRUE AND WHAT'S NOT

I'm not sure where to start with this. I've been embroiled with the Lumineaus and Paris since I first started work on *The Resistance Knitting Club* nearly two years ago.

For me a story needs an in, or a starting point if you like. A firing gun in my mind to send me on my way. For *The Secret Dressmaker* it was SOE operative Brian Stonehouse, MBE, even though he doesn't feature.

I happened upon the life and times of Stonehouse purely by accident when I decided to trawl through the list of SOE agents. Many of these heroes' lives have been well-catalogued and written about, but Torquay-born Brian Julian Warry Stonehouse piqued my interest solely because of one of his middle names. Warry. Mostly articles about him don't mention it but I was down a research rabbit hole by then. There was a book about him. I decided to read it.

Warry is a well-known local 'Guernsey' name. For those of you new to my writing, I have lived on the island for nearly forty years now. While Stonehouse wasn't born here, his mother was. His father moved his young family to France, where he became fluent and the reason for being picked as a special agent. This alone wouldn't have led me to writing the book. It was the fact that he was also an insanely talented fashion artist, published in the likes of *Vogue*. I drew hugely from his paintings when I was creating Lucien's talent with a piece of charcoal. Thank you, Brian Julian Warry Stonehouse.

Keeping on the fashion theme, Paul Poiret was a Parisian groundbreaking couturier at the start of the twentieth century. He had fallen out of fashion by 1942, dying in poverty in 1944. The fashion designer Elsa Schiaparell paid for his funeral. I have modelled Lucien on him in part, as well as on Madeleine Vionnet, but mainly in the designs they created.

Carrickfergus, Co Antrim, was heavily involved in WW2, serving as a base for US troops. It was also the temporary location for a Harland and Woolff tank factory. My story picks up the threads of its long history of spinning and cloth manufacture, which stretches back to the 1800s. During the war, the local mill was used for silk spinning and the manufacture of parachutes.

There are plenty of true-life stories about parachute wedding dresses, although usually the silks were recycled at the time for further chutes. Making a wedding dress from parachute fabric during the war would have been unusual, but it suited the storyline so...

Dobbins Inn still exists in Carrickfergus. Its origins can be traced back to the 1200s, and it might well be the oldest inn in Ulster. It has a fascinating history, which can be found in the *about* section of its website, and includes the ghostly tale of Maude and Buttoncap. During the war it had been split into two townhouses, only reconverted back to an inn shortly afterwards. That's where poetic licence comes in. The ghostly links to Carrickfergus Castle sold it for me. It currently has a beer garden.

Boneybefore is only a mile from Carrickfergus. It's also the ancestorial home of Andrew Jackson, the seventh US president. Much of Carrickfergus's coast has been redeveloped. It was here in Boneybefore, pronounced Bonnybefore, that I found the traditional thatched cottage I wanted for Flora's home.

I read about Edith Piaf staying at Madame Billy's early on.

Much is written about Piaf, but not so very much about her stay at the brothel, certainly not in translated biographies, with only a few notable exceptions. As with all my historical fiction novels, I drew on primary eyewitness testimonies instead of biographies, unless autobiographical accounts weren't available. There are also many contradictions between biographers for this French national hero. While this book isn't about Piaf and the scenes with Flora are fictitious, everything else is based on fact. For instance, it's a well-known fact that Piaf was a passionate knitter. She used to always knit her boyfriend of the day a jumper but rarely finished it. Piaf was only twenty-six when she went to live in one of the three rented rooms on the top floor of Madame Billy's in the winter of 1942 – the establishment was renowned for its warmth and Piaf suffered from the cold. It was here that she played the piano late into the night, often necessitating a visit by the authorities. It's also reported that she wasn't the tidiest of individuals. At Madame Billy's she resided with her cousin, but I haven't included that here. Edith's Piaf's hair caused some research. Brown, black or red. Impossible to tell with the black and white images available at the time. I finally decided on the rust red mentioned in an article by AJ Liebling, published in the *New Yorker*, November 8, 1947. The Parisian sparrows are well known – a little foreshadowing for this acclaimed Little Sparrow.

Madame Billy, or Aline Soccodato, ran L'Etoile de Kleber, a brothel situated along Rue de Villejust. This road was renamed after the war to Rue Paul Valery. (As an aside, Valery was an acclaimed poet, essayist and philosopher, and nominated for the Nobel prize for literature no less than twelve times.) Madame Billy employed a Chinese chef, hence my idea for the oriental garden. I read that L'Etoile de Kleber was meant to have a luxurious garden – from what I can make out from the images available, it's not there now. It's also recorded that Madame Billy, who acted like a headmistress in her own home, used to spend her days knitting. Her physical description is drawn from the only image of her that I could find.

The Café de Palmier on the Place Blanche, directly opposite Le Moulin Rouge, is long gone. All I had was a mention in an out-of-print book and an old photograph.

The Café de la Rotonde, on the other hand, exists and is thriving. In the early days it was a meeting place for the likes of Picasso, Matisse and Hemingway. The story about the owner, Victor Libion, accepting sketches and paintings, often drawn on napkins from artists as collateral until they could meet their bar bill, is true, as is the fact that some customers settled the artist's bill and earned the artwork. It was in the café somewhere between 1911 and 1920 that Picasso would have rubbed shoulders with the likes of Lucien Lumineau, although the latter is fictitious.

Picasso was in Paris during the war. He was photographed by Lee Miller in 1944, which influenced what he was wearing in the book. His inclusion came by accident when I was searching for a Left Bank café that was open in the 1940's and is still open today. Café de la Rotonde. As a Spanish national living in France, he was of great interest to the occupiers and therefore I think it unlikely he would have travelled outside of Paris, for instance, to attend a wedding in Ancinnes. I particularly wanted to include Ancinnes as this was a site for Special Operations Executive (SOE) parachute drops, albeit later in the war. On the flip side, Picasso was acquainted with the German sculpture Arno Breker before the war. According to Breker's memoirs, he smoothed Picasso's time in occupied France. This might have included the odd foray outside of Paris. Who knows.

The Nazis were interested in art, particularly removing it to Germany. It's estimated that over 21,000 pieces of art from artists such as Rembrandt, Vermeer and Gainsborough were looted by the Reich. Picasso and Matisse took over the three vaults at the National Bank for Trade and Industry to secure their collections, containing both their artwork and the art of others. Matisse had already left Paris when two German soldiers demanded access to the bank vaults and it was here that Picasso managed to convince them that the artwork inside was worthless.

It is this period that I tapped into for the painting, *The Weeping Woman*.

The Weeping Woman, *La Femme qui Pleure*, is a series of oils on canvas featuring Picasso's partner and muse, Dora Maar. He painted them in 1937 as a statement to the bombing of Guernica in the Spanish Civil War. What interested me is that there are three paintings, as well as numerous preliminary sketches and watercolours. My version of *The Weeping Woman* draws on poetic licence. It's an undiscovered and uncatalogued fourth painting (in other words, fictitious).

When I wanted to include a German nun working undercover in France, I looked to the history books to see if there were any records I could draw from. I didn't have to look very far to find Sister Cläre Barwitzky. Sister Cläre was fluent in French and cared for thirty Jewish refugee children only a stone's throw away from the enemy. Everything else about Sister Maria Clara is fictitious apart from her forenames. See the acknowledgements page for more.

Do nun's habits have pockets? Some do. Some even have secret pockets but some don't. My fictitious order of Sainte-Marthe-des-Anges doesn't.

Triplets. Initially this book was going to be about twins. As a mother to twins, I do tend to write about them, but the idea for Lili cropped up early and it was impossible for me not to run with it. Going back to the drawing board, I researched the likelihood of triplets surviving in the 1920s and quickly discovered numerous references. Elisabeth Kübler, one of a set of triplets, was born in Switzerland in 1926. Interestingly, her and her sister were identical like Marguerette and Lili – and where the idea came from.

Le Moulin Rouge. This was the most difficult part to write about. While much has been written about the dance hall, there seems to be a blanket over information during the war years. I did contact their press officer – I'm still waiting for a reply. The information included is based on true-life accounts, some of which are included below, apart from the opening times. The dance hall opened at 9 pm, during war time, the same time as curfew. I had to bring this forward to tie in with the plot.

Otto Reiner. It's always difficult naming someone like Otto Reiner. Otto first appeared in *The Resistance Knitting Club*. Otto was also the name of our next-door neighbour's cat. It gave me a great deal of pleasure naming someone like Otto after a beautiful grey, longhaired cat with attitude. Sadly, Otto died while I was writing this book. I miss him popping in to say hello. Reiner was a random pick from a telephone-book-like-list I keep of names, crossing them off when I do.

Flora started life as Fleur until I came across Titian's Flora. I did think to change it back when a couple of writers announced books with the name, but I decided not to. The flower theme was too strong to think to change it.

Lucien, a small character that grew and grew to almost take over the book, first appeared in *The Resistance Knitting Club*, as did Sabine. The name of Maison Lumineau came when I made his father a lamplighter.

Sabine posed the biggest difficulty. Her surname was Marin until a vineyard decided to announce a new vineyard of that name while I was working on the book. It was back to the drawing board to name a vineyard that hadn't already been taken. There are a lot of vineyards around. Then a stroke of genius. No writer likes to mess with their manuscript during the final stages. Beau Marin is original and fit the bill. That it translates to Beautiful Sailor... No comment.

Patchwork quilts. Quilts weren't going to feature until I heard about a brilliant new Guernsey charity called Little Quilts, Big Hugs. This initiative was set up to bring warmth and comfort to those who need it the most. It reminded me of the quilt I made many years ago and got me thinking about all the things people use quilts for. The memories weaved between the stitches. There are numerous examples of patchwork across the centuries, too numerous to include here. Instead, I plan to write a blog post about the subject (on jennyobrienwriter.wordpress). The Calendar Quilt is my invention. I haven't made one yet, but I have purchased the material. I'll post a photo on my crafting group (The Resistance Knitting Club / Facebook) when (if) I finish it.

Finally, as someone who lives in jeans, I'm probably the least likely person imaginable to write a book that revolves around haute couture and yet... My father was a tailor. He trained in London as a pattern maker and spent most of his life in the bespoke men's tailoring industry. Like Lucien, he didn't sew. I learnt in school and, when one of his tailors went off sick, I used to run up a few seams for him.

He would have loved this book.

The dressmaking part of this is all my own work apart from researching metric over Imperial measuring systems and silk sewing pins. Any mistakes in this, and the rest of the book are all mine.

All any writer can say is that they tried to do their best.

Jenny O'Brien

Playlist

I don't listen to music when I'm working, but these are a few of the songs that I had playing on repeat while I was thinking about the book. I hope you enjoy.

Gary Moore – 'Parisienne Walkways'

Peter Sarstedt – 'Boulevard'

Francis Cabrel – 'Je L'aime à Mourir' (I love her so much I could die)

Alain Souchon – 'Le Baiser' (The Kiss)

Gerard Presgurvic – 'Les Rois du Monde' (The kings of the world, from *Romeo and Juliette* – the musical.)

And, last but not *least* – 'L'Étranger', by Edith Piaf

Further reading

A Cry from the Heart Margaret Crosland
 Paris Nights: My Year at Le Moulin Rouge Cliff Simons
 Les Parisiennes Anne Sebba
 Piaf, Le Livre d'Edith Silvain Reiner
 Le Moulin Rouge Jean Castaréde
 WW2 People's War BBC

BOOK CLUB QUESTIONS

1. What drew you to read *The Secret Dressmaker*? Was it
   the true-life inspiration or something else?
2. Who was your favourite character? How did they
   resonate with you?
3. Flora gives up her daughters thinking it's best for them,
   but it doesn't work out well. Could you relate to her
   actions?
4. Lucien seems like the villain at first, but he becomes
   someone much more sympathetic. When did your
   feelings about him start to change?
5. Sewing and knitting appear throughout the book: from
   parachutes to coded patterns to the wedding dress. Did
   you know about this true-life war history before or was
   it new to you?
6. Would you agree to Tomas' plan to spy in wartime
   Paris?
7. Which part of Flora's double life in Paris did you find
   most tense or surprising?
8. Flora and Marguerette's reunion is difficult and
   complex. What was the moment you felt things shift
   between them?

9. How effective was setting Flora's journey in wartime France? Did it add tension to her quest to find her daughters?

10. If you were casting the film adaptation, who would play Violette, Tomas, Lucien and Marguerette?

ACKNOWLEDGMENTS

Thank you for choosing to read *The Secret Dressmaker*. This has been one of my favourite books to write. I adored researching high fashion in Paris.

As always, the dedication first. Kari Clayton-Johns, thank you for the coffee and bookish chat and thank you for your expertise in French champagne, even though it didn't make the edits. You made the book in style this time!

This book wouldn't have happened without the support of Claire Bord, my amazing editor at Storm Publishing. Writing one book takes a village, writing the first in a series requires a good deal of faith, along with a firm hand at the helm to ensure my writing doesn't venture too far away from my scrappy outline. Thank you, Claire, truly.

The team at Storm Publishing is magnificent; from Oliver Rhodes and Alexandra Begley to Ariell Cacciola, Elke Desanghere, Naomi Knox and Maheen Mehmood. Thanks also to copyeditor Dushi Horti and proofreader Shirley Khan. If you're listening to the audio version, you'll know already what a great narrator Shelley Atkinson is. And as for the cover designer Sara Simpson... Thank you both!

In 2024, I was interviewed by the fabulous local historian, Nick Le Huray, for the Guernsey Literary Festival, during which there was a raffle. I didn't manage to sneak in an Irish character in *The Resistance Knitting Club*. This time I made an extra special effort, although only with the surname in the end. Thank you, Sinead Granville. Maria Clara Soler: Thank you, MC, for allowing me to turn you into a nun. I'll bet there aren't many people who get to say/write that.

Valerie Keogh. I don't think I would still be writing without you egging me on from the sidelines. You make writing far more fun than it's meant to be. I hope we get to meet up in 2026.

Thanks too to fellow writers, Luisa Jones, Pam Lecky, Jane Mosse, Theresa Le Flem, S E Lynes, Sam Tonge, RJ Verity, Jill Bray and Kelly Priaulx and last but not least Kelvin Whelan, writer and owner of the Writer's Block bookshop on the Island. If you haven't read their books, do give them a look.

Thank you, CHOG. If you know, you know.

Also thank you to my very special Dream Team. In no particular order, thanks to Beverley, Michele, Diane, Elaine, Susan, Lesley, Tracy, Amanda, Sarah, Sharon, Jo, Daniela, Carol, Madeleine, Tracey, Terri, Maggie, Lynda, Hayley, Donna and finally Maureen.

A final mention as always to my family.

Buns for tea!